Little Women

Little Women

By LOUISA MAY ALCOTT

Illustrated by Arvis Stewart

Modern Abridged Edition

A WHITMAN BOOK

Western Publishing Company, Inc.

Racine, Wisconsin

Contents

1 Playing Pilgrims 13

2 A Merry Christmas 23

3 The Laurence Boy 31

4 Being Neighborly 39

5 Beth Finds the Palace Beautiful 52

6 Amy's Valley of Humiliation 58

7 Jo Meets Apollyon 65

8 Meg Goes to Vanity Fair 75

9 Experiments 85

10 Camp Laurence 94

11 Secrets 102

12 A Telegram 111

13 Letters 122

14 Little Faithful 130

15 Dark Days 137

16 Amy's Will 144

17 Confidential 153

18 Laurie Makes Mischief 160

19 Aunt March Settles a Question 166

20 The First Wedding 171

21 Experiences 179

22 Tender Troubles 185

23 Jo's Journal 195

24 A Friend 203

25 Heartache 212

26 New Impressions 220

27 The Valley of the Shadow 233

28 Learning to Forget 240

29 All Alone 247

30 Surprises 254

31 My Lord and Lady 264

32 Under the Umbrella 270

at your dresses, and label your father if he isn't rich, and insult you when your nose isn't nice."

"If you mean *libel*, I'd say so and not talk about *labels* as if Papa were a pickle bottle," advised Jo, laughing.

"I know what I mean, and you needn't be *statirical* about it. It's proper to use good words and improve your *vocabilary*," returned Amy with dignity.

"Don't peck at one another, children. Don't you wish we had the money Papa lost when we were little, Jo? Dear me, how happy and good we'd be, if we had no worries," said Meg, who could remember better times.

"You said the other day you thought we were a deal happier than the King children, for they were fighting and fretting all the time, in spite of their money."

"So I did, Beth. Well, I guess we are, for, though we do have to work, we make fun for ourselves and are a pretty jolly set, as Jo would say."

"Jo does use such slang words," observed Amy, with a reproving look at the long figure stretched on the rug. Jo immediately sat up, put her hands in her apron pockets, and began to whistle.

"Don't, Jo; it's so boyish."

"That's why I do it."

"I detest rude, unladylike girls."

"I hate affected, niminy-piminy chits."

"'Birds in their little nests agree,'" sang Beth, the peacemaker, with a funny face that made both girls laugh.

"Really, girls, you are both to be blamed," said Meg, beginning to lecture in her elder-sisterly fashion. "You are old enough to leave off boyish tricks and behave better, Josephine. It didn't matter so much when you were a little girl, but now that you are so tall and turn up your hair, you should remember that you are a young lady."

"I'm not! And if turning up my hair makes me one, I'll wear it in two tails till I'm twenty," cried Jo, pulling off her net and shaking down a chestnut mane. "I hate to think I've got to grow up and be Miss March and wear long gowns and look as prim as a China aster. It's bad enough to be a girl, anyway, when I like boys' games and work and manners. I can't get over my disappointment in not being a boy, and it's worse than ever now, for I'm dying to go and fight with Papa, and I can only stay at home and knit like a poky old woman!" And Jo shook the blue army sock till the needles rattled like castanets and her ball bounded across the room.

"Poor Jo, it's too bad! But it can't be helped. So you must try to be contented with making your name boyish and playing brother to us girls," said Beth.

"As for you, Amy," continued Meg, "you are altogether too particular and prim. Your airs are funny now, but you'll grow up an affected little goose if you don't take care. I like your nice manners and refined ways of speaking, when you don't try to be elegant, but your absurd words are as bad as Jo's slang."

"If Jo is a tomboy and Amy a goose, what am I, please?" asked Beth.

"You're a dear, and nothing else," answered Meg warmly; and no one contradicted her, for the "Mouse" was the pet of the family.

The four sisters sat knitting away in the twilight while the December snow fell quietly without, and the fire crackled cheerfully within. It was a comfortable old room, though the carpet was faded and the furniture very plain, for a good picture or two hung on the walls, books filled the recesses, chrysanthemums and Christmas roses bloomed in the windows, and a pleasant atmosphere of a peaceful home pervaded it.

Margaret, the eldest of the four, was sixteen and very pretty. Fifteen-year-old Jo was very tall, thin, and brown, and reminded one of a colt. Her long, thick hair was her one beauty. Elizabeth—or Beth—was a rosy, smooth-haired, bright-eyed girl of thirteen, with a shy manner, a timid voice, and a peaceful expression. Amy was a regular snow maiden, with blue eyes, and yellow hair curling to her shoulders, pale and slender, and always carrying herself like a young lady mindful of her manners.

The clock struck six, and, having swept up the hearth, Beth put a pair of slippers down to warm. Mother was coming. Everyone brightened to welcome her. Meg stopped lecturing and lit the lamp. Amy got out the easy chair without being asked. Jo forgot how tired she was as she sat up to hold the slippers nearer to the blaze.

"They are quite worn out. Marmee must soon have a new pair."

"I thought I'd buy her some with my dollar," said Beth quietly.

"No, I shall!" cried Amy.

"But I'm the oldest—" began Meg.

"I'm the man of the family," cut in Jo, "now that Papa is away. I shall provide the slippers, for he told me to take special care of Mother while he was gone."

"I'll tell you what we'll do," said Beth. "Let's each get her something pretty for Christmas, and not get anything for ourselves."

"That's like you, dear! What will we get?" exclaimed Jo.

"I shall give her a nice pair of gloves," said Meg.

"Army shoes, best to be had," cried Jo.

"Some handkerchiefs, all hemmed," said Beth.

"I'll get a little bottle of cologne. She likes it, and it won't cost much—so I'll have some money left to buy my pencils," added Amy.

"How will we give the things?" asked Meg.

"Put 'em on the table and bring her in and see her open the bundles. Don't you remember how we used to do on our birthdays?" answered Jo.

"Let Marmee think we are getting things for ourselves, and then surprise her. We must go shopping tomorrow afternoon, Meg. There is so much to do about the play for Christmas night."

"I don't mean to act anymore after this time. I am getting too old for such things," observed Meg.

"You won't stop, I know, as long as you can trail round in a white gown with your hair down, and wear gold-paper jewelry. You are the best actress we've got," said Jo. "We ought to rehearse tonight. Come here, Amy, and do the fainting scene. You are as stiff as a poker in that."

"I can't help it! I never saw anyone faint, and I don't choose to make myself all black and blue tumbling flat as you do," returned Amy.

"Do it this way: Clasp your hands so, and stagger across the room, crying frantically, 'Roderigo! Save me! Save me!'" And away went Jo, with a melodramatic scream.

Amy followed, but she poked her hands out stiffly before her and jerked herself along as if she went by machinery. Her "Ow!" was more suggestive of pins being run into her than of fear and anguish.

"It's no use! Do the best you can when the time comes, and if the audience laughs, don't blame me. Come on."

18

Then things went smoothly, for Don Pedro defied the world in a speech of two pages without a single break; Hagar, the witch, chanted an awful incantation over her kettleful of simmering toads; Roderigo rent his chains asunder manfully; and Hugo died in agonies of remorse and arsenic.

"It's the best we've had yet," said Meg as the dead villain sat up and rubbed his elbows.

"I don't see how you can write and act such splendid things, Jo. You're a regular Shakespeare!" exclaimed Beth proudly.

"Not quite," replied Jo modestly.

The rehearsal ended in a general burst of laughter.

"Glad to find you so merry, my girls," said a cheery voice at the door. The actors and audience turned to welcome a tall, motherly lady.

"Well, dearies, how have you got on today? There was so much to do, getting the boxes ready to go tomorrow, that I didn't come home to dinner. Has anyone called, Beth? How is your cold, Meg? Jo, you look tired to death. Come here and kiss me, baby."

Mrs. March got her wet things off, her hot slippers on, and, sitting down in the easy chair, drew Amy to her lap. The girls flew about. Meg arranged the tea table; Jo brought wood and set chairs; Beth trotted to and fro; while Amy gave directions to everyone.

As they gathered about the table, Mrs. March said, with a particularly happy face, "I've got a treat for you after supper."

Jo tossed up her napkin, crying, "A letter! A letter! Three cheers for Father!"

"Yes, a nice long letter," said Mrs. March, patting her

pocket as if she had a treasure there.

"Hurry up and get done. Don't stop to quirk your little finger and prink over your plate, Amy," cried Jo, dropping her bread, butter side down, on the carpet, in her haste to get at the treat.

Beth ate no more, but crept away to sit in her shadowy corner and brood over the delight to come.

"I think it was so splendid of Father to go as a chaplain, when he was too old to be drafted and not strong enough for a soldier," said Meg warmly.

"Don't I wish I could go as a drummer or a nurse, so I could be near him and help him!" exclaimed Jo with a groan.

"It must be very disagreeable to sleep in a tent, and eat all sorts of bad-tasting things, and drink out of a tin mug," sighed Amy.

"When will he come home, Marmee?" asked Beth.

"Not for many months, dear, unless he is sick. Now come and hear the letter."

They all drew near the fire. In a low voice Mrs. March read the letter from Father. Little was said of the hardships endured, the dangers faced, or the homesickness conquered; it was a cheerful, hopeful letter, full of lively descriptions of camp life, marches, and military news. It ended with fatherly love and longing for the little girls at home.

" 'Give them all my dear love and a kiss. Tell them I think of them by day, pray for them by night, and find my best comfort in their affection at all times. I know that when I come back to them I may be fonder and prouder than ever of my little women.' "

Everybody sniffed when they came to that part. Amy

hid her face on her mother's shoulder and sobbed out, "I *am* a selfish pig! But I'll try to be better, so he mayn't be disappointed in me by and by."

"We all will!" cried Meg. "I think too much of my looks, and hate to work—but I won't anymore, if I can help it."

"I'll try and be what he loves to call me, 'a little woman,' and not be rough and wild," said Jo.

Beth said nothing, but began to knit with all her might, while she resolved in her quiet little soul to be all that Father hoped to find her.

Mrs. March broke the silence that followed Jo's words by saying in her cheery voice, "Do you remember how you used to play *Pilgrim's Progress* when you were little things? Nothing delighted you more than to have me tie my piece bags on your backs for burdens, give you hats and sticks and rolls of paper, and let you travel through the house from the cellar, which was the City of Destruction, clear up to the housetop, where you had all the lovely things you could collect to make a Celestial City."

"What fun it was!" said Jo.

Mrs. March went on, "It is a play we are playing all the time in one way or another. Our burdens are here, our road is before us, and the longing for goodness and happiness is the guide that leads us through many troubles and mistakes to the peace which is a true Celestial City. Now, my little Pilgrims, suppose you begin again—not in play, but in earnest—and see how far on you can get before Father comes home."

"Really, Mother? Where are our bundles?" asked Amy.

"Each of you told what your burden was just now, except Beth."

"Mine is dishes and dusters, and envying girls with nice

pianos, and being afraid of people," sighed Beth.

"Let us do it," said Meg thoughtfully. "It is only another name for trying to be good, and maybe *Pilgrim's Progress* will help us."

"We were in the Slough of Despond tonight, and Mother came and pulled us out as Help did in the book. We ought to have our roll of directions, like Christian," said Jo.

"Look under your pillows Christmas morning, and you will find your guidebook," replied Mrs. March.

They talked over the new plan while old Hannah cleared the table. Then out came the four little workbaskets, and the needles flew as the girls made sheets for Aunt March. It was uninteresting sewing, but tonight no one grumbled. They adopted Jo's plan of dividing the long seams into four parts, and calling the quarters Europe, Asia, Africa, and America.

At nine they stopped work and sang, as usual, before they went to bed. No one but Beth could get much music out of the old piano, but she had a way of touching the yellow keys and making a very pleasant accompaniment to the simple songs they sang. They had done this since they could lisp, and it had become a household custom, for the mother was a born singer. The first sound in the morning was her voice, and the last sound at night was the same cheery sound, for the girls never grew too old for that familiar lullaby.

2 · A Merry Christmas

Jo was the first to wake in the gray dawn of Christmas morning. No stockings hung at the fireplace, and for a moment she felt disappointed. Then she remembered her mother's promise and, slipping her hand under her pillow, drew out a little crimson-covered book. It was that beautiful old story of the best life ever lived. Jo felt it was a true guidebook for any pilgrim going the long journey. She woke Meg with a "Merry Christmas" and bade her see what was under her pillow. A green-covered book appeared, with the same picture inside. Presently Beth and Amy woke to rummage and find their little books, also—one dove-colored, the other blue.

"Girls," said Meg seriously, "Mother wants us to read and love and mind these books, and we must begin at once. I shall keep my book on the table here and read a little every morning as soon as I wake, for I know it will do me good and help me through the day."

Then she opened her new book and began to read. Jo put her arm around her and, leaning cheek to cheek, read also, with the quiet expression so seldom seen on her restless face.

"Where is Mother?" asked Meg as she and Jo ran down

to thank her for their gifts half an hour later.

"Goodness only knows. Some poor creeter come a-beggin', and your ma went right off to see what was needed. There never *was* such a woman for givin' away vittles and drink, clothes and firin'," replied Hannah, who had lived with the family since Meg was born and was considered by them all more as a friend than a servant.

"She will be back soon, I guess. So do your cakes and have everything ready," said Meg, looking over the presents, which were collected in a basket and kept under the sofa. "Why, where is Amy's bottle of cologne?"

"She took it out a minute ago and went off with it to put a ribbon on it, or some such notion," replied Jo.

"How nice my handkerchiefs look, don't they? I marked them all myself," said Beth, looking proudly at the uneven letters which had cost her such labor.

"There's Mother—hide the basket, quick!" cried Jo as a door slammed and steps sounded in the hall.

Amy came in hastily and looked rather abashed when she saw her sisters all waiting for her.

"Where have you been, and what are you hiding behind you?" asked Meg, surprised to see, by her hood and cloak, that lazy Amy had been out so early.

"Don't laugh at me, Jo. I didn't mean anyone should know till the time came. I only meant to change the little bottle for a big one, and I gave *all* my money to get it, and I'm truly trying not to be selfish anymore."

Amy showed the handsome flask which replaced the cheap one. Meg hugged her and Jo pronounced her 'a trump.' Beth ran to the window and picked her finest rose to ornament the stately bottle.

Another bang of the street door sent the basket under

the sofa and the girls to the table, eager for breakfast.

"Merry Christmas, Marmee! Lots of them! Thank you for our books. We read some, and mean to every day," they cried in chorus.

"Merry Christmas, little daughters! I'm glad you began at once and hope you will keep on. Not far away from here lies a poor woman with a little newborn baby. Six children are huddled into one bed to keep from freezing, for they have no fire. There is nothing to eat over there. My girls, will you give them your breakfast as a Christmas present?"

They were all unusually hungry, having waited nearly an hour, and for a minute no one spoke; only a minute, for Jo exclaimed impetuously, "I'm so glad you came before we began to eat!"

"May I go and help carry the things to the poor little children?" asked Beth eagerly.

"I thought you'd do it," said Mrs. March, smiling as if satisfied. "You shall all go and help me, and when we come back we will have bread and milk for breakfast, and make it up at dinner time."

They were soon ready, and the procession set out.

A poor, bare, miserable room it was, with broken windows, no fire, ragged bedclothes, a sick mother, a wailing baby, and a group of pale, hungry children.

"*Ach, mein Gott!* It is good angels come to us!" cried the poor woman.

In a few minutes it really did seem as if kind spirits had been at work there. Hannah, who had carried wood, made a fire. Mrs. March gave the mother tea and gruel and dressed the baby tenderly. The girls set the children round the fire and fed them like so many hungry birds.

"*Die Engelkinder!*" cried the poor things as they ate, warming their purple hands at the blaze.

That was a very happy breakfast, though the March girls didn't get any of it.

"That's loving our neighbor better than ourselves," said Meg later as they ate their own Christmas breakfast of bread and milk. Then they set out their presents while their mother was upstairs collecting clothes for the poor Hummels.

The tall vase of red roses, white chrysanthemums, and trailing vines, which stood in the middle, gave quite an elegant air to the table.

"She's coming!" cried Jo. "Three cheers for Marmee!"

Beth played her gayest march, Amy threw open the door, and Meg escorted her mother to the seat of honor. Mrs. March was both surprised and touched. The slippers went on at once; a new handkerchief, well scented with Amy's cologne, was slipped into her pocket; the rose was fastened at her bosom; and the nice gloves were pronounced "a perfect fit."

The rest of the day was devoted to preparations for the Christmas play.

No gentlemen were admitted, so Jo played the male parts.

On Christmas night a dozen girls piled onto the bed, which was the "dress circle," and sat before the blue and yellow chintz curtains in a most flattering state of expectancy. Soon a bell rang, the curtains flew apart, and the Operatic Tragedy began.

A gloomy wood was represented by a few shrubs in pots, a green baize on the floor, and a cave in the distance. The cave was made with a wooden clotheshorse for a roof,

bureaus for walls; in it was a small furnace in full blast, with a black pot on it and an old witch bending over it.

Then Hugo, the villain, stalked in. He struck his forehead and burst out in a wild strain, singing of his hatred for Roderigo, his love for Zara, and his resolution to kill the one and win the other. He stole to the cavern and ordered the witch, Hagar, to come forth, with a commanding "What ho, minion! I need thee!"

Out came Meg, with gray horsehair hanging about her face, a red and black robe, a staff, and cabalistic signs upon her cloak. Hugo demanded a potion to make Zara adore him, and one to destroy Roderigo. Dark bottles were tossed at Hugo. Putting the bottles into his boots, he departed. Hagar then informed the audience that she had cursed Hugo and intended to thwart his plans.

In the second act Zara appeared in a lovely blue and silver dress. She waited for Roderigo, who made his entrance in gorgeous array.

He sang to her a serenade in melting tones. Don Pedro, her father, rushed in and ordered Roderigo banished from the kingdom. Roderigo defied the old gentleman. Zara also defied him. Thereupon the father ordered both of them to the deepest dungeon of the castle.

In act three Hagar appeared, having come to free the lovers and finish Hugo. Hugo dutifully drank of her poisoned wine and, after a good deal of clutching and stamping, fell flat and died. The lovers were freed.

The final curtain fell upon the lovers kneeling to receive a penitent Don Pedro's blessing, in attitudes of the most romantic grace.

Tumultuous applause followed. Then, suddenly and surprisingly, the bed on which the "dress circle" was built, shut up and extinguished the enthusiastic audience. Roderigo and Don Pedro flew to the rescue. The excitement had hardly subsided when Hannah appeared, with "Mrs. March's compliments, and would the ladies walk down to supper."

There was ice cream, two dishes of it—pink and white—and cake and fruit and distracting French bonbons, and in the middle of the table four great bouquets of hothouse flowers!

"Is it Santa Claus?" asked Beth breathlessly.

"Wrong. Old Mr. Laurence sent it," replied Mrs. March, smiling.

"The Laurence boy's grandfather! What in the world put such a thing into his head? We don't know him," exclaimed Meg, her eyes wide with surprise.

"Hannah told one of his servants about your breakfast party. He is an odd old gentleman, but that pleased him. He knew my father years ago, and he sent me a polite note this afternoon, saying he hoped I would allow him to express his friendly feeling toward my children by sending them a few trifles in honor of the day. I could not refuse, and so you have a little feast at night to make up for the bread-and-milk breakfast this morning."

"That boy put it into his head—I know he did! He's a capital fellow, and I wish we could get acquainted. He looks as if he'd like to know us. But he's bashful, and Meg is so prim she won't let me speak to him when we pass," said Jo as the plates went round.

"You mean the people who live in the big house next door, don't you?" asked one of the girls. "My mother says old Mr. Laurence is very proud. He keeps his grandson shut up when he isn't riding or walking with his tutor.

We invited him to our party, but he didn't come."

"Our cat ran away once and he brought her back, and we talked over the fence and were getting along capitally, all about cricket, and so on, when he saw Meg coming and walked off. I mean to know him some day, for he needs fun; I'm sure he does," said Jo decidedly.

"I like his manners, and he looks like a little gentleman. So I've no objection to your knowing him if a proper opportunity comes," smiled Mrs. March.

It was Beth who nestled up to her mother and said, a little later, "How I wish Father were here. I'm afraid he isn't having such a merry Christmas as we are."

3 • The Laurence Boy

Jo! Jo! WHERE are you?" cried Meg, at the foot of the garret stairs.

"Here," answered a husky voice from above; and, running up, Meg found her sister eating apples and crying over *The Heir of Redclyffe*. This was Jo's favorite refuge, and here she loved to retire with half a dozen russets and a nice book.

"Such fun! Only see! A regular note of invitation from Mrs. Gardiner for tomorrow night!" cried Meg. She read:

" 'Mrs. Gardiner would be happy to see Miss March and Miss Josephine at a little dance on New Year's Eve.' Marmee is willing we should go. Now what *shall* we wear?"

"What's the use of asking that, when you know we shall wear our poplins, because we haven't anything else?" answered Jo, with her mouth full.

"If I only had a silk!" sighed Meg. "Mother says I may when I'm eighteen, perhaps, but two years is an everlasting time to wait."

"I'm sure our pops look like silk, and they are nice enough for us. Yours is as good as new, but I forgot the burn and the tear in mine. Whatever shall I do? The burn shows horridly, and I can't take any out."

"You must sit still all you can, and keep your back out of sight; the front is all right. I shall have a new ribbon for my hair, and Marmee will lend me her little pearl pin, and my new slippers are lovely, and my gloves will do, though they aren't as nice as I'd like."

"Mine are spoiled with lemonade, and I can't get any new ones—so I shall have to go without," said Jo, who never troubled herself much about dress.

"You *must* have gloves, or I won't go," cried Meg decidedly. "Gloves are more important than anything else. You can't dance without them. If you don't have them I shall be *so* mortified."

"Then I'll stay still. I don't care much for company dancing; it's no fun to go sailing around."

"You can't ask Mother for new ones—they are so expensive, and you are so careless. Can't you fix them any way?" asked Meg anxiously.

"I can hold them crunched up in my hand. No! Each wear one good one and carry a bad one, don't you see?"

"Your hands are bigger than mine, and you will stretch my glove dreadfully," said Meg petulantly.

"Then I'll go without," said Jo, taking up her book.

"You may have it, you may! Only don't stain it, and do behave nicely. Don't put your hands behind you, or stare, or say 'Christopher Columbus!' Will you?"

"I'll be as prim as a dish."

So Meg went away happily to "accept with thanks," look over her dress, and sing blithely as she did up her one real lace frill, while Jo finished reading her story and eating her apples.

On New Year's Eve the two younger March sisters

played dressing maids, and the two elder were absorbed in "getting ready for the party." There was a great deal of running up and down. Meg wanted a few curls about her face, and Jo undertook to pinch the papered locks with a pair of hot tongs.

"What a queer smell! It's just like burned feathers," observed Amy.

"There! Now I'll take off the papers and you'll see a cloud of little ringlets," said Jo, putting down the tongs.

No cloud of ringlets appeared. The hair came off with the papers, and the horrified hairdresser laid a row of little scorched bundles on the bureau.

"Oh, oh, oh! I'm spoiled! I can't go!" wailed Meg, looking with despair at the uneven frizzle on her forehead.

"Just my luck!" groaned poor Jo.

"It isn't spoiled," soothed Amy. "Tie your ribbons so the ends come on your forehead a bit, and it will look like the latest fashion."

"Serves me right for trying to be fine. I wish I'd let my hair alone," cried Meg.

She was finished at last, and Jo's hair was got up and her dress on. Each put on one light glove and carried one soiled one, and all pronounced the effect "quite easy and nice." Meg's high-heeled slippers hurt dreadfully, and Jo's nineteen hairpins all seemed stuck straight into her head, which was not exactly comfortable; but, dear me, let us be elegant or die.

As the gate clashed behind them, a voice cried from a window, "Girls, girls! *Have* you both got nice handkerchiefs?"

"Yes, yes, spandy nice," laughed Jo. "And Meg has cologne on hers."

Mrs. Gardiner, a stately old lady, greeted them kindly and handed them over to the eldest of her six daughters. Meg knew Sallie and was at her ease very soon, but Jo, who didn't care much for girls or girlish gossip, stood about with her back carefully against the wall. Half a dozen jovial lads were talking about skates, and she longed to go and join them, for skating was one of the joys of her life. She could not roam about and amuse herself, for the burned breadth would show. Jo saw a big redheaded youth approaching her corner, and, fearing he meant to ask her to dance, she slipped into a curtained recess. Another bashful person had chosen the same refuge. The Laurence boy!

"Dear me, I didn't know anyone was here!" stammered Jo.

The boy laughed and said pleasantly, "Don't mind me. Stay if you like."

The boy sat down and looked at his boots, till Jo said, "I think I've had the pleasure of seeing you before. You live near us, don't you?"

"Next door."

Jo laughed, pleased.

"We had such a good time over your nice Christmas gift."

"Grandpa sent it."

"But you put it into his head, didn't you, now?"

"How is your cat, Miss March?" The boy's black eyes shone with fun.

"Nice, thank you, Mr. Laurence," returned Jo mischievously. "But I am not Miss March—I'm only Jo."

"I'm not Mr. Laurence—I'm only Laurie." Then he added, "Don't you like to dance, Miss Jo?"

"I like it well enough if there is plenty of room, and everyone is lively. In a place like this I'm sure to upset something or tread on people's toes. Don't you dance?"

"Sometimes. You see I've been abroad a good many years, and I haven't been about enough yet to know how you do things here."

"Abroad!" cried Jo. "Oh, do tell me about it!"

He told her about how he had been at a school in Vevey, Switzerland.

Laurie's bashfulness soon wore off, for Jo's boyish demeanor amused him and set him at his ease. Jo was her merry self again. She liked the "Laurence boy" better than ever and took several good looks at him so she might describe him to the girls.

Curly black hair, brown skin, big black eyes, long nose, nice teeth, little hands and feet, tall as I am, very polite for a boy, and altogether jolly. Wonder how old he is, she thought.

With unusual tact, she tried to find out.

"I suppose you are going to college soon. I see you pegging away at your books—no, I mean studying hard." And Jo blushed at the dreadful "pegging" which had escaped her.

Laurie smiled, but didn't seem shocked.

"Not for two or three years yet. I won't go before seventeen, anyway."

"Aren't you but fifteen?" He seemed older.

"Sixteen, next month."

Jo, having found out what she wanted, changed the subject by saying, as her foot kept time, "That's a splendid polka. Why don't you go and try it?"

"Yes, indeed I will, if you will come, too," Laurie

answered with a queer little French bow.

"I can't!" There Jo stopped. She was undecided whether to tell or to laugh.

"Why?"

"You won't tell?"

"Never!"

"Well, I have a bad trick of standing before the fire, and so I burn my frocks, and I scorched this one. If I dance it will show."

"Never mind that," said Laurie gently. "I'll tell you how we can manage. There's a long hall out there, and we can dance grandly, and no one will see us. Please come."

The hall was empty and they had a grand polka, which delighted Jo, who was full of swing and spring. When the music stopped, they sat down on the stairs to get their breath. Meg appeared. She beckoned, and Jo reluctantly followed her.

"I've sprained my ankle," said Meg as they entered a side room. "That stupid high heel turned and gave me a horrid wrench. I don't know how I'm ever going to get home," she added, rocking to and fro in pain.

"I don't see what you can do, except get a carriage or stay here all night," answered Jo, softly rubbing the poor aching ankle.

"I can't have a carriage without its costing ever so much. I daresay I can't get one at all, for most people come in their own, and it's a long way to the stable, and no one to send."

"I'll go."

"No, indeed! It's past ten, and dark as Egypt. I can't stop here, for the house is full. I'll rest till Hannah comes, and then do the best I can."

"I'll ask Laurie—he will go," said Jo, looking relieved as the idea occurred to her.

"Mercy, no! Don't ask or tell anyone. Watch for Hannah, and tell me the minute she comes."

"I'll stay with you! I'd rather."

"No, dear. Run along and bring me some coffee. I'm so tired I can't stir."

Jo went blundering away to the dining room. She secured the coffee, which she immediately spilled, making the front of her dress as bad as the back.

"Oh, dear, what a blunderbuss I am!" exclaimed Jo, finishing Meg's glove by scrubbing her gown with it.

"Can I help you?" There was Laurie, with a full cup in one hand and a plate of ice in the other.

"I was trying to get something for Meg, my sister, who is very tired," answered Jo, glancing dismally from the stained skirt to the coffee-colored glove.

"Too bad! I was looking for someone to give this to. May I take it to your sister?"

"Oh, thank you. I'll show you where she is."

Jo led the way. Laurie drew up a little table and got more coffee and ice for Jo. Meg pronounced him a "nice boy." They were having a merry time when Hannah appeared. Meg forgot her foot and rose so quickly that she was forced to catch hold of Jo, with an exclamation of pain.

Whereupon Laurie gallantly offered them his grandfather's carriage to take them home.

"It's so early—you can't mean to go yet," began Jo, relieved, but hesitating to accept the offer.

"I always go early. I do, truly. Please allow me to take you home."

So they rolled away in the luxurious closed carriage, feeling very festive and elegant.

"I had a capital time," said Jo later as they were getting ready for bed. "Did you, Meg?"

"Yes, until I hurt my foot," answered Meg. "Sallie Gardiner's friend, Annie Moffat, took a fancy to me and asked me to spend a fortnight with her when Sallie does.

"I declare, it really seems like being a fine young lady, to come home from the party in a carriage, and have a maid to wait on me," Meg added as Jo bound up her foot with arnica.

"I don't believe fine young ladies enjoy themselves a bit more than we do," Jo said soberly, "in spite of our burned hair, old gowns, one glove apiece, and tight slippers that sprain our ankles when we are silly enough to wear them."

Meg gave her hair one last stroke with her brush. "I think you are quite right, Jo." She smiled.

4 • Being Neighborly

As MEG SAID, she *was* "fond of luxury," and her chief trouble was poverty. She found it harder to bear than the others, because she could remember a time when home was beautiful, life full of ease and pleasure, and want of any kind unknown. She tried not to be envious or discontented, but it was very natural that the young girl should long for pretty things, gay friends, accomplishments, and a happy life.

When Mr. March lost his property in trying to help an unfortunate friend, the two oldest girls begged to be allowed to do something toward their own support, at least. Believing that they could not begin too early to cultivate energy, industry, and independence, their parents consented, and both fell to work with the hearty goodwill which, in spite of everything, is sure to succeed at last.

Margaret found a place as a nursery governess. At the Kings' she daily saw all she wanted, for the children's older sisters were just out, and Meg caught frequent glimpses of dainty ball dresses and bouquets, heard lively gossip about theaters, concerts, sleighing parties, and merrymakings of all kinds, and saw money that would have been so precious to her lavished on trifles. Poor Meg seldom complained, but a sense of injustice made her feel bitter toward everyone sometimes.

Jo happened to suit Aunt March, who was lame and needed an active person to wait upon her. In her heart Jo rather liked the peppery old lady, though the real attraction might have been the large library of fine books, which was left to dust and spiders after Uncle March died. The moment Aunt March took her nap or was busy with company, Jo hurried to this quiet place and, curling herself up in the big chair, devoured poetry, romance, history, travels, and pictures, like a regular bookworm.

Jo's ambition was to do something very splendid; what it was she had no idea, but left it for time to tell her, and, meanwhile, found her greatest affliction in the fact that she couldn't read, run, and ride as much as she liked. But the thought that she was doing something to support herself made her happy in spite of Aunt March's perpetual "Josy-phine!"

Beth was too bashful to go to school; it had been tried, but she suffered so much it was given up, and she did her lessons at home with her father. Even when he went away, and her mother was called to devote her skill and energy to Soldiers' Aid Societies, Beth went faithfully on by herself and did the best she could. She was a housewifely little creature, and helped Hannah keep home neat and comfortable. There were her dolls, six of them, to be taken up and dressed every morning, and this she did faithfully. All had been outcasts till Beth took them in, for when her sisters outgrew these idols, they passed to her.

Beth had her troubles, as well as the others, and often

"wept a little weep" because she couldn't take music lessons and have a fine piano. She loved music dearly, tried so hard to learn, and practiced away so patiently at the jingling old instrument that it did seem as if someone (not to hint Aunt March) ought to help her. Day after day she said hopefully to herself, "I know I'll get my music sometime, if I'm good."

If anybody had asked Amy what the greatest trial of her life was, she would have answered at once, "My nose." When she was a baby, Jo had accidentally dropped her into the coal hod, and Amy insisted that the fall had ruined her nose forever. It was rather flat and not the Grecian nose that Amy wished it was.

Amy had a decided talent for drawing and was never so happy as when copying flowers, designing fairies, or illustrating stories with queer specimens of art. Her little airs and graces were much admired, as were her accomplishments; for, besides her drawing, she could play twelve tunes, crochet, and read French without mispronouncing more than two-thirds of the words. Her long words were considered "perfectly elegant" by the girls. Amy was in a fair way to being spoiled.

Meg was Amy's confidante and monitor, and, by some strange attraction of opposites, Jo was gentle Beth's. The two older girls were a great deal to one another, but each took one of the younger into her keeping, "playing mother," as they called it.

"What in the world are you going to do now, Jo?" asked Meg one snowy afternoon.

"Going out for exercise," answered Jo, with a mischievous twinkle in her eyes.

"I should think two long walks this morning would

have been enough. It's cold and dull out, and I advise you to stay warm and dry by the fire, as I do," said Meg with a shiver.

"Never take advice; can't keep still all day, and, not being a pussycat, I don't like to doze by the fire. I like adventures, and I'm going to find some."

Meg went back to toast her feet and read *Ivanhoe*, and Jo began to dig paths with great energy. The snow was light, and with her broom she soon swept a path all round the garden. Now, the garden separated the Marches' house from that of Mr. Laurence. A low hedge parted the two estates. On one side was an old brown house, looking rather bare and shabby, robbed of the vines that in summer covered its walls and the flowers which then surrounded it. On the other side was a stately mansion, plainly betokening every sort of comfort and luxury. Yet it seemed a lonely, lifeless sort of house, for no children frolicked on the lawn, no motherly face ever smiled at the windows, and few people went in and out, except the old gentleman and his grandson.

Jo had long wanted to behold the hidden glories of that mansion and to know the "Laurence boy," who looked as if he would like to be known, if he only knew how to begin. Since the party she had been more eager than ever. When the snowy afternoon came, Jo resolved to try what could be done. She saw Mr. Laurence drive off, and then sallied out to dig her way down to the hedge, where she paused and took a survey. All quiet; curtains down at the lower windows; nothing human visible but a curly black head leaning on a thin hand, at the upper window.

There he is, thought Jo. *Poor boy!*

Up went a handful of soft snow. The head turned at once, showing a face which lost its listless look in a minute as the big eyes brightened and the mouth began to smile. Jo nodded and laughed and flourished her broom as she called out, "How do you do? Are you sick?"

Laurie opened the window and croaked out as hoarsely as a raven, "Better, thank you. I've had a horrid cold and been shut up a week."

"I'm sorry. What do you amuse yourself with?"

"Nothing. It's as dull as tombs up here."

"Don't you read?"

"Not much. They won't let me."

"Can't somebody read to you?"

"Grandpa does, sometimes; but my books don't interest him, and I hate to ask Brooke all the time."

"Have someone come and see you, then."

"There isn't anyone I'd like to see. Boys make such a row, and my head is weak."

"Isn't there some nice girl who'd read and amuse you? Girls are quiet, and they like to play nurse."

"Don't know any."

"You know us," began Jo, then laughed and stopped.

"So I do! Will you come, please?" cried Laurie.

"I'm not quiet and nice, but I'll come if Mother will let me. I'll go ask her. Shut that window, like a good boy, and wait till I come."

With that Jo shouldered her broom and marched into the house, wondering what they would all say to her.

Laurie was in a little flutter of excitement at the idea of having company, and flew about to get ready. He did honor to the coming guest by brushing his curly pate, putting on a fresh collar, and trying to tidy up the room, which, in spite of half a dozen servants, was anything but neat.

"All right, show her up—it's Miss Jo," he said to the servant who announced that a young lady was calling. Jo appeared, looking rosy and kind and quite at her ease, with a covered dish in one hand and Beth's three kittens in the other.

"Here I am, bag and baggage," she said briskly. "Mother sent her love, Meg wanted me to bring some of her blancmange, and Beth thought her cats would be quite comforting."

Laurie laughed heartily at the three kittens.

"That looks too pretty to eat," he said, smiling with pleasure as Jo uncovered the dish and showed the blancmange, surrounded by a garland of green leaves and the scarlet flowers of Amy's pet geranium.

"It isn't anything, only they all felt kindly and wanted to show it. Tell the girl to put it away for your tea. It's so simple you can eat it, and, being soft, it will slip down without hurting your sore throat.

"What a cozy room this is!"

"It might be if it was kept nice, but the maids are lazy and I don't know how to make them mind. It worries me, though."

"I'll right it up in two minutes, for it only needs to have the hearth brushed, so—

"And the things made straight on the mantelpiece, so—

"And the books put here, and the bottles there, and your sofa turned from the light, and the pillows plumped up a bit. Now then, you're fixed."

And so he was, for as she laughed and talked, Jo had whisked things into place and given quite a different air to the room. Laurie watched her in respectful silence, and, when she finished, he sat down and heaved a sigh of satisfaction.

"How kind you are!" he said gratefully. "Yes, that's what it wanted. Now please take the big chair and let me do something to amuse my company."

"No, I came to amuse you. Shall I read now?" Jo looked affectionately toward some inviting books nearby.

"Thank you, but I've read all those, and, if you don't mind, I'd rather talk," said Laurie.

"Not at all. I'll talk all day if you'll only set me going. Beth says I never know when to stop."

"Is Beth the rosy one, who stays at home a good deal, and sometimes goes out with a little basket?" Laurie asked with eager interest.

"Yes, that's Beth. She's my girl, and a regular good one she is, too."

"The pretty one is Meg, and the curly-haired one is Amy, I believe?"

"How did you find that out?"

Laurie colored up, but answered frankly, "Why, you see, I often hear you calling to one another, and when I'm alone up here, I can't help looking over at your house. You all seem to be having such good times." His voice was wistful.

So Laurie was lonely. Jo's brown face was very friendly and her voice unusually gentle as she said, "I just wish you'd come over and see us. Mother would do you heaps of good, and Beth would sing to you if I begged her to, and Amy would dance, and Meg and I would make you laugh over some of our funny stage properties. Wouldn't your grandpa let you?"

"I think he would if your mother asked him. He lets me do as I like pretty much," said Laurie, brightening. "Only he's afraid I might be a bother to strangers."

"We aren't strangers; we are neighbors, and you needn't think you'd be a bother."

"Do you like your school?" asked the boy, after a little pause. Then he added, "I have a tutor, Mr. Brooke, you know."

Jo had been looking around much pleased. But she turned back at the question.

"Don't go to school. I'm a businessman—girl, I mean. I go to wait on my great-aunt, and a dear, cross old soul she is, too."

Jo proceeded to give him a lively description of the fidgety old lady, her fat poodle, the parrot that talked Spanish, and the library where she reveled. Laurie enjoyed that immensely.

"Oh, that does me lots of good! Tell on, please," he said, his face red and shining with merriment.

She "told on." Then Laurie offered to show her the house.

"I should love to see it," said Jo eagerly.

Laurie led the way from room to room, letting Jo stop to examine whatever struck her fancy. At last they came to the library, where she clapped her hands and pranced, as she always did when especially delighted. It was lined with books, and it had Sleepy Hollow chairs and a great open fireplace.

"Theodore Laurence, you ought to be the happiest boy in the world," Jo whispered, half to herself. "Such richness!"

"A fellow can't live on books," said Laurie.

A bell rang. Jo flew up, exclaiming with alarm, "Mercy me! It's your grandpa, Laurie!"

"Well, what if it is? You are not afraid of anything, you know," returned the boy, looking wicked.

"I think I'm a little afraid of your grandpa," said Jo, keeping her eyes on the door.

But it was Laurie's doctor.

"Would you mind if I left you for a minute? I suppose I must see him," said Laurie.

"Don't mind me. I'm as happy as a cricket here," answered Jo, smiling.

She was standing before a fine portrait of old Mr. Laurence when the door opened again. She was saying softly to herself, "He isn't as handsome as my grandfather, but I think I could like him."

"Thank you, ma'am," said a gruff voice behind her; and there, to her great dismay, stood old Mr. Laurence.

For a minute a wild desire to run away possessed Jo. But that would be cowardly; so she resolved to stay and get out of the scrape as best she could.

The voice was gruffer than ever as the old gentleman said, "So you don't think me quite as handsome as your grandfather?"

"Not quite, sir."

"But you like me in spite of it?"

"Yes, I do, sir."

That answer pleased the old gentleman; he gave a short laugh and shook hands with her. "You've got your grandfather's spirit," he said. "He *was* a fine man, my dear. But what's better, he was a brave and honest one, and I was proud to be his friend."

"Thank you, sir," said Jo, relieved.

"What have you been doing to this boy of mine, hey?" was the next question, sharply put.

"Only trying to be neighborly, sir." And Jo told how her visit came about.

"You think he needs cheering up a bit, do you?"

"Yes, sir. He seems a little lonely, and young folks would do him good, perhaps. We are only girls, but we should be glad to help if we could, for we don't forget the splendid Christmas present you sent us," said Jo eagerly.

"Tut, tut, tut! That was the boy's affair. How is the poor woman?"

"Doing nicely, sir." And off went Jo, talking very fast, as she told all about the Hummels, in whom her mother had interested friends richer than they were.

"Just her father's way of doing good. I shall come and see your mother some fine day. Tell her so," said Mr. Laurence. "Hey! What the dickens has come to the fellow?" he demanded as Laurie came running downstairs.

"I didn't know you'd come, sir," he began as Jo gave him a triumphant little glance.

"That's evident by the way you racket downstairs. Tea is being served," said the old gentleman as a bell tinkled not far away.

"Come, young man, and behave like a gentleman."

Mr. Laurence offered Jo his arm with great courtesy.

The old gentleman did not say much as he drank his four cups of tea, but he watched the young people, who soon chatted away like old friends, and the change in his grandson did not escape him.

She is right, he thought. *The lad is lonely. I'll see what these little girls can do for him.*

After tea Laurie took Jo away to the conservatory,

which had been lighted for her benefit. It seemed quite fairy-like to Jo as she went up and down the walks, enjoying the blooming walls on either side—the soft light, the damp, sweet air, and the wonderful vines and trees that hung above her—while her new friend cut the finest flowers. Then he tied them up, saying, "Please take these to your mother."

They found Mr. Laurence standing before the fire in the great drawing room, but Jo's attention was entirely absorbed by a grand piano which stood open.

"Do you play?" she asked, turning to Laurie.

"Sometimes," he answered modestly.

"Please do now. I want to hear it, so I can tell Beth."

"Won't you first?"

"Don't know how! Too stupid to learn, but I love music dearly."

So Laurie played and Jo listened, with her nose luxuriously buried in heliotrope and tea roses. She praised him till he was quite abashed.

His grandfather spoke up. "That will do, young lady. Too many sugarplums are not good for him. Going? Well, I'm much obliged to you, and I hope you'll come again."

He shook hands kindly, but looked as if something did not please him. When they got into the hall, Jo asked Laurie if she had said anything amiss. He shook his head.

"No, it was me! He doesn't like to hear me play."

"Why not?"

"I'll tell you someday."

"Good night, Laurie."

"Good night, Jo, good night."

When the afternoon's adventures had been told, the March family felt inclined to go visiting in a body, for each found something very attractive in the big house on the other side of the hedge. Mrs. March wanted to talk of her father with the old man who had not forgotten him; Meg longed to walk in the conservatory; Beth sighed for the grand piano; and Amy was eager to see the fine pictures and statues.

"Mother, why didn't Mr. Laurence like to have Laurie play?" asked Jo.

"I am not sure, but I think it was because his son, Laurie's father, married an Italian lady, a musician, which displeased the old man, who is very proud. The lady was good and lovely and accomplished, but he did not like her and never saw his son after he married. They both died when Laurie was a little child, and then his grandfather took him home. Laurie's playing probably reminded Mr. Laurence of the woman he did not like, and so he 'glowered,' as Jo said."

Beth had been looking dreamily into the fireplace. She turned and said, "I was thinking about our *Pilgrim's Progress*. I was thinking of how maybe we are out of the Slough and through the Wicket Gate because we resolved to be good, and up the steep hill because we tried. Maybe the house next door, full of all those splendid things, is going to be our Palace Beautiful."

"We have got to get by the lions first," said Jo, as if she rather liked the prospect.

5 · Beth Finds the Palace Beautiful

THE BIG HOUSE did prove a Palace Beautiful, though it took some time for all to get in, and Beth found it very hard to pass the lions. Old Mr. Laurence was the biggest one; but, after he had called, said something funny or kind to each one of the girls, and talked over old times with their mother, nobody felt much afraid of him except timid Beth. The other lion was the fact that they were poor and Laurie rich, for this made them shy of accepting favors which they could not return. But after a while they found that he considered them the benefactors and could not do enough to show how grateful he was for Mrs. March's motherly welcome, their cheerful society, and the comfort he took in that humble home of theirs; so they soon began interchanging kindnesses without stopping to think which was doing the most.

What good times they had! Such plays and tableaux, such sleigh rides and skating frolics, such pleasant evenings in the old parlor, and now and then such gay little parties at the great house. Meg could walk in the conservatory whenever she liked and revel in bouquets; Jo browsed over the new library voraciously, and convulsed the old gentleman with her criticisms; Amy copied pictures and enjoyed beauty to her heart's content; and Laurie played "lord of the manor" in the most delightful style.

But Beth, though yearning for the grand piano, could not pluck up courage to go to the "Mansion of Bliss," as Meg called it. That fact, coming to Mr. Laurence's ear, caused him to set about mending matters. During one of the brief calls he made, he artfully led the conversation to music. Beth, all ears, stood back of his chair.

Mr. Laurence, knowing she was there, said, "Laurie does not play much now. The piano suffers for want of use. Wouldn't some of your girls like to run over and practice on it now and then, just to keep it in tune, you know, ma'am?"

Timid Beth pressed her hands tightly together. The thought of practicing on that splendid instrument quite took her breath away.

Mr. Laurence went on, "They needn't see or speak to anyone, but run in at any time." He rose. "Please tell the young ladies, and if they don't care to come, why, never mind."

Here a little hand slipped into his, and Beth looked up at him with a face full of gratitude as she said in her earnest, yet timid, way, "Oh, sir, they do care, very, very much!"

"Are you the musical girl?" he asked ever so gently.

"I'm Beth. I love it dearly, and I'll come if you are quite sure nobody will hear me—or be disturbed," she added, fearing to be rude and trembling at her own boldness.

"Not a soul, my dear. The house is empty half the day. So come and drum away as much as you like, and I shall be obliged to you."

"How kind you are, sir."

Beth was not frightened now. She gave the big hand a grateful squeeze. The old man softly stroked the hair off her forehead, and, stooping down, he kissed her, saying, "I had a little girl once with eyes like these. God bless you, my dear. Good day, madam." And away he went, in a great hurry.

So next day, having seen both the old and young gentleman out of the house, Beth, after two or three retreats, fairly got in at the side door and made her way as noiselessly as any mouse to the drawing room, where her idol stood. Quite by accident, of course, some pretty, easy music lay on the piano; and, with trembling fingers and frequent stops to listen and look about, Beth at last touched the great instrument, and straightway forgot her fear, herself, and everything else but the unspeakable delight which the music gave her.

After that, the little brown hood slipped through the hedge nearly every day, and the great drawing room was haunted by a tuneful spirit that came and went unseen. She never knew that Mr. Laurence often opened his study door to hear the old-fashioned airs he liked; she never saw Laurie mount guard in the hall to warn the servants away; she never suspected that the exercise books and new songs which she found in the rack were put there for her special benefit.

"Mother, I'm going to work Mr. Laurence a pair of slippers. He is so kind to me I must thank him, and I know of no other way. Can I do it?" asked Beth, a few weeks after the old gentleman's call.

"Yes, dear; it will please him very much, and be a nice way of thanking him. The girls will help you about them, and I will pay for the making up," replied Mrs. March, who took peculiar pleasure in granting Beth's requests, because she so seldom asked anything for herself.

After many serious discussions with Meg and Jo, the pattern was chosen, the materials bought, and the slippers begun. A cluster of grave yet cheerful pansies on a deeper purple ground was pronounced very appropriate and pretty, and Beth worked early and late. When finished she wrote a very short, simple note and, with Laurie's help, got them smuggled up to the study one morning before the old gentleman was up.

When this excitement was over, Beth waited to see what would happen. All that day passed and a part of the next before any acknowledgment arrived, and she was beginning to fear she had offended her crotchety friend. On the afternoon of the second day she went out to do an errand and give poor Joanna, the invalid doll, her daily exercise. As she came up the street on her return she saw three, yes, four heads popping in and out of the parlor windows; and the moment they saw her, several hands were waved and several joyful voices screamed, "Here's a letter from the old gentleman! Come quick and read it!"

"Oh, Beth! He's sent you—" began Amy, gesticulating with unseemly energy. But she got no further, for Jo quenched her by slamming down the window.

Beth hurried on in a twitter of suspense. At the door her sisters seized her and bore her to the parlor in a triumphal procession, all pointing and all saying at once, "Look there! Look there!" Beth did look and turned pale with delight and surprise; for there stood a little cabinet piano, with a letter lying on the glossy lid, directed, like a signboard, to "Miss Elizabeth March."

"For me?" gasped Beth.

"Yes, all for you, my precious! Isn't it splendid of him? Don't you think he's the dearest old man in the world?" cried Jo, hugging her sister. "Here, read this note."

"You read it. I can't—I feel so queer. Oh, it is too lovely!"

Jo read:

"Miss March:

"I have had many pairs of slippers in my life, but I never had any that suited me so well as yours. Heartsease is my favorite flower, and these will always remind me of the gentle giver. I like to pay my debts, so I know you will allow 'the old gentleman' to send you something which once belonged to the little granddaughter he lost. With hearty thanks and best wishes, I remain,

"Your grateful friend and humble servant,
"James Laurence

"There, Beth, that's an honor to be proud of, I'm sure!" exclaimed Jo. "Laurie told me how fond Mr. Laurence used to be of the child who died, and how he kept all her little things carefully. Just think, he's given you her piano!"

"See the cunning brackets to hold candles, and the nice green silk, all puckered up with a gold rose in the middle, and the pretty rack and stool, all complete," added Meg, opening the instrument and displaying its beauties.

"Try it, honey; let's hear the sound of the baby pianny," said Hannah, who always shared in family joys and sorrows.

So Beth tried it, and everyone pronounced it the most remarkable piano ever heard. It had evidently been newly tuned and put in apple-pie order.

"You'll have to go and thank him," said Jo, by way of

a joke; for the idea of the child's going never entered her head.

"Yes, I mean to." To the utter amazement of the family, Beth walked down the garden, through the hedge, and in at the Laurences' door.

She went and knocked at the study door, and when a gruff voice called out, "Come in!" she did go in, right up to Mr. Laurence, who looked quite taken aback. She held out her hand, saying, with only a small quaver in her voice, "I came to thank you, sir, for—" But she didn't finish, for he looked so friendly that she forgot her speech; and only remembering that he had lost the little girl he loved, she put both arms round his neck and kissed him.

Mr. Laurence was so touched and pleased by that confiding little kiss that all his crustiness vanished; and he set her on his knee and laid his wrinkled cheek against her rosy one, feeling as if he had got his own little granddaughter back again. Beth ceased to fear him from that moment, and sat there talking to him as cozily as if she had known him all her life; for love casts out fear, and gratitude can conquer pride. When she went home, he walked with her to her own gate, shook hands cordially, and touched his hat as he marched back again, looking very stately and erect, like a handsome, soldierly old gentleman, as he was.

"Well!" cried Meg as she and the others saw this. "I do believe the world is coming to an end!"

6 • Amy's Valley of Humiliation

THAT BOY is a perfect Cyclops, isn't he?" said Amy one day as Laurie clattered by on horseback, with a flourish of his whip as he passed.

"How dare you say that, when he's got both his eyes! And exceedingly handsome ones they are, too!" cried Jo indignantly.

"I didn't say anything about his eyes, and I don't see why you need fire up when I admire his riding."

"Oh, my goodness! The little goose means a centaur!" Jo burst into laughter.

"You needn't be so rude. It's only a 'lapse of lingy,' as Mr. Davis says," retorted Amy. "I just wish I had a little of the money Laurie spends on that horse," she added.

"Why?" asked Meg kindly, for Jo had gone off in another laugh at Amy's second blunder.

"I need it so much. I'm dreadfully in debt, and it won't be my turn to have the rag-money for a month."

"In debt, Amy! What do you mean?" And Meg looked sober.

"Why, I owe at least a dozen pickled limes, and I can't pay them, you know, till I have money, for Marmee forbade my having anything charged at the shop."

"Tell me about it. Are limes the fashion now? It used to be pricking bits of rubber to make balls."

"Why, you see," said Amy, looking grave and important, "the girls are always buying them, and unless you want to be thought mean, you must do it, too. It's nothing but limes now, for everyone is sucking them in their desks in schooltime, and trading them off for pencils, bead rings, paper dolls, or something else at recess. If one girl likes another, she gives her a lime. If she's mad with her, she eats one before her face and doesn't offer even a suck. They treat by turns, and I've had ever so many but haven't returned them, and I ought, for they are debts of honor, you know."

"How much would pay them off and restore your credit?" asked Meg, taking out her purse.

"A quarter would more than do it, and leave a few cents over for a treat for you. Don't you like limes?"

"Not much; you may have my share. Here's the money. Make it last as long as you can, for it isn't very plentiful, you know."

Next day Amy was rather late at school, but could not resist displaying a moist brown paper parcel before she consigned it to the inmost recesses of her desk. During the next few minutes the rumor that Amy March had got twenty-four delicious limes (she ate one on the way) and was going to treat circulated through her "set," and the attentions of her friends became quite overwhelming. Katy Brown invited her to her next party on the spot; Mary Kingsley insisted on lending her her watch till recess; and Jenny Snow, a satirical young lady who had basely twitted Amy upon her limeless state, promptly buried the hatchet. But Amy had not forgotten Miss

Snow's cutting remarks. She instantly crushed "that Snow girl's" hopes by a withering telegram: "You needn't be so polite of a sudden, for you won't get any."

A distinguished personage happened to visit the school that morning, and Amy's beautifully drawn maps received praise, which honor to her foe rankled in the soul of Miss Snow and caused Miss March to assume the airs of a young peacock. Whereupon the revengeful Snow turned the tables with disastrous success. No sooner had the guest paid the usual stale compliments and bowed himself out than Jenny, under pretense of asking an important question, informed Mr. Davis, the teacher, that Miss Amy March had some pickled limes in her desk.

Now, Mr. Davis had declared limes a contraband article and had vowed to ferule publicly the first person who was found breaking the law. With face flushed angrily, he rapped on his desk.

"Young ladies, attention, if you please!"

The buzz ceased.

"Miss March, come to my desk."

Amy rose to comply with outward composure, but a secret fear oppressed her, for the limes weighed upon her conscience.

"Bring with you the limes you have in your desk," was the unexpected command which arrested her before she got out of her seat.

"Don't take all," whispered her neighbor, a young lady of great presence of mind.

Amy hastily shook out half a dozen and laid the rest down before Mr. Davis, feeling that any man possessing a human heart would relent when that delicious perfume met his nose. Unfortunately, Mr. Davis particularly detested the odor of the fashionable pickled lime, and disgust added fresh fuel to his wrath.

"Is that all?"

"Not quite," stammered Amy.

"Bring the rest, immediately."

With a despairing glance at her set she obeyed.

"You are sure there are no more?"

"I never lie, sir."

"So I see. Now, take these disgusting things, two by two, and throw them out of the window."

There was a simultaneous sigh from the girls. Scarlet with shame and anger, Amy went to and fro twelve mortal times; and as each doomed couple, looking, oh, so plump and juicy, fell from her reluctant hands, a shout from the street completed the anguish of the girls, for it told them that their feast was being exulted over by the little Irish children who were their sworn foes.

As Amy returned from her last trip, Mr. Davis gave a "hem" and said sternly, "Young ladies, you remember what I said to you a week ago. I never allow my rules to be infringed, and I *never* break my word. Miss March, hold out your hand."

Amy started, and put both hands behind her, and turned on him an imploring look. She was rather a favorite of Mr. Davis', and he might have broken his word if one irrepressible young lady had not hissed. That hiss, faint as it was, irritated the irascible gentleman and sealed the culprit's fate.

"Your hand, Miss March!" Too proud to cry or beseech, Amy set her teeth, threw back her head defiantly, and bore without flinching several tingling blows on her little palm. They were neither many nor heavy, but that made

61

no difference to her. For the first time in her life she had
been struck, and the disgrace, in her eyes, was as deep as
if she had been knocked down.

"You will now stand on the platform till recess," said
Mr. Davis, resolved to do the thing thoroughly, since he
had begun it.

During the fifteen minutes that followed, the proud and
sensitive little girl suffered a shame and pain which she
never forgot. During the twelve years of her life she had
been governed by love alone, and a blow of that sort had
never touched her before. The smart of her hand and the
ache of her heart were forgotten in the sting of one
thought: *I shall have to tell at home, and Mother and the
girls will be so disappointed in me!*

Recess came. Amy went, without a word to anyone,
straight into the anteroom, snatched her things, and left.

At the March home, not long after, an indignation meet-
ing was held. The result was that, just before school was
out, Jo appeared wearing a grim expression, stalked up
to the desk and delivered a letter from her mother, then
collected Amy's property and departed.

"Yes, you can have a vacation from school, but I want
you to study a little every day with Beth," said Mrs. March
that evening. "I don't approve of corporal punishment,
especially for girls."

"It's perfectly maddening to think of those lovely
limes," sighed Amy with the air of a martyr.

"I am not sorry you lost them, for you broke the rules
and deserved some punishment for disobedience," was
the severe reply, which rather disappointed the young
lady, who expected nothing but sympathy.

"Do you mean you are glad that I was disgraced before

the whole school?" cried Amy.

"I should not have chosen that way of mending a fault," replied her mother, "but I am not sure that it won't do you good. You are getting altogether too conceited and important, my dear. You have a good many little gifts and virtues, but there is no need of parading them. The consciousness of possessing and using them should satisfy you, and the great charm of all power is modesty."

"So it is," cried Laurie, who was playing chess in a corner with Jo. "I knew a girl, once, who had a really remarkable talent for music, and she didn't know it—never guessed what sweet little things she composed when she was alone."

"I wish I'd known that nice girl. Maybe she would have helped me; I'm so stupid," said Beth quietly.

"You do know her, and she helps you better than anyone else could," answered Laurie, looking at her with such mischievous meaning in his merry black eyes that Beth turned red and hid her face in the sofa cushion.

Jo let Laurie win the game, to pay for that praise of her Beth, who could not be prevailed upon to play for them after her compliment. So Laurie sang, and delightfully, too. When he was gone, Amy, who had been pensive all the evening, asked suddenly, as if busy with some new idea, "Is Laurie an accomplished boy?"

"Yes, he has had an excellent education and has much talent. He will make a fine man, if not spoiled by petting," replied her mother.

"And he isn't conceited, is he?" asked Amy.

"Not in the least. That is why he is so charming and why we all like him so much."

"I see. It's nice to have accomplishments and be elegant,

but not to show off or get perked up," said Amy thoughtfully.

"These things are always seen and felt in a person's manner and conversation if modestly used, but it is not necessary to display them," said Mrs. March.

"Any more than it's proper to wear all your bonnets and gowns and ribbons at once, that folks may know you've got them," added Jo, and the lecture ended in a laugh.

7 • Jo Meets Apollyon

GIRLS, WHERE are you going?" asked Amy one Saturday afternoon, coming into their room and finding Jo and Meg ready to go out.

"Never mind; little girls shouldn't ask questions," returned Jo sharply.

Amy bridled up at this insult. Turning to Meg, who never refused her anything very long, she coaxed, "Do tell me! I should think you might let me go, too. Beth is fussing over her dolls, and I haven't anything to do and am *so* lonely."

"I can't, dear, because you aren't invited," began Meg.

But Jo broke in impatiently, "Now, Meg, be quiet, or you will spoil it all. You can't go, Amy. So don't be a baby now and whine about it."

"You are going somewhere with Laurie, I know you are. You were whispering and laughing together on the sofa last night, and you stopped when I came in. You are going with him, aren't you?"

"Yes, we are. Now, do be still and stop bothering."

Amy held her tongue but used her eyes and saw Meg slip a fan into her pocket.

"I know! I know! You're going to the theater to see the

Seven Castles!" she cried, adding resolutely, "and I *shall* go, for Mother said I might see it, and I've got my rag-money, and it was mean not to tell me in time."

"Just listen to me a minute, and be a good child," said Meg soothingly. "Mother doesn't wish you to go this week, because your eyes are not well enough yet to bear the light of this fairy piece. Next week you can go with Beth and Hannah, and have a nice time."

"I don't like that half as well as going with you and Laurie. Please let me! I've been sick with this cold so long and shut up, I'm dying for some fun. Do, Meg! I'll be ever so good," pleaded Amy, looking as pathetic as she could.

"Suppose we take her. I don't believe Mother would mind, if we bundle her up well," began Meg.

"If *she* goes, I shan't, and if I don't, Laurie won't like it. And it will be very rude, after he invited only us, to go and drag in Amy. I'd think she'd hate to poke herself where she isn't wanted," said Jo crossly.

Her tone and manner angered Amy. She began to put on her boots, saying, "I *shall* go—Meg says I may. And if I pay for myself, Laurie hasn't anything to do with it."

"You can't sit with us, for our seats are reserved, and you mustn't sit alone. So Laurie will give you his place, and that will spoil our pleasure. Or he'll get another seat for you, and that isn't proper, when you weren't asked. You shan't stir a step. So you may just stay where you are," scolded Jo, crosser than ever, having just pricked her finger in her hurry to get started.

Amy began to cry and Meg to reason with her, when Laurie called from below.

Just as the party was setting out, Amy called over the banisters, "You'll be sorry for this, Jo! See if you aren't."

"Fiddlesticks!" returned Jo, slamming the door.

They had a charming time. But Jo's pleasure had a drop of bitterness in it. Between acts she wondered what Amy would do to make her "sorry for it." She and Amy had had many lively skirmishes. Amy teased Jo, and Jo irritated Amy, and semi-occasional explosions occurred, of which both were much ashamed afterward.

When they got home, they found Amy reading in the parlor. She assumed an injured air as they came in; never lifted her eyes from her book or asked a single question. On going up to put away her best hat, Jo's first look was toward the bureau, for in their last quarrel Amy had soothed her feelings by turning Jo's top drawer upside down on the floor. Everything was in its place. Jo decided that Amy had forgiven and forgotten her wrongs.

But next day Jo burst into the room where Meg, Beth, and Amy were sitting, and demanded breathlessly, "Has anyone taken my story?"

Meg and Beth said, "No."

"Amy, you've got it!"

"No, I haven't."

"You know where it is, then!"

"No, I don't."

"That's a fib!" cried Jo, taking her by the shoulders.

"It isn't. I haven't got it, don't know where it is now, and don't care."

"You know something about it, and you'd better tell at once, or I'll make you, Amy March!" And Jo gave her a slight shake.

"Scold as much as you like, you'll never get your silly old story again," cried Amy.

"Why not?"

"I burned it up."

"What! My little book I was so fond of, and worked over, and meant to finish before Father got home? Have you really burned it?" said Jo, turning very pale.

"Yes, I did! I told you I'd make you pay for being so cross yesterday, and I have, so—"

Amy got no further, for Jo's hot temper mastered her, and she shook Amy till her teeth chattered in her head, crying in a passion of grief and anger, "You wicked, wicked girl! I never can write it again, and I'll never forgive you!"

Meg flew to rescue Amy, and Beth to pacify Jo, but Jo was quite beside herself; and, with a parting box on her sister's ear, she rushed out of the room up to the old sofa in the garret and finished her fight alone.

The storm cleared up below, for Mrs. March came home, and, having heard the story, soon brought Amy to a sense of the wrong she had done her sister. Jo's book was the pride of her heart, and was regarded by her family as a literary sprout of great promise. It was only half a dozen fairy tales, but Jo had worked over them patiently, putting her whole heart into her work, hoping to make something good enough to print. She had just copied them with great care, and had destroyed the old manuscript, so that Amy's bonfire had consumed the loving work of several years. It seemed a small loss to others, but to Jo it was a dreadful calamity, and she felt that it never could be made up to her.

When the tea bell rang, Jo appeared, looking so grim and unapproachable that it took all Amy's courage to say meekly, "Please forgive me, Jo. I'm very, very sorry."

"I shall never forgive you," was Jo's stern answer, and

from that moment she ignored Amy entirely.

It was not a happy evening. As Jo received her good-night kiss, Mrs. March whispered gently, "My dear, don't let the sun go down upon your anger. Forgive each other, help each other, and begin again tomorrow."

But Jo felt so deeply injured that she really *couldn't* forgive quite yet. So she winked hard, shook her head, and said gruffly, for Amy was listening, "It was an abominable thing, and she doesn't deserve to be forgiven."

With that she marched off to bed, and there was no merry or confidential gossip that night.

Amy was much offended that her overtures of peace had been repulsed, and began to wish she had not humbled herself. Jo looked like a thundercloud, and nothing went well all next day.

"Everybody and everything is against me. I'll ask Laurie to go skating. He is always so kind and jolly and will put me to rights, I know," said Jo to herself, and off she went.

Amy heard the clash of skates, and looked out with an impatient exclamation. "There! She promised I should go next time, for this is the last ice we shall have. But it's no use to ask such a crosspatch to take me."

"Don't say that. You *were* very naughty, and it *is* hard to forgive the loss of her precious book. But I think she might do it now, and I guess she will, if you try her at the right minute," said Meg. "Go after them. Don't say anything till Jo has got good-natured with Laurie. Then take a quiet minute and just kiss her, or do some kind thing, and I'm sure she'll be friends again."

"I'll try," said Amy.

Jo saw her coming and turned her back. Laurie did not see, as he was carefully skating along the shore, sounding the ice, for a warm spell had preceded the cold snap.

"I'll go on to the first bend and see if it's all right, before we begin to race," Amy heard him say.

Jo heard Amy panting after her run, stamping her feet, and blowing her fingers as she tried to put her skates on; but Jo never turned, and went slowly zigzagging down the river, taking a bitter, unhappy satisfaction in her sister's troubles.

Laurie shouted back, "Keep near the shore; it isn't safe in the middle."

Jo heard, but Amy did not catch a word. Jo glanced over her shoulder, and the little demon she was harboring said in her ear, *No matter whether she heard or not, let her take care of herself.*

Laurie had vanished round the bend; Jo was just at the turn, and Amy, far behind, struck out toward the smoother ice in the middle of the river. Then something held Jo, made her turn around, just in time to see Amy throw up her hands and go down. Jo's heart stood still with fear. She tried to rush forward, but her feet seemed to have no strength in them. She could only stand motionless, staring with a terror-stricken face at the little blue hood above the black water. Something rushed swiftly by her, and Laurie's voice cried out, "Bring a rail! Quick! Quick!"

For the next few minutes she worked as if possessed, blindly obeying Laurie. Together they got the child out, more frightened than hurt.

They got Amy home, shivering, dripping, and crying; and after an exciting time of it, she fell asleep, rolled in blankets, before a hot fire.

When Amy was comfortably asleep, Mrs. March called Jo to her, beside Amy's bed.

"Are you sure she is safe?" whispered Jo, looking remorsefully at the golden head, which might have been swept away from her sight forever under the treacherous ice.

"Quite safe, dear. She is not hurt and won't even take cold, I think, you were so sensible in covering her and getting her home quickly," replied her mother cheerfully.

"Laurie did it all; I only let her go. Mother, if she *should* die, it would be my fault." And Jo dropped down beside the bed in a passion of penitent tears.

"It's my dreadful temper! I try to cure it. I think I have, and then it breaks out worse than ever. Oh, Mother! What shall I do?"

"Watch and pray, dear. Never get tired of trying, and never think it is impossible to conquer your fault," said Mrs. March, drawing Jo close to her. Then she added softly, "You think your temper is the worst in the world, but mine used to be just like it."

"Yours, Mother? Why, you are never angry!"

"It has taken me twenty years to control it. I am angry nearly every day, Jo, but I have learned not to show it. And I still hope to learn not to feel it, though it may take me another forty years."

"Mother, are you angry when you fold your lips tight together and go out of the room sometimes, when Aunt March scolds or people worry you?" asked Jo, feeling nearer and dearer to her mother than ever before.

"Yes, I've learned to check the hasty words that rise to my lips," answered Mrs. March with a smile.

"I wish I could. The sharp words fly out before I know what I'm about. Tell me how you do it, Marmee dear."

"My good mother used to help me—"

"As you do us—" interrupted Jo with a grateful kiss.

"But I lost her when I was a little older than you are, and for years I had to struggle on alone. Then your father came, and I was so happy I found it easy to be good. But by and by, when I had four little daughters round me and we were poor, then the old trouble began again. For I am not patient by nature, and it tried me very much to see my children wanting for anything."

"Poor Mother! What helped you then?"

"Your father, Jo. He never loses patience. And the love, respect, and confidence of my children is the sweetest reward I could receive for my efforts to be the woman I would have them copy."

"Oh, Mother, if I'm ever half as good as you, I shall be satisfied!" cried Jo, much touched.

"I hope you will be a great deal better, my dear. But, speaking of Father, it reminded me how much I miss him, how much I owe him, and how faithfully I should watch and work to keep his little daughters safe and good for him."

"You told him to go, Mother, and didn't cry when he went, and never complain now, or seem as if you needed any help," said Jo, wondering.

"I gave my best to the country I love, and kept my tears till he was gone. Why should I complain when we both have merely done our duty? If I don't seem to need help, it is because I have a better Friend, even than Father, to comfort and sustain me. My child, the troubles and temptations of your life are beginning, and may be many. Go to God with all your little cares and hopes and sins and sorrows as freely and confidingly as you come to your mother."

Jo's only answer was to hold her mother close, and, in the silence which followed, the sincerest prayer she had ever prayed left her heart without words. Led by her mother's hand, she had drawn nearer to the Friend who welcomes every child with a love stronger than that of any father, tenderer than that of any mother.

Amy stirred and sighed in her sleep. She opened her eyes. Seeing Jo's penitent expression, she held out her arms with a smile that went straight to Jo's heart. Neither said a word, but they hugged one another close, in spite of the blankets, and everything was forgiven and forgotten in one hearty kiss.

8 · Meg Goes to Vanity Fair

I DO THINK it was the most fortunate thing in the world that those children should have the measles just now," said Meg one April day as she stood packing the "go abroady" trunk in her room, surrounded by her sisters.

"And so nice of Annie Moffat not to forget her promise. A fortnight of fun will be regularly splendid," replied Jo, looking like a windmill as she folded skirts with her long arms.

"And such lovely weather. I'm so glad of that," added Beth, tidily sorting neck and hair ribbons in her best box, lent for the great occasion.

"I wish I was going to have a fine time and wear all these nice things," said Amy, with her mouth full of pins, as she artistically replenished her sister's cushion.

"I wish you were all going. But as you can't, I shall keep my adventures to tell you when I come back. I'm sure it's the least I can do, when you have been so kind, lending me things and helping me get ready," said Meg, glancing round the room at the very simple outfit, which seemed nearly perfect in their eyes. "There, now, the trays are ready and everything in but my ball dress, which I shall leave for Mother." She glanced from the half-filled

trunk to the many-times pressed and mended white tarlatan, which she called her "ball dress," with an important
air.

The next day was fine, and Meg departed in style for a
fortnight of novelty and pleasure. Mrs. March had consented to the visit rather reluctantly, fearing that Margaret would come back more discontented than she went.
But she begged so hard, and Sallie had promised to take
good care of her, and a little pleasure seemed so delightful after a winter of hard work, that the mother yielded,
and the daughter went to take her first taste of fashionable life.

The Moffats *were* very fashionable, and simple Meg
was rather daunted at first by the splendor of the house
and the elegance of its occupants. But soon she began to
imitate the manners and conversation of those about her,
to put on little airs and graces, use French phrases, crimp
her hair, take in her dresses, and talk about the fashions,
as well as she could. The more she saw of Annie Moffat's
pretty things, the more she envied her and sighed to be
rich. Home now looked bare and dismal.

When the evening for the "small party" came, she found
that her simple poplin dress wouldn't do at all, for the
other girls were putting on thin dresses and making themselves very fine indeed; so out came the tarlatan, looking
older, limper, and shabbier than ever beside Sallie's crisp
new one. Meg saw the girls glance at it and then at one
another, and her cheeks began to burn; for, with all her
gentleness, she was very proud. No one said a word about
it, but Sallie offered to do her hair, and Annie to tie her
sash, and Belle, the engaged sister, praised her white
arms; but in their kindness Meg saw only pity for her

poverty, and her heart felt very heavy as she stood by herself, while the others laughed and chattered and flew about like gauzy butterflies.

Then the maid brought in a box of flowers.

"These are for Miss March," she said, giving Meg the flowers and a note.

"What fun! Who are they from? Didn't know you had a lover," cried the girls, surprised.

"The note is from Mother, and the flowers from Laurie," said Meg, pleased.

"Oh, indeed!" said Annie, with a funny look.

Feeling happy again, Meg laid by a few ferns and roses for herself and quickly made up the rest in dainty bouquets for her friends. Somehow the kind act finished her despondency. She was happy and bright-eyed as she laid her ferns against her rippling hair and fastened the roses in the dress that didn't strike her as so *very* shabby now.

She enjoyed herself very much that evening. That is, she did until she overheard a bit of conversation. She was waiting in the conservatory for her partner to bring her an ice, when she heard a voice ask, on the other side of the flowery wall, "How old is she?"

"Sixteen or seventeen, I should say," replied another voice.

"It would be a grand thing for one of those girls, wouldn't it? Sallie says they are very intimate now, and the old man quite dotes on them."

"Mrs. M. has laid her plans, I daresay, and will play her cards well, early as it is. The girl evidently doesn't think of it yet," said Mrs. Moffat.

"She told that fib about the note from her mamma, and colored up when she opened up the box of flowers. Poor thing! She'd be so nice if she was only got up in style. Do you think she'd be offended if we offered to lend her a dress for Thursday?" asked another voice.

"She's proud, but I don't believe she'd mind, for that dowdy tarlatan is all she has. She may tear it tonight, and that will be a good excuse for offering a decent one."

"We'll see. I shall ask that Laurence, as a compliment to her, and we'll have fun about it afterward."

Meg's partner appeared, finding her much flushed and rather agitated. Innocent and unsuspicious as she was, she could not help understanding the gossip of her friends. She did her best to seem gay. But she was very glad when it was over, and she was quiet in her bed.

Her innocent friendship with Laurie was spoiled by the silly speeches she had overheard in the conservatory; even her faith in her mother was a little shaken by the worldly plans attributed to her by Mrs. Moffat.

Poor Meg had a restless night and got up heavy-eyed, unhappy, and half-resentful toward her friends. But something in their manner struck her at once; they treated her with more respect, she thought, took quite a tender interest in what she said, and looked at her with eyes that plainly betrayed curiosity. All this surprised and flattered her, though she did not understand it till Miss Belle said, "Meg, dear, I've sent an invitation to your friend, Mr. Laurence, for Thursday. We should like very much to know him, and it's only a proper compliment to you."

"You are very kind, but I'm afraid he won't come." Suddenly Meg had a mischievous fancy to tease the girls.

"Why not, *chérie?*" asked Miss Belle.

"He's too old."

"My child, what do you mean? What is his age?"

"Nearly seventy, I believe," answered Meg, counting stitches to hide the merriment in her eyes.

"You sly creature! Of course we meant the young man," exclaimed Miss Belle, laughing.

"There isn't any. Laurie is only a little boy." And Meg laughed at the queer look the sisters exchanged as she thus described her supposed lover.

"About your age," Annie said.

"Nearer my sister Jo's; I'm seventeen in August." Meg tossed her head.

"It's very thoughtful of him to send you flowers, isn't it?" said Annie.

"He often does, to all of us, for their house is full and we are so fond of them. My mother and old Mr. Laurence are friends, you know. So it is quite natural that we children should play together." And Meg hoped they would say no more.

"I've got a sweet blue silk laid away, which I've outgrown," said Sallie. "You shall wear it Thursday, Meg, to please me. Won't you, dear?"

"You are very kind, but I don't mind my old dress, if you don't. It does very well for a little girl like me," said Meg.

But Meg couldn't refuse the offer for long. So, on Thursday evening, Belle shut herself up with her maid; and, between them, they turned Meg into a fine lady. They crimped and curled her hair, they polished her neck and arms with some fragrant powder, touched her lips with coralline salve to make them redder, and Hortense would have added "a *soupçon* of rouge" if Meg had not rebelled. They laced her into a sky-blue dress, which was so tight she could hardly breathe and so low in the neck that modest Meg blushed at herself in the mirror. A set of silver filigree was added—bracelets, necklace, brooch, and earrings. A pair of high-heeled blue silk boots satisfied the last wish of Meg's heart.

"I'm afraid to go down, I feel so queer and stiff and half-dressed," said Meg to Sallie when Mrs. Moffat sent to ask the young ladies to appear at once.

"You don't look a bit like yourself, but you are very nice. I'm nowhere beside you, for Belle has heaps of taste, and you're quite French, I assure you," returned Sallie, trying not to care that Meg was prettier than herself.

"Margaret March—father a colonel in the army—one of our first families, but reverses of fortune, you know; intimate friends of the Laurences; sweet creature, I assure you; my Ned is quite wild about her," Meg heard Mrs. Moffat say later to one of the guests.

Meg did her best to act the fine lady, and got on pretty well, though the tight dress gave her a side ache, the train kept getting under her feet, and she was in constant fear lest her earrings should fly off and get lost or broken. She was flirting her fan, and laughing at the feeble jokes of a young gentleman who tried to be witty, when she suddenly stopped laughing; for, just opposite, she saw Laurie. He was staring at her with undisguised surprise, and disapproval, also, she thought. Something in his honest eyes made her blush and wish she had her old dress on. She saw Belle nudge Annie, and both glance from her to Laurie.

Silly creatures, to put such thoughts into my head! I won't let it change me a bit, thought Meg, and she rustled across the room to shake hands with her friend.

"I'm glad you came, for I was afraid you wouldn't," she

said, with her most grown-up air.

"Jo wanted me to come and tell her how you looked."

"What shall you tell her?" asked Meg, full of curiosity.

"I shall say I didn't know you. For you look so grown-up and unlike yourself, I'm quite afraid of you," he said, fumbling at his glove button.

"Don't you like me so?"

"No, I don't," was the blunt reply.

"Why not?" in an anxious tone.

"I don't like fuss and feathers."

That was altogether too much from a lad younger than herself; and Meg walked away, saying petulantly, "You are the rudest boy I ever saw."

She went and stood at a quiet window to cool her cheeks. As she stood there, Major Lincoln passed by; and a minute after, she heard him say to his mother; "They are making a fool of that little girl. I wanted you to see her, but they have spoiled her entirely. She's nothing but a doll tonight."

"Oh, dear!" sighed Meg. "I wish I'd been sensible and worn my own things. Then I should not have disgusted other people or felt so uncomfortable and ashamed of myself."

Laurie appeared, looking penitent, and with his very best bow said, "Please forgive my rudeness, and dance with me."

"I'm afraid it will be too disagreeable to you," said Meg, trying to look offended and failing entirely.

"Not a bit of it. I don't like your gown, but I do think you are—just splendid." And he waved his hands, as if words failed to express his admiration.

Meg smiled and relented and whispered, as they stood

waiting to catch the time, "Take care my skirt doesn't trip you up. It's the plague of my life, and I was a goose to wear it."

Away they went, fleetly and gracefully.

"Laurie, I want you to do me a favor, will you?" said Meg, as they twirled merrily round and round.

"Won't I!" said Laurie, with alacrity.

"Please don't tell them at home about my dress tonight. They won't understand the joke, and it will worry Mother. I shall tell them myself when I get home."

"Silence *à la mort*," said Laurie.

Later Laurie saw Meg drinking champagne with Ned Moffat.

"You'll have a splitting headache tomorrow if you drink too much of that. I wouldn't, Meg. Your mother doesn't like it, you know," he whispered, leaning over her chair as Ned turned to refill her glass.

Meg answered, with an affected little laugh, "I'm not Meg tonight. I'm a doll who does all sorts of crazy things. Tomorrow I shall put away my 'fuss and feathers' and be desperately good again."

"Wish tomorrow was here, then," muttered Laurie, walking off, ill pleased at the change he saw in her.

Meg danced and flirted, chattered and giggled; after supper she undertook the German, and blundered through it, nearly upsetting her partner with her long skirt, and romping in a way that scandalized Laurie.

She was sick all the next day and on Saturday went home, quite used up with her fortnight's fun and feeling that she had sat in the lap of luxury long enough.

"It does seem pleasant to be quiet and not have company manners on all the time," she said as she sat with her mother and Jo on Sunday evening.

"I'm glad to hear you say so, dear, for I was afraid home would seem dull and poor to you, after your fine quarters," replied her mother.

As the clock struck nine and Jo proposed bed, Meg suddenly left her chair and, taking Beth's stool, leaned her elbows on her mother's knee, saying bravely, "Marmee, I want to ''fess.'"

"What is it, dear?"

"Shall I go away?" asked Jo discreetly.

"Of course not. Don't I always tell you everything? I was ashamed to speak of it before the children, but I want you to know all the dreadful things I did at the Moffats'."

"We are prepared," said Mrs. March, smiling but looking a little anxious.

"I told you they rigged me up, but I didn't tell you that they powdered and squeezed and frizzled, and made me look like a fashion plate. Laurie thought I wasn't proper. They flattered me and said I was a beauty—and quantities of nonsense. So I let them make a fool of me."

"Is that all?" asked Jo as Mrs. March looked silently at the downcast face of her pretty daughter and could not find it in her heart to blame her little follies.

"No, I drank champagne, and romped, and tried to flirt, and was altogether abominable," said Meg self-reproachfully.

"There is something more, I think." And Mrs. March smoothed the soft cheek, which suddenly grew rosy, as Meg answered slowly, "Yes, it's very silly, but I want to tell it, because I hate to have people say and think such things about us and Laurie."

Then she told the various bits of gossip she had heard

at the Moffats'. Her mother's lips tightened.

"I was very unwise," said Mrs. March gravely, "to let you go among people of whom I know so little—kind, I daresay, but worldly, ill bred, and full of these vulgar ideas about young people."

"Mother, do you have 'plans,' as Mrs. Moffat said?" asked Meg bashfully.

"Yes, my dear, I do, a great many—all mothers do, but mine differ somewhat from Mrs. Moffat's, I suspect. I want you to listen to my 'plans.' I want my daughters to be beautiful, accomplished, and good; to be admired, loved, and respected; to have a happy youth; to be well and wisely married; and to lead useful, pleasant lives. Your father and I trust and hope that our daughters, whether married or single, will be the pride and comfort of our lives."

"We will, Marmee, we will!" cried Meg and Jo with all their hearts as she bade them good night.

9 · Experiments

THE FIRST of June! The Kings are off to the seashore tomorrow, and I'm free! Three months' vacation! How I shall enjoy it!" exclaimed Meg.

"Aunt March went today, for which, oh, be joyful!" said Jo. "I was mortally afraid she'd ask me to go with her. I quaked till she was fairly in the carriage, and had a final fright, for, as it drove off, she popped out her head, saying, 'Josy-phine, won't you—?' I didn't hear any more, for I basely turned and fled. I did actually run, and whisked round the corner, where I felt safe."

"Poor old Jo! She came in looking as if bears were after her," said Beth.

"Aunt March is a regular samphire, is she not?" observed Amy, who was making lemonade for them all.

"She means *vampire*, but it doesn't matter," murmured Jo.

"What shall you do all your vacation?" asked Amy.

"I shall lie abed late and do nothing," replied Meg. "I've been routed up early all winter, and had to spend my days working for other people. So now I'm going to rest and revel to my heart's content."

"Don't let us do any lessons, Beth, for a while, but play

all the time, and rest, as the girls mean to," proposed Amy.

"Well, I will, if Mother doesn't mind," said Beth.

"May we, Mother?" asked Meg, turning to Mrs. March, who sat sewing in what they called "Marmee's corner."

"You may try your experiment for a week and see how you like it. I think by Saturday night you will find that all play and no work is as bad as all work and no play."

"Oh, dear, no! It will be delicious, I'm sure," said Meg complacently.

Jo raised a glass of lemonade. "Fun forever," she cried, "and no grubbage!"

Next morning Meg did not appear till ten o'clock. Jo spent the morning on the river with Laurie, and the afternoon reading and crying over *The Wide, Wide World* up in the apple tree. Beth rummaged everything out of the big closet and then went to her music. Amy sat down to draw under the honeysuckle bower, hoping someone would see and inquire who the young artist was.

At teatime they compared notes, and all agreed that it had been a delightful, though unusually long, day. But they assured their mother that the experiment was working fine. Mother smiled, said nothing, and, with Hannah's help, did their neglected work, keeping home pleasant and the domestic machinery working smoothly.

The week wore on. It was astonishing what a peculiar and uncomfortable state of things was produced by the "resting and reveling" process. The days kept getting longer and longer; tempers kept getting shorter and shorter. As the height of luxury, Meg put out some of her sewing and then found time hanging so heavily that she fell to snipping and spoiling her clothes, in her attempts to furbish them *à la* Moffat. Jo read till her eyes gave out and she was sick of books. Beth got on pretty well, for she was constantly forgetting that it was to be *all play and no work*, and fell back into her busy ways now and then. Amy fared worst of all, for her resources were small—she didn't like dolls, fairy tales were childish, and one couldn't draw all the time.

No one would own that she was tired of the experiment; but by Friday night each acknowledged to herself that she was glad the week was nearly done. Hoping to impress the lesson more deeply, Mrs. March, who had a good deal of humor, resolved to finish off the trial in an appropriate manner; so she gave Hannah a holiday, and let the girls enjoy the full effect of the play system.

When they got up on Saturday morning, there was no fire in the kitchen, no breakfast in the dining room, and no Mother anywhere to be seen.

Meg ran upstairs and soon came back again.

"Mother isn't sick," she said. "But she says it *has* been a hard week for her. So we mustn't grumble, but take care of ourselves."

It was an immense relief to them all to have a little work. But they soon realized the truth of Hannah's saying, "Housekeeping ain't no joke."

While Beth and Amy set the table, Meg and Jo cooked the breakfast together.

"I shall take some up to Mother," said Beth.

So a tray was fitted out and taken up before anyone began to eat. The tea was bitter, the omelette scorched, and the biscuits speckled with saleratus; but Mrs. March received her repast with thanks and laughed heartily over it after Beth was gone.

Many were the complaints below, and great the chagrin of the head cook at her failures. "Never mind! I'll get the dinner and be servant. You be missus, keep your hands nice, see company, and give orders," said Jo, who knew still less than Meg about culinary matters.

This obliging offer was gladly accepted, and Margaret retired to the parlor, which she hastily put in order by whisking the litter under the sofa and shutting the blinds to save the trouble of dusting. Jo, with perfect faith in her own powers, put a note in their post office inviting Laurie to dinner.

Now, this post office was an old martin house, set in the hedge in the lower corner of the garden by Laurie. Letters, books, manuscripts, and bundles were passed in there. Each had a key to it. But I fancy that if Laurie could have foretold what he was letting himself in for this day, he would never have put it there.

"I'll have corned beef and plenty of potatoes," mused Jo, "and I shall get some asparagus and a lobster, 'for a relish,' as Hannah says. We'll have lettuce and make a salad—I don't know how, but the book tells. I'll have blancmange and strawberries for dessert, and coffee, too, if you want to be elegant."

"I'm going out to dinner," said Mrs. March when she heard of Jo's plan. "I never enjoyed housekeeping, and I'm going to take a vacation today and read, write, visit, and amuse myself. Get what you like for dinner."

An earthquake or a volcanic eruption could have seemed no stranger to Jo.

"Everything is out of sorts," she said, going downstairs. "There's Beth crying. That's a sure sign something is wrong with this family."

Jo hurried into the parlor to find Beth sobbing over Pip, the canary, who lay dead in his cage.

"It's all my fault. I forgot him. There isn't a seed or drop left—oh, Pip! Oh, Pip! How could I be so cruel to you?" Beth took the poor thing in her hands and tried to restore him.

"Put him in the oven, and maybe he will get warm and revive," said Amy hopefully.

"He's been starved, and he shan't be baked, now he's dead. I'll make him a shroud, and he shall be buried in a grave," murmured Beth.

"The funeral will be this afternoon, and we'll all go. Now, don't cry, Bethy. After the dinner party we'll have a nice little funeral," said Jo, beginning to feel as if she had undertaken a great deal.

Mrs. March went out, after peeping here and there to see how matters went. A strange sense of helplessness fell upon the girls as the gray bonnet vanished around the corner; and despair seized them, when, a few minutes later, Miss Crocker appeared and said she'd come to dinner. Now, this lady was a thin, inquisitive spinster with a sharp nose, who saw everything and gossiped about all she saw.

Language cannot describe the anxieties, experiences, and exertions which Jo underwent that morning; and the dinner she served up became a standing joke.

She rang the bell half an hour later than usual and stood hot, tired, and dispirited, surveying the messy feast spread for Laurie, accustomed to all sorts of elegance, and Miss Crocker, whose curious eyes would mark all her failures and whose tattling tongue would surely report them far and wide.

Poor Jo would gladly have gone under the table, as one thing after another was tasted and left, while Amy giggled, Meg looked distressed, Miss Crocker pursed her lips, and Laurie talked and laughed with all his might, to give a cheerful tone to the scene. Jo's one strong point was the strawberries, for she had sugared them well and had a pitcher of rich cream to eat with them. Her hot cheeks cooled a trifle, and she drew a long breath as the pretty glass plates went round and everyone looked graciously at the little rosy islands floating in a sea of cream. Miss Crocker tasted first, made a wry face, and drank some water hastily. Jo, who had refused, thinking there might not be enough, for they dwindled sadly after the picking over, glanced at Laurie, who was eating away manfully, though there was a slight pucker at his mouth, and he kept his eyes fixed on his plate. Amy, who was fond of delicate fare, took a heaping spoonful, choked, hid her face in her napkin, and left the table precipitately.

"Oh, what is it?" exclaimed Jo, trembling.

"Salt instead of sugar, and the cream is sour," replied Meg, with a tragic gesture.

Jo uttered a groan and fell back in her chair, remembering that she had given a last hasty powdering to the berries out of one of the two boxes on the kitchen table and had neglected to put the milk in the refrigerator. She turned scarlet and was on the verge of crying, when she met Laurie's eyes, which *would* look merry in spite of his heroic efforts; the comical side of the affair suddenly struck her, and she laughed till the tears ran down her cheeks. So did everyone else, even "Croaker," as the girls called the old lady; and the unfortunate dinner ended gaily, with bread and butter, olives, and fun.

91

"I haven't the strength of mind to clear up now. So we will sober ourselves with a funeral," said Jo as they rose and Miss Crocker made ready to go.

Laurie dug a grave under the ferns in the grove, little Pip was laid in, with many tears by his tenderhearted mistress, and covered with moss, while a wreath of violets and chickweed was hung on the stone, which bore this epitaph, composed by Jo while she struggled with the dinner:

> Here lies Pip March,
>   Who died the 7th of June;
> Loved and lamented sore,
>   And not forgotten soon.

Mrs. March came home to find the girls hard at work in the middle of the afternoon, making beds, straightening up and clearing away; and a glance at the closet gave an idea of the success of one part of the experiment.

As twilight fell, one by one the girls gathered on the porch, where the June roses were budding beautifully.

"What a dreadful day this has been!" groaned Jo.

"It has seemed shorter than usual, but *so* uncomfortable," said Meg.

"Not a bit like home," added Amy.

"It can't seem so without Marmee and little Pip," sighed Beth, glancing at the empty cage above her head.

"Here's Mother, dear, and you shall have another bird tomorrow if you want it."

As she spoke, Mrs. March came and took her place among them, looking as if her holiday had not been much pleasanter than theirs.

"Are you satisfied with your experiment, girls, or do you want another week of it?" she asked.

"I don't!" cried Jo decidedly.

"Nor I," echoed the others.

"Lounging and larking doesn't pay," observed Jo. "I'm tired of it, and mean to go to work at something right off."

"Suppose you learn plain cooking. That's a useful accomplishment," said Mrs. March. She had met Miss Crocker and heard an account of the dinner party.

"Mother! Did you go away and let everything be, just to see how we'd get on?" cried Meg, who had had suspicions all day.

"Yes, I wanted you to see how the comfort of all depends on each doing her share faithfully. Let me advise you to take up your little burdens again. Work is wholesome, and there is plenty for everyone. It keeps us from ennui and mischief, is good for health and spirits, and gives us a sense of power and independence better than money or fashion. Make each day both useful and pleasant, and prove that you understand the worth of time by employing it well. Then youth will be delightful, old age will bring few regrets, and life will become a beautiful success, in spite of poverty."

"We'll remember, Mother!" And they did.

10 · Camp Laurence

BETH WAS postmistress, for, being most at home, she could attend to it regularly and dearly liked the daily task of unlocking the little door and distributing the mail. One July day she came in with her hands full.

"Here's your posy, Mother! Laurie never forgets that," she said, putting the nosegay in the vase that stood in "Marmee's corner" and was kept supplied by the affectionate boy.

"Miss Meg March, one letter and a glove," continued Beth, delivering the articles to her sister, who sat near her mother, stitching wristbands.

"Why, I left a pair over there, and here is only one," said Meg. "Didn't you drop the other in the garden?"

"No, I'm sure I didn't, for there was only that one in the post office."

"I hate to have odd gloves! Never mind, the other may be found. My letter is only a translation of the German song I wanted. I guess Mr. Brooke did it; it isn't Laurie's writing."

Mrs. March glanced at Meg, who was looking very pretty in her gingham morning gown, with the little curls blowing about her forehead. And she looked very womanly as she sat sewing at her little worktable full of tidy white rolls.

"Two letters for Doctor Jo, a book, and a funny old hat that covered the whole post office, stuck outside," said Beth, laughing, as she went into the study where Jo sat writing.

"What a sly fellow Laurie is! I said I wished bigger hats were the fashion, because I burn my face every hot day. He said, 'Why mind the fashion? Wear a big hat and be comfortable!' I said I would if I had one, and he has sent me this, to try me. I'll wear it for fun and show him I *don't* care for the fashion." And, hanging the antique broadbrim on a bust of Plato, Jo read her letters.

One from her mother made her cheeks glow, for it said:

My dear:

I write a little word to tell you with how much satisfaction I watch your efforts to control your temper. I now believe heartily in the sincerity of your resolution, since it begins to bear fruit. Go on, dear, patiently and bravely, and always believe that no one sympathizes more tenderly with you than your loving

Mother

"That does me good!" cried Jo. "Oh, Marmee, I will keep on trying and not get tired, since I have you to help me."

In a big, dashing hand, Laurie wrote:

Dear Jo, What ho!

Some English boys and girls are coming to see me tomorrow, and I want to have a jolly time. If it's fine, I'm going to pitch my tent in Longmeadow, and row up the whole crew to lunch and croquet; have a fire, make messes, gypsy fashion, and all sorts of larks.

They are nice people and like such things. Brooke will go, to keep us boys steady, and Kate Vaughn is to play propriety for the girls. I want you all to come; can't let Beth off, at any price, and nobody shall worry her. Don't bother about rations. I'll see to that and everything else. Only do come, there's a good fellow!

In a tearing hurry,
Yours ever, Laurie

"Here's richness!" cried Jo, flying in to tell the news to Meg. "Of course we can go, Mother? It will be such a help to Laurie, for I can row, and Meg see to the lunch, and the children be useful some way."

"I hope the Vaughns are not fine, grown-up people. Do you know anything about them, Jo?" asked Meg.

"Only that there are four of them. Kate is older than you, Fred and Frank, twins about my age, and a little girl, Grace, who is nine or ten. Laurie knew them abroad and liked the boys. I fancied, from the way he primmed up his mouth in speaking of her, that he didn't admire Kate much. You'll come, Bethy?"

"I like to please Laurie," said Beth, "and I'm not afraid of Mr. Brooke—he is so kind. But I don't want to play, or sing, or say anything. I'll work hard, and not trouble anyone. And you'll take care of me, Jo—so I'll go."

"That's my good girl! You do try to fight off your shyness, and I love you for it. Fighting faults isn't easy, as I know, and a cheery word kind of gives a lift. Thank you, Mother." And Jo gave the thin cheek a grateful kiss.

"I had a box of chocolate drops and the picture I wanted to copy," said Amy, showing her mail.

"And I got a note from Mr. Laurence, asking me to come over and play to him tonight before the lamps are lighted, and I shall go," added Beth, whose friendship with the old gentleman prospered finely.

A bright sun next morning promised a fine day.

"Oh, oh, Jo! You aren't going to wear that awful hat! It's too absurd! You shall *not* make a guy of yourself," remonstrated Meg as Jo tied down with a red ribbon the broad-brimmed, old-fashioned leghorn Laurie had sent for a joke.

"I just will, though! It's capital, so shady, light, and big. It will make plenty of fun, and I don't mind being a guy, if I'm comfortable."

With that Jo marched straight away and the rest followed, a bright little band of sisters, all looking their best, in summer suits, with happy faces under the jaunty hat brims.

Laurie ran to meet them and present them to his friends in the most cordial manner. The lawn was the reception room, and for several minutes a lively scene was enacted there. Meg was grateful to see that Miss Kate, though twenty, was dressed with a simplicity which American girls would do well to imitate; and she was much flattered by Mr. Ned Moffat's assurances that he came especially to see her. Jo understood why Laurie "primmed up his mouth" when speaking of Kate, for that young lady had a stand-off-don't-touch-me air, which contrasted strongly with the free and easy demeanor of the other girls. Fred was nice, and Frank, who was lame, was gentle and frail. Amy found Grace a well-mannered, merry little person; they suddenly became very good friends.

Tents, lunch, and croquet utensils having been sent on beforehand, the party soon embarked, and the two boats pushed off together, leaving Mr. Laurence on the shore, waving good-bye with his hat.

It was not far to Longmeadow; but by the time they arrived, the tent was pitched and the wickets down in a pleasant green field with three wide-spreading oaks in the middle and a smooth strip of turf for croquet.

"Welcome to Camp Laurence!" said the young host. "Brooke is commander in chief; I am commissary general; the other fellows are staff officers; and you, ladies, are company. Now let's have a game before it gets hot, and then we'll see about fixing dinner."

Frank, Beth, Amy, and Grace sat down to watch the game played by the other eight. Mr. Brooke chose Meg, Kate and Fred; Laurie took Sallie, Jo, and Ned. The Englishers played well, but the Americans played better. Jo and Fred had several skirmishes, and once narrowly escaped high words. Jo was through the last wicket, and had missed the stroke, which failure ruffled her a good deal. Fred was close behind her, and his turn came before hers; he gave a stroke; his ball hit the wicket and stopped an inch on the wrong side. No one was very near, and, running up to examine it, he gave it a sly nudge with his toe, which put it just an inch on the right side.

"I'm through! Now, Miss Jo, I'll settle you and get in first," he cried, swinging his mallet for another blow.

"You pushed it! I saw you. It's my turn now," retorted Jo sharply.

"Upon my word, I didn't move it! It rolled a bit, perhaps, but that is allowed. So stand off, please, and let me have a go at the stake."

"We don't cheat in America, but *you* can, if you choose," said Jo angrily.

"Yankees are a deal the most tricky, everybody knows.

There you go," returned Fred, croqueting her ball far away.

Jo opened her lips to say something rude, but checked herself in time. Fred hit the stake and declared himself out, with much exultation. She went off to get her ball, and was a long time finding it; but she came back looking cool and quiet. It took several strokes to regain the place she had lost; and, when she got there, the other side had nearly won, for Kate's ball was the last but one and lay near the stake.

"By George, it's all up with us! Good-bye, Kate! Miss Jo owes me one. So you are finished," cried Fred excitedly as they all drew near to see the finish.

"Yankees have a trick of being generous to their enemies," said Jo, with a look that made the lad redden. "Especially when they beat them," she added as, leaving Kate's ball untouched, she won the game by a clever stroke.

Laurie threw up his hat, then remembered that it wouldn't do to exult over the defeat of his guests, and stopped in the middle of a cheer to whisper to his friend, "Good for you, Jo! He did cheat—I saw him. We can't tell him so, but he won't do it again; take my word for it."

"Time for lunch," said Mr. Brooke, looking at his watch. "Commissary general, will you make the fire and get water, while Miss March, Miss Sallie, and I spread the table? Who can make good coffee?"

"Jo can," said Meg, glad to recommend her sister. So Jo, feeling that her late lessons in cookery were to do her honor, went to preside over the coffeepot.

The tablecloth was soon spread with an inviting array of eatables and drinkables, prettily decorated with green leaves. Jo announced that the coffee was ready, and everyone settled themselves to a hearty meal.

"There's salt here, if you prefer it," said Laurie as he handed Jo a saucer of berries.

"Thank you! I prefer spiders," she replied, fishing up two unwary ones who had gone to a creamy death. "How dare you remind me of that horrid dinner party?" added Jo as they both laughed.

"What shall we do when we can't eat any more?" asked Laurie.

"Have games till it's cooler. I brought Authors, and I daresay Miss Kate knows something new and nice. Go and ask her. She's company, and you ought to stay with her more."

"Aren't you company, too? I thought she'd suit Brooke. But he keeps talking to Meg, and Kate just stares at them through that ridiculous glass of hers. I'm going, so you needn't try to preach propriety, for you can't do it, Jo."

Miss Kate did know several new games; and, as the girls would not, and the boys could not, eat any more, they all sat around on the grass to play Rigmarole.

"One person begins a story, any nonsense you like, and tells as long as he pleases, only taking care to stop short at some exciting point, when the next takes it up and does the same. It's very funny when well done, and makes a perfect jumble of tragical-comical stuff to laugh over. Please start it, Mr. Brooke," said Kate with a commanding gesture, which surprised Meg, who treated the tutor with as much respect as any other gentleman.

Mr. Brooke obediently began the story, and the others, one by one, took it up and carried it on.

"What a piece of nonsense we have made!" said Sallie,

after they had finished and laughed over their story. "Do you know how to play Truth?"

"What is it?" said Fred.

"Why, you pile up your hands, choose a number, and draw out in turn, and the person who draws at the number has to answer truly any questions put by the rest. It's great fun."

"Let's try it," said Jo. They did, but not for long. Jo stopped it with, "I think Truth is a very silly play. Let's have a sensible game of Authors, to refresh our minds."

An impromptu circus, fox and geese, and an amicable game of croquet finished the afternoon. At sunset the tent was struck, hampers packed, wickets pulled up, boats loaded, and the whole party floated down the river, singing at the tops of their voices.

On the lawn where it had gathered, the little party separated with cordial good-nights and good-byes, for the Vaughns were going to Canada. As the four sisters went home through the garden, Miss Kate looked after them, saying, without the patronizing tone in her voice, "In spite of their demonstrative manners, American girls are very nice when one really knows them."

"I quite agree with you," said Mr. Brooke.

11 • Secrets

Jo WAS VERY busy up in the garret, for the October days began to grow chilly, and the afternoons were short. For two or three hours the sun lay warmly in at the high window, showing Jo seated on the old sofa writing busily, with her papers spread out upon a trunk before her. Quite absorbed in her work, Jo scribbled away till the last page was filled, when she signed her name with a flourish and threw down her pen.

"There, I've done my best! If this doesn't suit, I shall have to wait till I can do better."

Lying back on the sofa, she read the manuscript carefully through, making dashes here and there and putting in many exclamation points; then she tied it up with a smart red ribbon and sat a minute looking at it with a sober, wistful expression, which plainly showed how earnest her work had been. Jo's desk up here was an old tin kitchen, which hung against the wall. In it she kept her papers and a few books. From this tin receptacle, Jo produced another manuscript and, putting both of them in her pocket, crept quietly downstairs.

She put on her hat and jacket as noiselessly as possible and, going to the back entry window, got out upon the roof of a low porch, swung herself down to the grassy bank, and took a roundabout way to the road. Once there, she composed herself, hailing a passing omnibus, and rolled away to town, looking very merry and mysterious.

On alighting, she went off at a great pace till she reached a certain number in a certain busy street. Having found the place with some difficulty, she went into the doorway, looked up the dirty stairs, and, after standing stock-still a minute, suddenly dived into the street and walked away as rapidly as she had come. This maneuver she repeated several times, to the great amusement of a black-eyed young gentleman lounging in the window of a building opposite. On returning for the third time, Jo gave herself a shake, pulled her hat over her eyes, and walked up the stairs, looking as if she were going to have all her teeth out.

There was a dentist's sign, among others, which adorned the entrance, and after staring a moment at the pair of artificial jaws which slowly opened and shut to draw attention to a fine set of teeth, the young gentleman put on his coat, took his hat, and went down to post himself in the opposite doorway, saying with a smile and a shiver, "It's like her to come alone, but if she has a bad time she'll need someone to help her home."

In ten minutes Jo came running downstairs with a very red face and the general appearance of a person who has just passed through a trying ordeal of some sort. When she saw the young gentleman she looked anything but pleased, and passed him with a nod.

But he followed, asking with an air of sympathy, "Did you have a bad time?"

"Not very."

"You got through quick."

"Yes, thank goodness!"

"Why did you go alone?"

"Didn't want anyone to know."

"You're the oddest fellow I ever saw. How many did you have out?"

Jo looked at her friend as if she did not understand him, then began to laugh, as if mightily amused at something.

"There are two which I want to have come out, but I must wait a week."

"What are you laughing at? You are up to some mischief, Jo," said Laurie, looking mystified.

"So are you. What were you doing, sir, up in that billiard saloon?"

"Begging your pardon, ma'am, it wasn't a billiard saloon, but a gymnasium, and I was taking a lesson in fencing."

"I'm glad of that!"

"Why?"

"You can teach me; and then, when we play *Hamlet*, you can be Laertes, and we'll make a fine thing of the fencing scene."

Laurie burst out into a hearty boy's laugh, which made several passersby smile.

Jo went on. "I am glad you were not in the saloon, Laurie, because I hope you never go to such places. Do you?"

"Not very often."

"I wish you wouldn't."

"It's no harm, Jo. I have billiards at home, but it's no fun unless you have good players. So, as I'm fond of it, I come sometimes and have a game with Ned Moffat or some of the other fellows."

"I did hope you'd stay respectable and be a satisfaction to your friends," said Jo, shaking her head.

"Can't a fellow take a little innocent amusement now and then without losing his respectability?" asked Laurie, looking nettled. "I like harmless larks now and then, don't you?"

"Yes, nobody minds them, so lark away. But don't get wild, will you?—or there will be an end to our good times. Mother wouldn't let us associate with fashionable young men."

"I'll be a double distilled saint."

"I can't bear saints. Just be a simple, honest, respectable boy, and we'll never desert you."

"Do you worry about me, Jo?"

"A little, when you look moody or discontented, as you sometimes do, for you've got such a strong will, if you once got started wrong, I'm afraid it would be hard to stop you."

Laurie walked on in silence a few minutes, and Jo watched him, wishing she had held her tongue, for his eyes looked angry, though his lips still smiled.

"Are you going to deliver lectures all the way home?" he asked presently.

"Of course not. Why?"

"Because if you are, I'll take a bus. If you are not, I'd like to walk with you and tell you something very interesting."

"I won't preach anymore, and I'd like to hear the news."

"Very well, then, come on. It's a secret, and if I tell you, you must tell me yours."

105

"I haven't got any," began Jo, but stopped suddenly, remembering that she had.

"You know you have. You can't hide anything—so up and ''fess,' or I won't tell," cried Laurie.

"Is your secret a nice one?"

"Oh, isn't it! All about people you know, and such fun! Come, you begin."

"You'll not say anything about it at home, will you?"

"Not a word."

"Well, I've left two stories with a newspaperman, and he's to give his answer next week," whispered Jo.

"Hurrah for Miss March, the celebrated American authoress!" cried Laurie, throwing up his hat and catching it again.

"Hush! It won't come to anything, I daresay. But I couldn't rest till I tried, and I said nothing about it, because I didn't want anyone else to be disappointed."

"It won't fail! Why, Jo, your stories are works of Shakespeare compared to half the rubbish that's published every day. Won't it be fun to see them in print! And shan't we feel proud of our authoress?"

Jo's eyes sparkled, for it's always nice to be believed in.

"What's your secret? Play fair, Teddy, or I'll never believe you again," she said.

"I may get into a scrape for telling. But I didn't promise not to, so I will, for I never feel easy in my mind till I've told you any plummy bit of news I get. I know where Meg's lost glove is."

"Is that all?"

"It's quite enough for the present, as you'll agree when I tell you where it is."

"Tell, then."

Laurie bent and whispered three words in Jo's ear, which produced a comical change. She stood and stared at him for a minute, looking both surprised and displeased, then walked on, saying sharply, "How do you know?"

"Saw it."

"Where?"

"Pocket."

"All this time?"

"Yes, isn't that romantic?"

"No, it's horrid."

"Don't you like it?"

"Of course I don't! It's ridiculous—it won't be allowed. My patience! What would Meg say?"

"I thought you'd be pleased."

"At the idea of anybody coming to take Meg away? No, thank you!" cried Jo. "I don't think secrets agree with me. I feel rumpled up in my mind since you told me all about that."

"Race down the hill with me, and you'll be all right," suggested Laurie.

No one was in sight; Jo darted away, leaving hat and comb behind her and scattering hairpins as she ran.

Laurie reached the goal first.

"I wish I were a horse," said Jo, dropping breathlessly down under a maple tree. "Then I could run for miles without getting out of breath. Go pick up my things, like the cherub you are."

Jo started bundling up her braids, hoping no one would pass by till she was tidy again. But Meg passed by, looking particularly ladylike in her state and festival suit.

"You have been running, Jo," she said reprovingly.

"How could you? When will you stop such romping ways?"

"Never till I'm old and stiff and have to use a crutch. Don't try to make me grow up before my time, Meg. It's hard enough to have you change so all of a sudden."

As she spoke, Jo bent over her work to hide the trembling of her lips; for lately she had felt that Margaret was fast getting to be a woman, and Laurie's secret made her dread the separation which must come sometime, and now seemed so near.

For a week or two Jo behaved so queerly that her sisters got quite bewildered. She rushed to the door when the postman rang; was rude to Mr. Brooke whenever they met; would sit looking at Meg with a woebegone face.

On the second Saturday Jo bounced into the room where the girls were sitting, sewing.

She laid herself on the sofa and affected to read from the newspaper she held.

"Have you anything interesting there?" asked Meg.

"Nothing but a story—doesn't amount to much, I guess," returned Jo, keeping the name of the newspaper hidden.

"You'd better read it aloud. That will amuse us and keep you out of mischief," said Amy in her most grown-up tone.

"What's the name?" asked Beth.

" 'The Rival Painters.' "

"That sounds well; read it," said Meg.

With a loud "hem!" and a long breath, Jo began to read very fast. The girls listened with interest, for the tale was romantic, and somewhat pathetic, as most of the characters died in the end.

109

"Who wrote it?" asked Beth, who had caught a glimpse of Jo's face.

Jo replied solemnly, "Your sister!"

"You?" cried Meg.

"It's very good," said Amy critically.

"I knew it! I knew it! Oh, my Jo, I *am* so proud!" And Beth ran to hug her sister and exult over her success.

"Tell us about it." "What will Father say?" "When did it come?" "How much did you get for it?" "Won't Laurie laugh?" cried the family all in one breath as they clustered about Jo, for these affectionate people made a jubilee over every little household joy.

"Stop jabbering, girls, and I'll tell you everything," said Jo. She told of how she had taken the stories to the newspaperman, and then added, "And when I went to get my answer the man said he liked them both, but they didn't pay beginners, only let them print in his paper, and noticed the stories. It was good practice, he said, and when the beginners improved, anyone would pay. So I let him have the two stories, and today this was sent to me, and I shall write more, and he's going to get the next paid for, and, oh, I am so happy, for in time I may be able to support myself and help the girls."

Jo's breath gave out here; and, wrapping her head in the paper, she bedewed her little story with a few natural tears, for to be independent and earn the praise of those she loved were the dearest wishes of her heart, and this seemed to be the first step toward that happy end.

12 • A Telegram

NOVEMBER is the most disagreeable month in the whole year," said Margaret, standing at the window one dull afternoon, looking out at the frostbitten garden.

"That's the reason I was born in it," observed Jo pensively, quite unconscious of the blot on her nose.

"If something very pleasant should happen now, we should think it a delightful month," said Beth, who took a hopeful view of everything, even November.

"I daresay, but nothing pleasant ever *does* happen in this family," said Meg, who was out of sorts. "We go grubbing along day after day, without a bit of change and very little fun. We might as well be in a treadmill."

"My patience, how blue we are!" cried Jo. "I don't much wonder, poor dear, for you see other girls having splendid times, while you grind, grind, year in and year out. Oh, don't I wish I could fix things for you as I do for my heroines! You're pretty enough and good enough, already, so I'd have some rich relation leave you a fortune unexpectedly. Then you'd dash out as an heiress, scorn everyone who had slighted you, go abroad, and come home My Lady Something, in a blaze of splendor and elegance."

111

"People don't have fortunes left them in that style nowadays. Men have to work, and women to marry for money. It's a dreadfully unjust world," said Meg bitterly.

"Jo and I are going to make fortunes for you all. Just wait ten years and see if we don't," said Amy, who sat in a corner making "mud pies," as Hannah called her little clay models of birds, fruit, and faces.

"Can't wait, and I'm afraid I haven't much faith in ink and dirt, though I'm grateful for your good intentions."

Meg sighed and turned to the frostbitten garden again; Jo groaned and leaned both elbows on the table in a despondent attitude; but Amy spatted away energetically; and Beth, who sat at the other window, said, smiling, "Two pleasant things are going to happen right away. Marmee is coming down the street, and Laurie is tramping through the garden as if he had something nice to tell."

In they both came, Mrs. March with her usual question, "Any letter from Father, girls?" and Laurie to say, in his persuasive way, "Won't some of you come for a drive? I've been pegging away at mathematics till my head is in a muddle, and I'm going to freshen my wits by a brisk turn. It's a dull day, but the air isn't bad, and I'm going to take Brooke home. So it will be gay inside, if it isn't out. Come, Jo, you and Beth will go, won't you?"

"Much obliged, but I'm busy." And Meg whisked out her workbasket, for she had agreed with her mother that it was best, for her at least, not to go driving too often with the young gentleman.

"We three will be ready in a minute," cried Amy, running away to wash her hands.

"Can I do anything for you, Madam Mother?" asked

Laurie, leaning over Mrs. March's chair with the affectionate look and tone he always gave her.

"No, thank you, except call at the office, if you'll be so kind. It's our day for a letter, and the penny postman hasn't been. Father is as regular as the sun, but there's some delay on the way, perhaps."

A sharp ring interrupted her, and, a minute after, Hannah came in with a letter.

"It's one of them horrid telegraph things, mum," she said, handling it as if she was afraid it would explode and do some damage.

At the word "telegraph," Mrs. March snatched it, read the two lines it contained, and dropped back into her chair as white as if the little paper had sent a bullet to her heart. Laurie dashed downstairs for water, while Meg and Hannah supported her, and Jo read aloud, in a frightened voice:

"Mrs. March:
　　"Your husband is very ill. Come at once.
　　　　　　　　　　　"S. Hale,
　　　　"Blank Hospital, Washington"

How still the room was as they listened breathlessly! How strangely the day darkened outside! And how suddenly the whole world seemed to change as the girls gathered about their mother, feeling as if all the happiness and support of their lives was about to be taken from them. Mrs. March was herself again directly, read the message over, and stretched out her arms to her daughters, saying, in a tone they never forgot, "I shall go at once, but it may be too late. Oh, children, children! Help me to bear it!"

For several minutes there was nothing but the sound

113

of sobbing in the room, mingled with broken words of comfort, tender assurances of help, hopeful whispers that died away in tears. Poor Hannah was the first to recover, and with unconscious wisdom she set all the rest a good example, for, with her, work was the panacea for most afflictions.

"The Lord keep the dear man! I won't waste no time a-cryin', but git your things ready right away, mum," she said heartily as she wiped her face on her apron, gave her mistress a warm shake of the hand with her own hard one, and went away to work like three women in one.

"She's right. There's no time for tears now. Be calm, girls, and let me think."

They tried to be calm, poor things, as their mother sat up, looking pale, but steady, and put away her grief to think and plan for them.

"Where's Laurie?" she asked presently, when she had collected her thoughts and decided on the first duties to be done.

"Here, ma'am. Oh, let me do something!" cried the boy, hurrying from the next room, whither he had withdrawn, feeling that their first sorrow was too sacred for even his friendly eyes to see.

"Send a telegram saying I will come at once. The next train goes early in the morning. I'll take that."

"What else? The horses are ready—I can go anywhere, do anything," he said, looking as if he was ready to fly to the ends of the earth.

"Leave a note at Aunt March's. Jo, give me that pen and some paper."

Tearing off the blank side of one of her newly copied pages, Jo drew the table before her mother, well knowing that money for the long, sad journey must be borrowed, and feeling as if she could do anything to add a little to the sum for her father.

"Now go, dear. But don't kill yourself driving at a desperate pace. There is no need of that."

Mrs. March's warning was evidently thrown away, for five minutes later Laurie tore by the window on his own fleet horse, riding as if for his life.

"Jo, run to the rooms and tell Mrs. King that I can't come. On the way get these things. I'll put them down. They'll be needed, and I must go prepared for nursing. Hospital stores are not always good. Beth, go and ask Mr. Laurence for a couple of bottles of old wine. I'm not too proud to beg for Father—he shall have the best of everything. Amy, tell Hannah to get down the black trunk. And Meg, come and help me find my things, for I am half bewildered."

Everyone scattered, like leaves before a gust of wind. Mr. Laurence came hurrying back with Beth, bringing every comfort he could think of for the invalid and friendliest promises of protection for the girls during the mother's absence, which comforted her very much.

Then came Mr. Brooke.

"I'm very sorry to hear of this, Miss March," he said to Meg in the kind, quiet tone which sounded very pleasant to her perturbed spirit. "I came to offer myself as escort for your mother. Mr. Laurence has commissions for me in Washington, and it will give me real satisfaction to be of some service to Mrs. March."

Down dropped the rubbers, and the tea was very near following as Meg put out her hand, with a face so full of gratitude that Mr. Brooke would have felt repaid for a much greater sacrifice than the trifling one of time and comfort which he was about to make.

"How kind you all are! Mother will accept, I'm sure, and it will be such a relief to know that she has someone to take care of her. Thank you very, very much."

Meg spoke earnestly and forgot herself entirely till something in the brown eyes looking down at her made her remember the cooling tea and lead the way into the parlor, saying she would call Mother.

Everything was arranged by the time Laurie returned with a note from Aunt March, enclosing the desired sum and a few lines repeating what she had often said before: that she had always told them it was absurd of March to go into the army, always predicted that no good would come of it, and she hoped they would take her advice next time.

The short afternoon wore away; all the other errands were done, and Meg and her mother were busy with some needlework, while Beth and Amy got tea and Hannah finished her ironing with what she called a "slap and a bang." But still Jo did not come. They began to get anxious; and Laurie went off to find her, for no one ever knew what freak Jo might take into her head. He missed her, however, and she came walking in with a very queer expression of countenance; for there was a mixture of fun and fear, satisfaction and regret in it, which puzzled the family as much as did the roll of bills she laid before her mother, saying, with a little choke in her voice, "That's to help make Father comfortable!"

"My dear, where did you get it? Twenty-five dollars! Jo, I hope you haven't done anything rash!"

"No, it's mine honestly. I didn't beg, borrow, or steal it.

I earned it, and I don't think you'll blame me, for I only sold what was my own."

As she spoke, Jo took off her bonnet, and a general outcry arose, for all her abundant hair was cut short.

"Your hair! Your beautiful hair!" "Oh, Jo, how could you? Your one beauty!" "My dear girl, there was no need of this!" "She doesn't look like my Jo anymore, but I love her all the more dearly for it!"

As everyone exclaimed and Beth hugged the cropped head tenderly, Jo assumed an indifferent air, which did not deceive anyone a particle, and said, rumpling up the brown bush and trying to look as if she liked it, "It doesn't affect the fate of the nation, so don't wail, Beth. It will be good for my vanity. I was getting too proud of my wig. It will do my brains good to have that mop taken off. My head feels deliciously light and cool. And the barber said I could soon have a curly crop, which will be boyish, becoming, and easy to keep in order. I'm satisfied. So please take the money and let's have supper, for I'm starved."

"Tell me all about it, Jo. I am not quite satisfied, but I can't blame you, for I know how willingly you sacrificed your vanity, as you call it, to your love. But, my dear, it was not necessary, and I'm afraid you will regret it one of these days," said Mrs. March.

"No, I won't!" returned Jo stoutly, feeling much relieved that her prank was not entirely condemned.

"What made you do it?" asked Amy, who would as soon have thought of cutting off her head as her pretty hair.

"Well, I was wild to do something for Father," replied Jo as they gathered about the table, for healthy young people can eat even in the midst of trouble. "I hate to borrow as much as Mother does, and I knew Aunt March would croak. She always does, if you ask for a ninepence. Meg gave all her quarterly salary toward the rent, and I only got some clothes with mine. So I felt wicked and was bound to have some money, if I sold the nose off my face to get it."

"You needn't feel wicked, my child. You had no winter things, and got the simplest, with your own hard earnings," said Mrs. March, with a look that warmed Jo's heart.

"I hadn't the least idea of selling my hair at first, but as I went along I kept thinking *what* I could do, and feeling as if I'd like to dive into some of the rich stores and help myself. In a barber's window I saw tails of hair with the prices marked. One black tail, longer but not so thick as mine, was forty dollars. It came over me all of a sudden that I had one thing to make money of, and without stopping to think, I walked in, asked if they bought hair, and what they would give for mine."

"I don't see how you dared to do it," said Beth in awe.

"Oh, the barber stared at first, as if he wasn't used to having girls bounce into his shop and ask him to buy their hair. He said he didn't care much about mine—it wasn't a fashionable color, and he never paid much for it in the first place; the work put into it made it dear, and so on. It was getting late, and I was afraid if it wasn't done right away that I shouldn't have it done at all, and you know, when I start to do a thing, I hate to give it up. So I begged him to take it, and told him why I was in such a hurry. It was silly, I daresay, but it changed his mind, for I got rather excited and told the story in my topsy-turvy way, and his wife heard and said so kindly, 'Take it, and oblige the young lady. I'd do as much for our Jimmy any day if I had a spire of hair worth selling.'"

119

"Who was Jimmy?" asked Amy.

"Her son, she said, who is in the army. How friendly such things make strangers feel, don't they? She talked away all the time the man clipped, and diverted my mind nicely."

"Didn't you feel dreadful when the first cut came?" asked Meg with a shiver.

"I took a last look at my hair while the man got his things, and that was the end of it. I never snivel over trifles like that. I will confess, though, I felt queer when I saw the dear old hair laid out on the table and felt only the short, rough ends on my head. The woman picked up a long lock for me to keep. I'll give it to you, Marmee, just to remember past glories by."

Mrs. March folded the wavy, chestnut lock and laid it away with a short gray one in her desk. She only said, "Thank you, deary," but something in her face made the girls change the subject and talk as cheerfully as they could about Mr. Brooke's kindness, the prospect of a fine day tomorrow, and the happy times they would have when Father came home.

No one wanted to go to bed when, at ten o'clock, Mrs. March put by the last finished job and said, "Come, girls." Beth went to the piano and played the father's favorite hymn; all began bravely but broke down one by one till Beth was left alone, singing with all her heart, for to her music was always a sweet consoler.

"Go to bed and don't talk, for we must be up early, and shall need all the sleep we can get. Good night, my darlings," said Mrs. March as the hymn ended, for no one cared to try another.

They kissed her quietly and went to bed as silently as

if the dear invalid lay in the next room.

The clocks were striking midnight and the rooms were very still as a figure glided quietly from bed to bed, smoothing a coverlid here, settling a pillow there, and pausing to look long and tenderly at each unconscious face, to kiss each with lips that mutely blessed, and to pray the fervent prayers which only mothers utter. As she lifted the curtain to look out into the dreary night, the moon broke suddenly from behind the clouds and shone upon her like a bright, benignant face, which seemed to whisper in the silence, "Be comforted, dear heart! There is always light behind the clouds."

13 • Letters

IN THE COLD, gray dawn the sisters lit their lamp and read their chapter with an earnestness never felt before, for now the shadow of a real trouble had come, showing them how rich in sunshine their lives had been. The little books were full of help and comfort; and, as they dressed, they agreed to say good-bye cheerfully, hopefully, and send their mother on her anxious journey unsaddened by tears or complaints from them. Everything seemed very strange when they went down, so dim and still outside, so full of light and bustle within. Breakfast at that early hour seemed odd, and even Hannah's familiar face looked unnatural as she flew about her kitchen with her nightcap on. The big trunk stood ready in the hall, Mother's cloak and bonnet lay on the sofa, and Mother herself sat trying to eat, but looking so pale and worn with sleeplessness and anxiety that the girls found it very hard to keep their resolution. Meg's eyes kept filling in spite of herself, Jo was obliged to hide her face in the kitchen roller more than once, and the little girls' young faces wore a grave, troubled expression, as if sorrow was a new experience to them.

Nobody talked much, but as the time drew very near

and they sat waiting for the carriage, Mrs. March said to the girls, who were all busied about her, one folding her shawl, another smoothing out the strings of her bonnet, a third putting on her overshoes, and a fourth fastening up her traveling bag: "Children, I leave you to Hannah's care, and Mr. Laurence's protection. Hannah is faithfulness itself, and our good neighbor will guard you as if you were his own. I have no fears for you, yet I am anxious that you should take this trouble in the right way.

"Don't grieve and fret when I am gone, or think that you can comfort yourselves by being idle and trying to forget. Go on with your work as usual, for work is a blessed solace. Hope and keep busy; and whatever happens, remember that you never can be fatherless."

"Yes, Mother."

"Meg, dear, be prudent, watch over your sisters, consult Hannah, and, in any perplexity, go to Mr. Laurence. Be patient, Jo, don't get despondent or do rash things; write to me often, and be my brave girl, ready to help and cheer us all. Beth, comfort yourself with your music and be faithful to the little home duties. And you, Amy, help all you can, be obedient, and keep happy safe at home."

"We will, Mother! We will!"

The rattle of an approaching carriage made them all start and listen. That was the hard minute, but the girls stood it well; no one cried; no one ran away or uttered a lamentation, though their hearts were very heavy as they sent loving messages to Father, remembering, all the while, that it might be too late to deliver them. They kissed their mother quietly, clung about her tenderly, and tried to wave their hands cheerfully when she drove away.

Laurie and his grandfather came over to see her off,

and Mr. Brooke looked so strong and sensible and kind that the girls christened him "Mr. Greatheart" on the spot.

"Good-bye, my darlings! God bless and keep us all," whispered Mrs. March as she kissed one dear little face after the other and hurried into the carriage.

As she rolled away, the sun came out, and, looking back, she saw it shining on the group at the gate, like a good omen. They saw it, also, and smiled and waved their hands; and the last thing she beheld, as she turned the corner, was the four bright faces and behind them, like a bodyguard, old Mr. Laurence, faithful Hannah, and devoted Laurie.

"How kind everyone is to us," she said, turning to find fresh proof of it in the respectful sympathy of the young man's face.

"I don't see how they can help it," returned Mr. Brooke, laughing so infectiously that Mrs. March could not help smiling; and so the long journey began with the good omens of sunshine, smiles, and cheerful words.

"I feel as if there had been an earthquake," said Jo as their neighbors went home to breakfast, leaving the girls to rest and refresh themselves.

"It seems as if half the house was gone," added Meg.

Beth opened her lips to say something, but could only point to the pile of nicely mended hose which lay on Mother's table, showing that even in her last hurried moments she had thought and worked for them. It was a little thing, but it went straight to their hearts; and in spite of their brave resolutions, they all broke down and cried bitterly.

Hannah wisely allowed them to relieve their feelings; and when the shower showed signs of clearing up, she came to the rescue, armed with a coffeepot.

"Now, my dear young ladies, remember what your ma said and don't fret. Come and have a cup of coffee all round, and then let's fall to work and be a credit to the family."

Coffee was a treat, and Hannah showed great tact in making it that morning. No one could resist her persuasive nods or the fragrant invitation issuing from the nose of the coffeepot. They drew up to the table, exchanged their handkerchiefs for napkins, and in ten minutes were all right again.

" 'Hope and keep busy'—that's the motto for us. So let's see who will remember it best. I shall go to Aunt March, as usual. Oh, won't she lecture, though!" said Jo as she sipped, with returning spirit.

"I shall go to my Kings, though I'd much rather stay at home and attend to things here," said Meg, wishing she hadn't made her eyes so red.

"No need of that. Beth and I can keep house perfectly well," put in Amy with an important air.

"Hannah will tell us what to do, and we'll have everything nice when you come home," added Beth, getting out her mop and dish tub without delay.

"I think anxiety is very interesting," observed Amy, eating sugar pensively.

The girls couldn't help laughing, and felt better for it, though Meg shook her head at the young lady who could find consolation in a sugar bowl.

When Jo and Meg went out to their daily tasks, they looked sorrowfully back at the window where they were accustomed to seeing their mother's face. It was gone; but Beth had remembered the little household ceremony, and there she was, nodding away at them like a rosy-faced mandarin.

"That's so like my Beth!" said Jo, waving her hat with a grateful face. "Good-bye, Meggy. I hope the Kings won't train today. Don't fret about Father, dear," she added as they parted.

"And I hope Aunt March won't croak. Your hair *is* becoming, and it looks very boyish and nice," returned Meg, trying not to smile at the curly head, which looked comically small on her tall sister's shoulders.

"That's my only comfort." And, touching her hat *à la* Laurie, away went Jo, feeling like a shorn sheep on a wintry day.

News from their father comforted the girls very much, for, though dangerously ill, the presence of the best and tenderest of nurses had already done him good. Mr. Brooke sent a bulletin every day, and, as the head of the family, Meg insisted on reading the dispatches, which grew more and more cheering as the week passed. At first everyone was eager to write, and plump envelopes were carefully poked into the letter box by one or other of the sisters, who felt rather important with their Washington correspondence. As one of these packets contained characteristic notes from the party, we will rob an imaginary mail and read them:

My dearest Mother,

It is impossible to tell you how happy your last letter made us, for the news was so good we couldn't help laughing and crying over it. How very kind Mr. Brooke is, and how fortunate that Mr. Laurence's business detains him near you so long, since he is so useful to you and Father. The girls are all as good as gold. Jo helps me with the sewing and insists on doing all sorts of hard jobs. I should be afraid she might overdo, if I didn't know that her "moral fit" wouldn't last long. Beth is as regular about her tasks as a clock. Amy minds me nicely, and I take great care of her. Mr. Laurence watches over us like a motherly old hen, as Jo says, and Laurie is very kind and neighborly. We are all well and busy, but we long, day and night, to have you back. Give my dearest love to Father, and believe me, ever your own

Meg

This note, prettily written on scented paper, was a great contrast to the next, which was scribbled on a big sheet of thin, foreign paper, ornamented with blots and all manner of flourishes and curly-tailed letters:

My precious Marmee,

Three cheers for dear old Father! Brooke was a trump to telegraph right off and let us know the minute he was better. I rushed up garret when the letter came and tried to thank God for being so good to us. We have such funny times; and now I can enjoy 'em, for everyone is so desperately good, it's like living in a nest of turtledoves. You'd laugh to see Meg head the table and try to be motherish. The children are regular archangels, and I—well, I'm Jo, and never shall be anything else. Oh, I must tell you that I came near having a quarrel with Laurie. I freed my mind about a silly little thing, and he was offended. I was right, but didn't speak as I ought, and he marched home, saying he wouldn't come again till I begged pardon. I declared I wouldn't, and got mad. It lasted all day. I felt bad and wanted you very much. Laurie and I are both so proud, it's hard to beg pardon; but I thought he'd come to it, for I was in the right. He didn't, and just at night I remembered what you had said when Amy fell into the river. I read my little book, felt better, resolved not to let the sun set on my anger, and ran over to tell Laurie I was sorry. I met him at the gate, coming for the same thing. We both laughed, begged each other's pardon, and felt all good and comfortable again.

I made a "pome" yesterday, when I was helping Hannah wash, and as Father likes my silly little things, I put it in to amuse him. Give him the lovingest hug that ever was, and kiss yourself a dozen times, for your

Topsy-Turvy Jo

Dear Mother,

There is only room for me to send my love and some pressed pansies from the root I have been keeping safe in the house for Father to see. I read every morning, try to be good all day, and sing myself to sleep with Father's tune. Everyone is very kind, and we are as happy as we can be without you. Amy wants the rest of the page, so I must stop. I didn't forget to cover the holders, and I wind the clock and air the rooms every day.

Kiss dear Father on the cheek he calls mine. Oh, do come soon to your loving

Little Beth

Ma Chere Mamma,

We are all well I do my lessons always and never corroberate the girls—Meg says I mean contradick so I put in both words and you can take the properest. Meg is a great comfort to me and lets me have jelly every night at tea. Laurie is not as respekful as he ought to be now I am almost in my teens, he calls me Chick and hurts my feelings by talking French to me very fast when I say Merci or Bon jour as Hattie King does. I do wish Hannah would put more starch in my aprons and have buckwheats every day. Can't she? Didn't I make that interrigation point nice? Meg says my punchtuation and spelling are disgraceful and I am mortyfied but dear me I have so many things to do, I can't stop. Adieu, I send heaps of love to Papa.

Your affectionate daughter,
Amy Curtis March

There were letters from Hannah and Laurie and Mr. Laurence, too, and you may be sure that they cheered the mother and sped the recovery of the father.

14 · Little Faithful

AFTER THE FIRST week, relieved of their first anxiety about their father, the girls insensibly relaxed and fell back into all the old ways—except Beth. All her little duties were faithfully done each day, and many of her sisters', also, for they were forgetful. They did not forget their motto, but hoping and keeping busy seemed to grow easier; and after such tremendous exertions, they felt that Endeavor deserved a holiday and gave it a good many.

"Meg, I wish you'd go and see the Hummels. You know Mother told us not to forget them," said Beth, ten days after Mrs. March's departure.

"I'm too tired to go this afternoon," replied Meg, rocking comfortably as she sewed.

"Can't you, Jo?" asked Beth.

"Too stormy for me. I've got a cold, you know."

"I thought it was most well."

"It's well enough for me to go out with Laurie, but not well enough to go to the Hummels'," said Jo, laughing but looking a little ashamed of her inconsistency.

"Why don't you go yourself?" asked Meg.

"I *have* been every day, but the baby is sick and I don't know what to do for it. Mrs. Hummel goes away to work, and Lottchen takes care of it. But it gets sicker and sicker; I think you or Hannah ought to go."

Beth spoke earnestly, and Meg promised that she would go tomorrow.

"Ask Hannah for some nice little mess and take it round, Beth. The air will do you good," said Jo, adding apologetically, "I'd go, but I want to finish my story."

"My head aches, and I'm tired. So I thought maybe some of you would go," said Beth.

"Amy will be in presently, and she will run down for us," suggested Meg.

"Well, I'll rest a little and wait for her."

So Beth lay down on the sofa, the others returned to their work, and the Hummels were forgotten. An hour passed. Amy did not come, Meg went to her room to try on a new dress, Jo was absorbed in her story, and Hannah was sound asleep before the kitchen fire when Beth quietly put on her hood, filled her basket with odds and ends for the poor children, and went out into the chilly air with a heavy head and a grieved look in her patient eyes. It was late when she came back, and no one saw her creep upstairs and shut herself in her mother's room.

Half an hour later, Jo went to "Mother's closet" for something and there found Beth sitting on the medicine chest, looking very grave, with red eyes and a camphor bottle in her hand.

"Christopher Columbus! What's the matter?" cried Jo. Beth put out her hand as if to warn her off, and asked quickly, "You've had scarlet fever, haven't you?"

"Years ago, when Meg did. Why?"

"Then I'll tell you—oh, Jo, the baby's dead!"

"What baby?"

"Mrs. Hummel's. It died in my lap before she got home," cried Beth, with a sob.

"My poor dear, how dreadful for you! I ought to have gone," said Jo, with a remorseful face, taking her sister in her lap as she sat down in her mother's big chair.

"It wasn't dreadful, Jo, only sad! I saw in a minute that it was sicker, but Lottchen said her mother had gone for a doctor. So I took the baby and let Lotty rest. It seemed asleep, but all of a sudden it gave a little cry, and trembled, and then lay very still. I tried to warm its feet, and Lotty gave it some milk, but it didn't stir, and I knew it was dead."

"Don't cry, dear! What did you do?"

"I just sat and held it softly till Mrs. Hummel came with the doctor. He said it was dead, and looked at Heinrich and Minna, who have got sore throats. 'Scarlet fever, ma'am; ought to have called me before,' he said crossly. Mrs. Hummel told him she was poor, and had tried to cure the baby herself, but now it was too late, and she could only ask him to help the others and trust to charity for his pay. He smiled then and was kinder, but it was very sad, and I cried with them till he turned round all of a sudden and told me to go home and take belladonna right away, or I'd have the fever."

"No, you won't!" cried Jo, hugging her close, with a frightened look. "Oh, Beth, if you should be sick I never could forgive myself! What *shall* I do?"

"Don't be frightened. I guess I shan't have it badly. I looked in Mother's book and saw that it begins with headache, sore throat, and queer feelings like mine. So I took some belladonna, and I feel better," said Beth, laying her hands on her hot forehead and trying to look well.

"If Mother were only at home!" exclaimed Jo, seizing the book and feeling that Washington was an immense way off. She read a page, looked at Beth, felt her head, peeped into her throat, and then said gravely, "You've been over to see the baby every day for more than a week and among the others who are going to have it. So I'm afraid you're going to have it, Beth. I'll call Hannah; she knows all about sickness."

"Don't let Amy come. She never had it, and I should hate to give it to her. Can't you and Meg have it over again?" asked Beth anxiously.

"I guess not. Don't care if I do. Serve me right, selfish pig, to let you go, and stay writing rubbish myself!" muttered Jo as she went to consult Hannah.

The good soul was wide-awake in a minute and took the lead at once, assuring Jo that there was no need to worry; everyone had scarlet fever, and, if rightly treated, nobody died; all of which Jo believed, and felt much relieved as they went up to call Meg.

"Now, I'll tell you what we'll do," said Hannah, when she had examined and questioned Beth. "We will have Dr. Bangs, just to take a look at you, dear, and see that we start right. Then we'll send Amy off to Aunt March's for a spell, to keep her out of harm's way, and one of you girls can stay at home and amuse Beth for a day or two."

"I shall stay, of course; I'm oldest," began Meg, looking anxious and self-reproachful.

"I shall, because it's my fault she is sick. I told Mother I'd do all the errands, and I haven't done as I promised," said Jo decidedly.

"Which will you have, Beth? There ain't no need of but one," said Hannah.

"Jo, please," said Beth, leaning her head against her sister.

"I'll go and tell Amy," said Meg, feeling a little hurt, yet rather relieved on the whole, for she did not like nursing, and Jo did.

Amy rebelled outright and passionately declared that she had rather have the fever than go to Aunt March. Laurie walked into the parlor to find Amy sobbing, with her head in the sofa cushions. She told the story, expecting to be consoled; but Laurie only put his hands in his pockets and walked about the room, whistling softly, as he knit his brows in deep thought. Presently he sat down beside her and said in his most wheedlesome tone, "Now, be a sensible little woman and do as they say. No, don't cry, but hear what a jolly plan I've got. You go to Aunt March's, and I'll come and take you out every day, driving or walking, and we'll have capital times. Won't that be better than moping here?"

"I don't wish to be sent off as if I was in the way," began Amy in an injured voice.

"Bless your heart, child! It's to keep you well. You don't want to be sick, do you?"

"No, I'm sure I don't. But I daresay I shall be, for I've been with Beth all this time."

"That's the very reason you ought to go away at once, so that you may escape it. Change of air and care will keep you well, I daresay. Or if it doesn't entirely, you will have the fever more lightly. I advise you to be off as soon as you can, for scarlet fever is no joke, miss."

"But it's dull at Aunt March's, and she is so cross," said Amy, looking rather frightened.

"It won't be dull with me popping in every day to tell

you how Beth is and take you out gallivanting. The old lady likes me, and I'll be as clever as possible to her, so she won't peck at us, whatever we do."

"Will you take me out in the trotting wagon with Puck?"

"On my honor as a gentleman."

"And come every single day?"

"See if I don't."

"And bring me back the minute Beth is well?"

"The identical minute."

"And go to the theater, truly?"

"A dozen theaters, if we may."

"Well—I guess—I will," said Amy slowly.

"Good girl! Sing out for Meg, and tell her you'll give in," said Laurie.

Meg and Jo came running down to behold the miracle which had been wrought.

"How is the little dear?" asked Laurie. Beth was his especial pet, and he felt much more anxious about her than he liked to show.

"She is lying down on Mother's bed and feels better. The baby's death troubled her, but I daresay she has only got cold. Hannah *says* she thinks so, but she *looks* worried, and that makes me fidgety," answered Meg.

"Tell me, Jo, if I shall telegraph to your mother, or do anything," said Laurie.

"That is what troubles me," said Jo. "I think we ought to tell her if Beth is really ill, but Hannah says we mustn't, for Mother can't leave Father, and it will only make them anxious."

"Suppose you ask Grandfather after the doctor has been here," suggested Laurie.

"We will," said Meg. "Jo, go and get Dr. Bangs at once.

135

We can't decide anything until he has been."

"Stay where you are, Jo. I'm errand boy in this establishment," said Laurie, taking up his cap.

"I'm afraid you are busy," began Meg.

"No, I've done my lessons for the day."

Dr. Bangs came, said Beth had symptoms of the fever, but thought she would have it lightly. Amy was ordered off at once; she departed in great state, with Jo and Laurie as escort.

Aunt March received them with her usual hospitality. Jo told her story.

"No more than I expected, if you are allowed to go poking about among poor folks. Amy can stay and make herself useful if she isn't sick."

Amy was on the point of crying, but Laurie slyly pulled the parrot's tail, which caused Polly to call out, "Go away. No boys allowed here!"

Amy laughed instead.

"What do you hear from your mother?" asked the old lady gruffly.

"Father is much better," replied Jo.

"Oh, is he? Well, that won't last long, I fancy. March never had any stamina," was the cheerful reply.

I don't think I can bear it, but I'll try, thought Amy as she was left alone with Aunt March.

"Get along, you're a fright!" screamed Polly, and at that rude speech Amy could not restrain a sniff.

15 · Dark Days

BETH DID HAVE the fever and was much sicker than any-one but Hannah and the doctor suspected. Meg stayed at home, lest she should infect the Kings, and kept house, feeling very anxious and a little guilty when she wrote letters in which no mention was made of Beth's illness. But Hannah wouldn't hear of "Mrs. March bein' told, and worried just for sech a trifle." Jo devoted herself to Beth day and night, not a hard task, for Beth was very patient and bore her pain uncomplainingly as long as she could control herself. But there came a time when during the fever fits she began to talk in a hoarse, broken voice, to play on the coverlet as if on her beloved little piano, and try to sing with a throat so swollen that there was no music left; a time when she did not know the familiar faces round her, but addressed them by wrong names and called imploringly for her mother. Then Jo grew frightened, Meg begged to be allowed to write the truth, and even Hannah said she "would think of it, though there was no danger *yet.*" A letter from Washington added to their trouble, for Mr. March had had a relapse and could not think of coming home for a long while.

How dark the days seemed now, how sad and lonely

the house, and how heavy the hearts of the sisters as they worked and waited, while the shadow of death hovered over the once happy home! Then it was that Margaret, sitting alone with tears dropping often on her work, felt how rich she had been in things more precious than any luxuries money could buy—in love, protection, peace, and health, the real blessings of life. Then it was that Jo learned to see the beauty and sweetness of Beth's nature, to feel how deep and tender a place she filled in all hearts. And Amy, in her exile, longed eagerly to be at home that she might work for Beth, feeling now that no service would be hard or irksome, and remembering with regretful grief how many neglected tasks those willing hands had done for her.

Laurie haunted the house like a restless ghost; Mr. Laurence locked the grand piano, because he could not bear to be reminded of the young neighbor who used to make the twilight so pleasant for him. The milkman, baker, grocer, and butcher inquired how she did; poor Mrs. Hummel came to beg pardon for her selfishness and to get a shroud for Minna; the neighbors sent all sorts of comforts and good wishes.

The first of December was a wintry day indeed to them, for a bitter wind blew, snow fell fast, and the year seemed getting ready for its death. When Dr. Bangs came that morning, he looked long at Beth, held the hot hand in both his own a minute, and laid it gently down, saying to Hannah in a low tone, "If Mrs. March *can* leave her husband, she'd better be sent for."

Hannah nodded without speaking; Meg dropped into a chair; and Jo ran to the parlor, snatched up the telegram, and throwing on her things, rushed out into the storm. She was soon back. and while she was noiselessly taking off her cloak, Laurie came in with a letter saying that Mr. March was mending again. Jo read it thankfully, but her face was so full of misery, anyway, that Laurie asked quickly, "What is it? Is Beth worse?"

"I've sent for Mother."

"Good for you, Jo! Did you do it on your own responsibility?" Laurie asked, helping her take off her boots.

"No, the doctor told us to."

"Oh, Jo, it's not so bad as that!" cried Laurie.

"Yes, it is. She doesn't know us. She doesn't even talk about the flocks of green doves, as she calls the vine leaves on the wall; she doesn't look like my Beth, and there's nobody to help us bear it—Mother and Father both gone, and God seems so far away I can't find Him."

As the tears streamed down poor Jo's cheeks, she stretched out her hand in a helpless sort of way, and Laurie took it in his, whispering, with a lump in his throat, "I'm here. Hold on to me, Jo!"

Soon she dried the tears and looked up with grateful face.

"Thank you, Teddy, I'm better now. I don't feel so forlorn, and will try to bear it if it comes."

"Poor girl! You're worn out. It isn't like you to be forlorn. Stop a bit. I'll hearten you up in a jiffy."

Laurie went off two stairs at a time, and Jo laid her wearied head down on Beth's little brown hood, which no one had thought to remove from the table where she had left it. It must have possessed some magic, for the submissive spirit of its gentle owner seemed to enter into Jo; and, when Laurie came running down with a glass of wine, she took it with a smile and said bravely, "I drink—

139

Health to my Beth! You are a good doctor, Teddy, and *such* a comfortable friend. How can I ever pay you?" she added as the wine refreshed her body and heartened her.

"I'll send in my bill by and by, and tonight I'll give you something that will warm the cockles of your heart better than quarts of wine," said Laurie, beaming at her with a face full of suppressed satisfaction at something.

"What is it?" cried Jo.

"I telegraphed to your mother yesterday, and Brooke answered she'd come at once, and she'll be here tonight, and everything will be all right. Aren't you glad I did it?"

"Oh, Laurie! Oh, Mother! I *am* so glad!" And Jo electrified Laurie by throwing her arms round his neck and clinging to him joyfully. Laurie, though decidedly amazed, patted her back reassuringly and, finding that she was recovering, followed it up with a bashful kiss or two, which brought Jo round to her senses. She put him gently away, saying breathlessly, "Oh, don't! I didn't mean to. It was dreadful of me. Tell me about it, and don't give me wine again. It makes me act so."

"I don't mind!" laughed Laurie as he settled his tie. "Why, you see I got fidgety, and so did Grandpa. We thought Hannah was overdoing the authority business, and your mother ought to know. Your mother will come, I know, and the train is in at two A.M. I shall go for her."

"Laurie, you're an angel! How shall I ever thank you?"

"Fly at me again. I rather like it," said Laurie, looking mischievous—a thing he had not done for a fortnight.

"That's the interferingest chap I ever see, but I forgive him and do hope Mrs. March is coming on right away," said Hannah, with an air of relief, when Jo told her the good news.

A breath of fresh air seemed to blow through the house; everything seemed to feel a hopeful change. All day Jo and Meg hovered over Beth, watching, waiting, hoping, and trusting in God and Mother; and all day the snow fell, the bitter wind raged, and the hours dragged slowly by. Every time the clock struck, the sisters, still sitting on either side of the bed, looked at each other with brightening eyes, for each hour brought help nearer. The doctor had been in to say that some change for better or worse would probably take place about midnight, at which time he would return.

Hannah, quite worn out, lay down on the sofa at the bed's foot and fell fast asleep. Mr. Laurence marched to and fro in the parlor; Laurie lay on the rug, staring into the fire.

Meg and Jo never forgot that night, for no sleep came to them as they kept their watch.

As the clock struck twelve, they fancied a change passed over Beth's wan face. Weary Hannah slept on, and no one but the sisters saw the pale shadow which seemed to fall upon the little bed. An hour went by and nothing happened except Laurie's quiet departure for the station.

It was past two when Jo, who stood at the window, thinking how dreary the world looked in its winding sheet of snow, heard a movement by the bed, and, turning quickly, saw Meg kneeling before their mother's easy chair, with her face hidden. A dreadful fear passed coldly over Jo as she thought, "Beth is dead, and Meg is afraid to tell me."

She went back to her post in an instant, and to her excited eyes a great change seemed to have taken place. The fever flush and the look of pain were gone, and the beloved little face looked so pale and peaceful in its utter repose that Jo felt no desire to weep or to lament. Leaning low over this dearest of her sisters, she kissed the damp forehead and softly whispered, "Good-bye, my Beth, good-bye!"

As if waked by the stir, Hannah started out of her sleep, hurried to the bed, looked at Beth, felt her hands, listened at her lips, and then, throwing her apron over her head, sat down to rock to and fro, exclaiming, under her breath, "The fever's turned, she's sleepin' natural, her skin's damp, and she breathes easy. Praise be given! Oh, my goodness me!"

The doctor soon came to confirm Hannah's diagnosis.

Never had the sun risen so beautifully, and never had the world seemed so lovely as it did to the heavy eyes of Meg and Jo as they looked out in the early morning, when their long, sad vigil was done.

"It looks like a fairy world," said Meg, smiling to herself as she stood behind the curtain watching the dazzling sight.

"Hark!" cried Jo, starting to her feet.

Yes, there was a sound of bells at the door below, a cry from Hannah, and then Laurie's voice, saying in a joyful whisper, "Girls, she's come! She's come!"

16 · Amy's Will

WHILE THESE things were happening at home, Amy was having hard times at Aunt March's. She felt her exile deeply and, for the first time in her life, realized how much she was beloved and petted at home. Aunt March never petted anyone; she did not approve of it; but she meant to be kind, for the well-behaved little girl pleased her very much, and Aunt March had a soft place in her old heart for her nephew's children, though she didn't think it proper to let anyone suspect it. She really did her best to make Amy happy, but what mistakes she made!

So Aunt March worried Amy most to death with her rules, her prim ways, and long, prosy talks. The old lady felt it her duty to try to counteract, as far as possible, the bad effects of home freedom and indulgence. She took Amy firmly in hand and taught her as she herself had been taught a full sixty years before.

Amy had to wash the cups every morning and polish up the old-fashioned spoons, the fat silver teapot, and the glasses till they shone. Then she must dust the room, and what a trying job that was! Not a speck escaped Aunt March's eye, and all the furniture had claw legs and much carving, which was never dusted to suit. Then Polly must be fed, the lapdog combed, and a dozen trips upstairs and down, to get things or deliver orders, for the old lady was very lame and seldom left her big chair. After these tiresome labors she must do her lessons, which were a daily trial of every possible virtue she possessed.

Then she was allowed an hour for exercise or play, and didn't she enjoy it! Laurie came every day and wheedled Aunt March till Amy was allowed to go out with him, when they walked and rode and had capital times. After dinner she had to read aloud and sit still while the old lady slept, which she usually did for an hour, as she dropped off over the first page or two.

Then patchwork or towels appeared, and Amy sewed them with outward meekness and inward rebellion till dusk, when she was allowed to amuse herself as she liked till teatime, The evenings were the worst of all, for Aunt March fell to telling long stories about her youth, which were so unutterably dull that Amy was always ready to go to bed, intending to cry over her hard fate, but usually going to sleep before she had squeezed out more than a tear or two.

If it had not been for Laurie and old Esther, the maid, she felt that she never could have got through that dreadful time. The parrot alone was enough to drive her distracted, for he soon felt that she did not admire him, and revenged himself by being as mischievous as possible. He pulled her hair whenever she came near him, made Mop bark by pecking at him while Madame dozed, and behaved in all respects like a reprehensible old bird. She could not endure the dog, a fat, cross beast; the cook was bad-tempered, the old coachman deaf, and Esther was the only one who ever took any notice of the young lady.

Esther was a Frenchwoman who had lived with "Madame" for many years and who rather tyrannized over the old lady, who could not get along without her. Her real name was Estelle; but Aunt March ordered her to change it, and she obeyed, on condition that she was never asked to change her religion. She took a fancy to *mademoiselle* and amused her very much with odd stories of her life in France when Amy sat with her while she got up Madame's laces. She also allowed her to roam about the great house and examine the curious and pretty things stored away in the big wardrobes and the ancient chests, for Aunt March had hoarded things away like a magpie.

Amy's delight was an Indian cabinet full of queer drawers, little pigeonholes, and secret places in which were kept all sorts of ornaments, some precious, some merely curious, all more or less antique. To examine these things gave Amy great satisfaction, especially the jewel cases, in which on velvet cushions reposed the ornaments which had adorned a belle of forty years ago. There was the garnet set which Aunt March wore when she came out, the pearls her father gave her on her wedding day, her lover's diamonds, the jet mourning rings and pins, the queer lockets with portraits of dead friends and weeping willows made of hair inside. There were the baby bracelets her one little daughter had worn; Uncle March's big watch, with the red seal so many childish hands had played with; and in a box all by itself, lay Aunt March's wedding ring, now too small for her fat finger, but put carefully away, like the most precious jewel of them all.

"Which would *mademoiselle* choose if she had her will?" asked Esther, who always sat near to watch over and lock up the valuables.

"I like the diamonds best, but there is no necklace among them, and I'm fond of necklaces; they are so becoming. I should choose this if I might," replied Amy, looking with great admiration at a string of gold and ebony beads, from which hung a heavy cross of the same.

"I, too, covet that, but not as a necklace. Ah, no! To me it is a rosary, and as such I should use it like a good Catholic," said Esther, eyeing the handsome thing wistfully.

"Is it meant to use as you use the string of good-smelling wooden beads hanging over your glass?" asked Amy.

"Truly, yes, to pray with. It would be pleasing to the saints if one used so fine a rosary as this, instead of wearing it as a vain *bijou*."

"You seem to take a deal of comfort in your prayers, Esther, and always come down looking quiet and satisfied. I wish I could feel like that."

"If *mademoiselle* was a Catholic, she would find true comfort. But, as that is not to be, it would be well if you went apart each day to meditate and pray, as did the good mistress whom I served before Madame. She had a little chapel, and in it found solacement for much trouble."

"Would it be right for me to do so, too?" asked Amy, who, in her loneliness, felt the need of help of some sort and found that she was apt to forget her little book, now that Beth was not there to remind her of it.

"It would be excellent and charming, and I shall gladly arrange the dressing room for you. While Madame is asleep, go you alone and sit a while to think good thoughts and ask the dear God to preserve your sister," said Esther.

Amy liked the idea and gave Esther leave to arrange the light closet next to her room, hoping that sitting there alone would do her good.

"I wish I knew where all these pretty things would go when Aunt March dies," she said as she slowly replaced the shining rosary and shut the jewel cases one by one.

"To you and your sisters. I know it. I witnessed Madame's will, and it is to be so," whispered Esther, smiling.

"How nice! But I wish she'd let us have them now," said Amy, taking a last look at the diamonds.

Esther went on softly, "I have a fancy that the little turquoise ring will be given to you when you go, for Madame tells me that she approves your good behavior and charming manners."

"Do you think so? Oh, I'll be a lamb, if I can only have that lovely ring! It's ever so much prettier than Kitty Bryant's. I do like Aunt March, after all." And Amy tried on the blue ring with a delighted face and a firm resolve in her heart to earn it.

From that day she was a model of obedience, and the old lady complacently admired the success of her training. Esther fitted up the closet with a little table, placed a footstool before it, and over it a picture, taken from one of the shut-up rooms. On the table Amy laid her little Testament and hymnbook, and she kept a vase there, too, always full of the best flowers Laurie brought her. Every day she came to the closet to "sit alone, thinking good thoughts and praying the dear God to preserve her sister."

Amy tried to forget herself, to keep cheerful and be satisfied with doing right, though no one saw or praised her for it. In her first effort at being very, very good, she decided to make her will, as Aunt March had done, so that if she *did* fall ill and die, her possessions might be justly and generously divided among her family and friends.

During one of her play hours she wrote out the important document as well as she could, with some help from Esther as to certain legal terms; and when the good-natured Frenchwoman had signed her name, Amy felt relieved and laid it by to show Laurie. She planned to ask him to sign it as a second witness.

As it was a rainy day, she went upstairs to amuse herself in one of the large rooms. In this room there was a wardrobe full of old-fashioned costumes with which Esther allowed her to play, and it was her favorite amusement to array herself in the faded brocades and parade up and down before the long mirror, making stately curtsies and sweeping her train about with a rustle which delighted her ears.

So busy was she on this particular day that she did not hear Laurie's ring, nor see his face peeping in at her as she gravely promenaded to and fro, flirting her fan and tossing her head, on which she wore a great pink turban, contrasting oddly with her blue brocade dress and yellow quilted petticoat.

Having with difficulty restrained an explosion of merriment, lest it should offend her majesty, Laurie tapped and was graciously received.

"Sit down and rest while I put these things away. Then I want to consult you about a very serious matter," said Amy, when she had shown her splendor.

A few minutes later she shut the wardrobe, took a paper from her pocket, and said, "I want you to read that, please, and tell me if it is legal and right. I feel that I ought to do it, for life is uncertain, and I don't want any ill feeling over my tomb."

Laurie bit his lips and, turning a little from the pensive

149

speaker, read the following document, with praiseworthy gravity, considering the spelling.

My Last Will and Testiment

I, Amy Curtis March, being in my sane mind, do give and bequeethe all my earthly property:—viz. to wit:—namely

To my father, my best pictures, sketches, maps, and works of art, including frames. Also my $100, to do what he likes with.

To my mother, all my clothes, except the blue apron with pockets,—also my likeness, and my medal, with much love.

To my dear sister Margaret, I give my turkquoise ring (if I get it), also my green box with the doves on it, also my piece of real lace for her neck, and my sketch of her as a memorial of her "little girl."

To Jo I leave my breast-pin, the one mended with sealing wax, also my bronze inkstand—she lost the cover,—and my most precious plaster rabbit, because I am sorry I burned up her story.

To Beth (if she lives after me) I give my dolls and the little bureau, my fan, my linen collars, and my new slippers if she can wear them being thin when she gets well. And I herewith also leave her my great regret that I ever made fun of her poor old Joanna.

To my friend and neighbor Theodore Laurence I bequeethe my paper marshay portfolio, my clay model of a horse, though he did say it hadn't any neck. Also in return for his great kindness in the hour of affliction any one of my artistic works he likes, Noter Dame is the best.

To our venerable benefactor Mr. Laurence I leave my purple box with a looking glass in the cover which will be nice for his pens and remind him of the departed girl who thanks him for his favors to her family, specially Beth.

I wish my favorite playmate Kitty Bryant to have the blue silk apron and my gold-bead ring with a kiss.

To Hannah I give the band-box she wanted and all the patchwork I leave hoping she "will remember me, when it you see."

And now having disposed of my most valuable property I hope all will be satisfied and not blame the dead. I forgive every one, and trust we may all meet when the trump shall sound. Amen.

To this will and testiment I set my hand and seal on this 20th day of Nov. Ammin Domino 1861.

AMY CURTIS MARCH

Witnesses:
ESTELLE VALNOR,
THEODORE LAURENCE

The last name was written in pencil, and Amy explained that he was to rewrite it in ink, and seal it up for her properly.

"What put it into your head? Did anyone tell you about Beth's giving away her things?" asked Laurie soberly as Amy laid a bit of red tape, with sealing wax, a taper, and a standish before him. She explained and then asked anxiously, "Laurie, what about Beth?"

"I'm sorry I spoke, but, as I did, I'll tell you. She felt so ill one day that she told Jo she wanted to give her piano to Meg, her bird to you, and the poor old doll to Jo, who would love it for her sake. She was sorry she had so little to give, and left locks of hair to the rest of us, and her best love to Grandpa. *She* never thought of a will."

Laurie was signing and sealing as he spoke and did not look up till a great tear dropped on the paper. Amy's face was full of trouble, but she only said, "Don't people put sort of postscripts to their wills sometimes?"

"Yes, 'codicils,' they call them."

"Put one in mine then—that I wish *all* my curls cut off and given round to my friends. I forgot it, but I want it done, though it will spoil my looks."

Laurie added it, smiling at Amy's last and greatest sacrifice. Then he amused her for an hour and was much interested in all her trials. But when he came to go, Amy held him back to whisper with trembling lips, "Is there really any danger about Beth?"

"I'm afraid there is, but we must hope for the best. So don't cry, dear." And Laurie put his arm about her with a brotherly gesture which was very comforting.

When he was gone, she went to her little chapel and, sitting in the twilight, prayed for Beth with streaming tears and an aching heart, feeling that a million turquoise rings would not console her for the loss of her gentle little sister.

17 · Confidential

When Beth woke from that long, healing sleep, the first object on which her eyes fell was her mother's face. Too weak to wonder at anything, she only smiled and nestled close into the loving arms about her, feeling that the hungry longing was satisfied at last. Then she slept again, and the girls waited upon their mother, for she would not unclasp the thin hand which clung to hers, even in sleep.

What a strange yet pleasant day that was! A Sabbath stillness reigned through the house; Hannah mounted guard at the door. With a blissful sense of burdens lifted off, Meg and Jo closed their weary eyes. Mrs. March would not leave Beth's side, but rested in the big chair.

Laurie, meanwhile, posted off to comfort Amy, and told his story so well that Aunt March actually "sniffed" herself and never once said, "I told you so." Amy came out so strong on this occasion that I think the good thoughts in the little chapel really began to bear fruit. She dried her tears quickly, restrained her impatience to see her mother, and never even thought of the turquoise ring when the old lady heartily agreed in Laurie's opinion that she behaved "like a capital little woman." Amy would very gladly have gone out to enjoy the bright, wintry weather; but, discovering that Laurie was dropping with sleep, in spite of manful efforts to conceal the fact, she persuaded him to rest on the sofa, while she wrote a note to her mother. She was a long time about it; and when she returned, he was stretched out with both arms under his head, sound asleep.

After a while they began to think he was not going to wake till night, and I'm not sure he would, had he not been effectually roused by Amy's cry of joy at sight of her mother. Amy was the happiest girl in the city that day when she sat in her mother's lap and told her trials, receiving consolation and compensation in the shape of approving smiles and fond caresses. They were alone together in the quiet little chapel, to which her mother did not object when its purpose was explained to her.

"On the contrary, I like it very much, dear," she said, looking from the dusty rosary to the well-worn book and the lovely picture with its garland of evergreen. "It is an excellent plan to have some place where we can go to be quiet when things vex or grieve us."

"Yes, Mother; and when I go home I mean to have a corner in the big closet to put my books and the copy of that picture which I've tried to make."

As Amy pointed to the picture, Mrs. March saw something on her daughter's hand that made her smile. She said nothing, but Amy understood the look and, after a minute's pause, added gravely, "I wanted to speak to you about this, but I forgot it. Aunt gave me the ring today. She gave me that funny guard to keep the turquoise on, as it's too big. I'd like to wear them, Mother. May I?"

"They are very pretty, but I think you're rather too young for such ornaments, Amy," said Mrs. March, looking at the plump little hand with the band of sky-blue stones on the forefinger, and the quaint guard, formed of two tiny golden hands clasped together.

"I'll try not to be vain," said Amy. "I don't think I like it only because it's so pretty. I want to wear it to remind me of something."

"Do you mean Aunt March?" asked her mother, laughing good-naturedly.

"No, to remind me not to be selfish." Amy looked so earnest and sincere about it that her mother stopped laughing and listened respectfully.

"I've thought a great deal lately about 'my bundle of naughties,' and being selfish is the largest one in it. So I'm going to try hard to cure it if I can, but I'm apt to forget my resolution. If I had something always about me to remind me, I guess I should do better. May I try this way?"

"Yes, but I have more faith in the corner of the big closet. Wear your ring, dear, and do your best. Now I must go back to Beth. Keep up your heart, little daughter, and we will soon have you home again."

That evening Jo slipped upstairs into Beth's room and, finding her mother in her usual place, stood a minute twisting her fingers, with a worried gesture and an undecided look.

"What is it, deary?" asked Mrs. March.

Jo settled herself at her mother's feet. "Last summer Meg left a pair of gloves over at the Laurences', and only one was returned. We forgot all about it, till Teddy told me that Mr. Brooke had it. He kept it in his waistcoat pocket, and once it fell out, and Teddy joked him about it, and Mr. Brooke owned that he liked Meg, but didn't dare say so, for she was so young and he so poor. Now, isn't that a *dreadful* state of things?"

"Do you think that Meg really cares for him?" asked Mrs. March anxiously.

"Mercy me! I don't know anything about love and such nonsense!" cried Jo. "But Meg doesn't blush or faint or refuse to eat like girls in love are supposed to do."

"Then you fancy that Meg is *not* interested in John?"

"Who?"

"Mr. Brooke. I call him 'John' now. We fell into the way of doing so at the hospital, and he likes it."

"Oh, dear! I know you'll take his part and let Meg marry him. Mean thing! To go petting Pa and truckling to you, just to wheedle you into liking him."

"My dear, John was perfectly open and honorable about Meg, for he told your father and me that he loved her. But I will not consent to Meg's engaging herself so young."

"Of course not. It would be idiotic! I knew there was mischief brewing!"

Mrs. March said gravely, "Jo, I confide in you and don't wish you to say anything to Meg yet. When John comes back and I see them together, I can judge better of her feelings toward him."

"She'll see his feelings in those handsome eyes of his. She'll go and fall in love, and there's an end of peace and fun and cozy times together. Oh, deary me! Why weren't we all boys? Then there wouldn't be any bother!"

Mrs. March sighed. Jo looked up with an air of relief.

"You don't like it, Mother? Let's send him about his business and not tell Meg a word of it, but all be jolly together as we always have been."

"I did wrong to sigh, Jo. It is natural and right you should all go to homes of your own in time. But Meg must not bind herself before she is twenty. If she and John love one another, they can wait and test the love by doing so."

"Hadn't you rather have her marry a rich man?" asked Jo.

"I'm not ambitious for a splendid fortune, a fashionable position, or a great name for my girls. If rank and money come with love and virtue, also, I should accept them gratefully, and enjoy your good fortune. But I know by experience how much genuine happiness can be had in a plain little house, where the daily bread is earned, and some privations give sweetness to the few pleasures."

"I'd planned for Meg to marry Teddy by and by."

"He is younger than she, you know."

"Oh, that doesn't matter. He's old for his age, and tall, and can be quite grown-up in his manners, if he likes. Then he's rich and generous and good and loves us all, and I say it's a pity my plan is spoiled."

"Don't make plans, Jo, but let time and their own hearts mate your friends."

"I won't, but I hate to see things going all crisscross. I wish wearing flatirons on our heads would keep us from growing up!"

"What's that about flatirons?" asked Meg as she crept into the room, a finished letter to Father in her hand.

"Only one of my stupid speeches. I'm going to bed," said Jo.

Mrs. March glanced over the letter and handed it back. "Please add my love to John," she said.

"Do you call him John?" asked Meg, smiling.

"Yes, he has been like a son to us, and we are very fond of him," replied Mrs. March, returning the look with a keen one of her own.

"I'm glad of that—he is so lonely. Good night, Mother dear. It is so inexpressibly comfortable to have you here," was Meg's quiet answer.

The kiss her mother gave her was a very tender one. And as she went away, Mrs. March said, with a mixture of satisfaction and regret, "She does not love John yet but will soon learn to."

18 · Laurie Makes Mischief

Jo's FACE WAS a study next day, for the secret rather weighed upon her, and she found it hard not to look mysterious and important. Meg observed it but did not trouble herself to make inquiries, for she had learned the best way to manage Jo was by the law of contraries. So she felt sure of being told everything if she did not ask. But the silence remained unbroken.

Laurie no sooner suspected a mystery than he set himself to finding it out, and led Jo a trying life of it. He wheedled, bribed, ridiculed, threatened, and scolded; and at last he satisfied himself that it concerned Meg and Mr. Brooke. Feeling indignant that he was not taken into his tutor's confidence, he set his wits to work to devise some proper retaliation for the slight.

Meg, meanwhile, had apparently forgotten the matter and was absorbed in preparations for her father's return; but all of a sudden a change seemed to come over her, and for a day or two she was quite unlike herself. She started when spoken to, blushed when looked at, was very quiet, and sat over her sewing with a timid, troubled look on her face. To her mother's inquiries she answered that she was quite well, and Jo's she silenced by begging to be let alone.

"She feels it in the air—love, I mean—and she's going very fast. She's got most of the symptoms. Whatever shall we do?" asked Jo, looking ready for any measures, however violent they might be.

"Nothing but wait. Father's coming will settle everything," replied her mother.

"Here's a note to you, Meg, all sealed up. How odd! Teddy never seals mine," said Jo, next day, as she distributed the contents of the little post office.

Mrs. March and Jo were deep in their own affairs, when a sound from Meg made them look up to see her staring at her note with a frightened face.

"My child, what is it?" cried her mother.

"It's all a mistake—he didn't send it—oh, Jo, how could you do it?" Meg hid her face in her hands.

"What's she talking about?" asked Jo, bewildered.

Meg's mild eyes kindled with anger as she pulled a crumpled note from her pocket and threw it at Jo, saying reproachfully, "You wrote it, and that bad boy helped you. How could you be so rude, so mean and cruel to us?"

Jo hardly heard her, for she and her mother were reading the note, which was written in a peculiar hand.

My dearest Margaret,

I can no longer restrain my passion, and must know my fate before I return. I dare not tell your parents yet, but I think they would consent if they knew we adored one another. Mr. Laurence will help me to some good place, and then, my sweet girl, you will make me happy. I implore you to say nothing to your family yet, but to send one word of hope through Laurie to

Your devoted,
John

"Oh, the little villain! That's the way he meant to pay me for keeping my word to Mother. I'll give him a hearty scolding, and bring him over to beg pardon," cried Jo. But her mother held her back, saying, with a look she seldom wore, "Stop, Jo, you must clear yourself first. You have played so many pranks that I am afraid you have had a hand in this."

"On my word, Mother, I haven't! I never saw that note before and don't know anything about it, as true as I live!" said Jo, so earnestly that they believed her. "I should think, Meg, that you'd have known Mr. Brooke wouldn't write such stuff as that."

"It's like his writing," faltered Meg, comparing it with the note in her hand.

"Oh, Meg, you didn't answer it?" cried Mrs. March quickly.

"Yes, I did!" And Meg hid her face again, overcome with shame.

"Do let me bring that wicked boy over to explain and be lectured." And Jo made for the door again.

"Hush! Let me manage this. Margaret, tell me the whole story," commanded Mrs. March.

"I received the first letter from Laurie, who didn't look as if he knew anything about it," began Meg without looking up. "I was worried at first and meant to tell you. Then I remembered how you liked Mr. Brooke, and so I thought you wouldn't mind if I kept my little secret for a few days. Oh, I can never look him in the face again!"

"What did you say to him?" asked Mrs. March.

"I only said I was too young to do anything about it yet, that I didn't wish to have secrets from you, and he must speak to Father. I was very grateful for his kindness, and would be his friend, but nothing more, for a long while."

Mrs. March smiled, as if well pleased, and Jo clapped her hands.

"What did he say to that?"

"He writes in a different way entirely, telling me that he never sent any love letter at all and is very sorry that my roguish sister, Jo, should take such liberties with our names. It's very kind and respectful, but think how dreadful for me!"

Jo caught up the two notes, and after looking at them closely, she said decidedly, "I don't believe Brooke ever saw either of these letters. Teddy wrote both, and keeps yours to crow over me with, because I wouldn't tell him my secret."

"Don't have any secrets, Jo. Tell it to Mother and keep yourself out of trouble, as I should have done," said Meg warningly.

"Jo, go get Laurie," said Mrs. March. "I shall sift the matter to the bottom and put an end to such pranks at once."

The sound of Mrs. March's and Laurie's voices in the parlor rose and fell for half an hour; and when Jo and Meg went in, Laurie was standing by their mother, with a penitent face. Meg received his humble apology and was much comforted by the assurance that Brooke knew nothing of the joke.

Everyone thought the matter ended and the little cloud blown over; but the mischief was done, for, though others forgot it, Meg remembered. She never alluded to a certain person, but she thought of him a great deal, dreamed dreams more than ever; and once Jo, rummaging her sister's desk for stamps, found a bit of paper scribbled over with the words, "Mrs. John Brooke"; whereat she groaned tragically and cast it into the fire, feeling that Laurie's prank had hastened the evil day for her.

Like sunshine after storm were the peaceful weeks that followed. The invalids improved rapidly, and Mr. March began to talk of returning early in the new year.

As Christmas approached, the usual mysteries began to haunt the house; several days of unusually mild weather fitly ushered in a splendid Christmas Day. Hannah "felt in her bones that it was going to be an unusually plummy day," and she proved herself a true prophetess.

Beth felt uncommonly well that morning and, being dressed in her mother's gift—a soft crimson merino wrapper—was borne in triumph to the window to behold the offering of Jo and Laurie, a stately snow maiden, crowned with holly, bearing a basket of fruit and flowers in one hand and a great roll of music in the other, standing in the garden.

How Beth laughed when she saw it!

"I'm so full of happiness that, if Father were only here, I couldn't hold one drop more," she sighed with contentment as Jo carried her off to the study to rest after the excitement.

"So am I," added Jo, slapping the pocket wherein reposed the long-desired *Undine and Sintram.*

"I'm sure I am," echoed Amy, poring over the engraved copy of the Madonna and Child, in a pretty frame, which her mother had given her.

"Of course I am," cried Meg, smoothing the silvery folds of her first silk dress; for Mr. Laurence had insisted on giving it.

"How can I be otherwise!" said Mrs. March gratefully

as her eyes went from her husband's letter to Beth's smiling face, and her hand caressed the brooch made of gray and golden and chestnut and dark brown hair, which the girls had just fastened on her breast.

Half an hour later Laurie opened the parlor door and popped his head in very quietly. He might just as well have turned a somersault and uttered a war whoop; for his face was so full of suppressed excitement, and his voice so treacherously joyful, that everyone jumped up, though he only said, in a queer, breathless voice, "Here's another Christmas present for the March family."

Before the words were well out of his mouth, he was whisked away somehow, and in his place appeared a tall man, muffled up to the eyes, leaning on the arm of another tall man, who tried to say something and couldn't. Of course there was a general stampede; and for several minutes everybody seemed to lose their wits, for the strangest things were done and no one said a word. Mr. March became invisible in the embrace of four pairs of loving arms.

Mrs. March was the first to recover herself, and held up her hand with a warning, "Hush! Remember Beth!"

But it was too late; the study door flew open, the little red wrapper appeared on the threshold, joy put strength into the feeble limbs, and Beth ran straight into her father's arms. Never mind what happened just after that; for the full hearts overflowed, washing away the bitterness of the past, and leaving only the sweetness of the present.

19 • Aunt March Settles a Question

MR. MARCH, the next day, was in a fair way to being killed by kindness; nothing more seemed needed to complete the March family's happiness. But something *was* needed, and the elder ones felt it, though no one confessed the fact.

Jo had sudden fits of sobriety and was seen to shake her fist at Mr. Brooke's umbrella, which had been left in the hall; Meg was absentminded, shy and silent, started when the bell rang, and colored when John's name was mentioned; Amy said "everyone seemed waiting for something and couldn't settle down, which was queer, since Father was safe at home."

Jo couldn't help smiling at the important air which Meg had unconsciously assumed, and which was as becoming as the pretty color varying in her cheeks.

"Would you mind telling me what you'd say if John asked for your hand?" asked Jo respectfully.

Meg spoke as if to herself, "Oh, I should merely say, quite calmly and decidedly, 'Thank you, Mr. Brooke, you are very kind, but I agree with Father that I am too young to enter into any engagement at present. So please say no more, but let us be friends as we were.'"

Meg rose as she spoke and was just going to rehearse a dignified exit, when a step in the hall made her fly into her seat and begin to sew as if her young life depended on it. Jo smothered a laugh at the sudden change and, when someone gave a modest tap, opened the door with a grim aspect which was anything but hospitable.

"Good afternoon. I came for my umbrella," said Mr. Brooke.

Jo said, "It's in the rack," and slipped out of the room to give Meg a chance to make her speech and air her dignity. But the instant she vanished, Meg began to sidle toward the door, murmuring, "Mother will like to see you. Pray sit down—I'll call her."

"Don't go. Are you afraid of me, Margaret?" said Mr. Brooke gently.

"How can I be afraid when you have been so kind to Father? I only wish I could thank you for it."

"Shall I tell you how?" Holding the small hand fast, John looked down at Meg with love in his brown eyes.

"Oh, no, please don't—I'd rather not," she said, trying to withdraw her hand.

"I won't trouble you. I only want to know if you care for me a little, Meg. I love you so much, dear."

This was the moment for the calm, proper speech, but Meg didn't make it.

"I don't know," she said, so softly that John had to stoop down to catch the foolish little reply.

He smiled to himself, as if quite satisfied.

"I'll wait, and in the meantime you could be learning to like me. Would it be a very hard lesson, dear?"

"Not if I chose to learn it, but—"

"Please choose to learn, Meg. I would love to teach,

167

and this is easier than learning German."

His tone was properly beseeching; but, stealing a shy look at him, Meg saw his eyes were merry as well as tender and that he wore the satisfied smile of one who had no doubt of his success. This nettled her. Withdrawing her hand, she said petulantly, "I *don't* choose. Please go away and let me be!"

Poor Mr. Brooke! "Do you really mean that?" he asked in an anxious tone.

"Yes, I do. I don't want to be worried about such things. Father says I needn't. It's too soon, and I'd rather not."

John was grave and pale now, and looked decidedly more like the novel heroes whom she admired. What could have happened next, I cannot say, for Aunt March came hobbling in at this interesting minute. Meg started as if she had seen a ghost, and Mr. Brooke vanished into the library.

"Bless me! What's all this?" cried the old lady.

"It's Father's friend. I'm *so* surprised to see you!" stammered Meg.

"That's evident," returned Aunt March. "But what is Father's friend saying, to make you look like a peony?"

"We were merely talking. Mr. Brooke came to get his umbrella."

"Brooke? That boy's tutor? Ah! I understand now. I know all about it. You haven't gone and accepted him, child?" cried Aunt March, looking scandalized. She went on impressively, "If you do marry this Cook, not one penny of my money ever goes to you."

"I shall marry whom I please, Aunt March, and you can leave your money to anyone you like," said the usually gentle Meg, nodding her head resolutely.

Aunt March, surprised, made a fresh start, saying as mildly as she could, "My dear, I only want you to marry well."

"I couldn't do better if I waited half my life! John is good and wise, he's got heaps of talent, he's willing to work and sure to get on, and I'm proud to think he cares for me, though I'm so poor and young and silly," said Meg, looking prettier than ever in her earnestness.

Meg stopped there, suddenly remembering that she hadn't made up her mind and that John might be over-hearing her inconsistent remarks.

Aunt March was very angry, for she had set her heart on having this pretty niece make a fine match.

"Well, I wash my hands of the whole affair!" she cried and, slamming the door in Meg's face, drove off in a high dudgeon.

Then Meg was taken possession of by a smiling Mr. Brooke, who said, "I couldn't help overhearing, Meg. You *do* care for me a little bit."

"I didn't know how much until she abused you," said Meg, hiding her face on Mr. Brooke's waistcoat.

Fifteen minutes later Jo came downstairs, confident that by now Meg had sent her would-be lover about his business. How shocked she was to behold her strong-minded sister enthroned upon her archenemy's knee! They rose at sight of her, and John, adding insult to injury, came forward and said happily, "Sister Jo, congratulate us!"

"I don't approve of the match," Jo later told Laurie, "but I've made up my mind to bear it." She continued with a quiver in her voice, "I've lost my dearest friend."

That evening Father and Mother sat together, quietly

169

reliving the first chapter of the romance which for them began some twenty years ago. Amy was drawing the lovers, who sat apart in a beautiful world of their own. Beth lay on her sofa talking cheerily with her old friend. Jo lounged in her favorite low seat; and Laurie, leaning on the back of her chair, his chin on a level with her curly head, smiled with his friendliest aspect and nodded at her in the long glass which reflected them both.

20 • The First Wedding

THREE YEARS have passed and brought few changes to the quiet March family. The war is over and Mr. March safely at home, busy with his books and the small parish which found in him a minister by nature as by grace—a quiet, studious man, rich in the wisdom that is better than learning, the charity which calls all mankind "brother," the piety that blossoms into character, making it august and lovely.

Mrs. March is as brisk and cheery, though rather grayer than when we saw her last, and just now so absorbed in Meg's affairs that the hospitals and homes, still full of wounded "boys" and soldiers' widows, decidedly miss the motherly missionary's visits.

John Brooke did his duty manfully for a year, got wounded, was sent home, and not allowed to return. He received no stars or bars, but he deserved them, for he cheerfully risked all he had; and life and love are very precious when both are in full bloom. Perfectly resigned to his discharge, he devoted himself to getting well, preparing for business, and earning a home for Meg. With the good sense and sturdy independence that characterized him, he refused Mr. Laurence's more generous offers and accepted the place of under bookkeeper, feeling better satisfied to begin with an honestly earned salary than to run any risks with borrowed money.

Meg had spent the time in working as well as waiting, growing womanly in character, wise in housewifely arts, and prettier than ever; for love is a great beautifier. She had her girlish ambitions and hopes, and felt some disappointment at the humble way in which the new life must begin. Ned Moffat had just married Sallie Gardiner, and Meg couldn't help contrasting their fine house and carriage, many gifts, and splendid outfit with her own, and secretly wishing she could have the same. But when she and John sat together in the twilight, talking over their small plans, the future always grew so beautiful and bright that she forgot Sallie's splendor and felt herself the richest, happiest girl in Christendom.

Jo never went back to Aunt March, for the old lady took such a fancy to Amy that she bribed her with the offer of drawing lessons from one of the best teachers going; and for the sake of this advantage, Amy would have served a far harder mistress.

As long as *The Spread Eagle* paid her a dollar a column for her "rubbish," as she called it, Jo felt herself a woman of means, and spun her little romances diligently. But great plans fermented in her busy brain and ambitious mind, and the old tin kitchen in the garret held a slowly increasing pile of blotted manuscript which was one day to place the name of March upon the roll of fame.

Laurie, having dutifully gone to college to please his grandfather, was now getting through it in the easiest manner possible. A universal favorite, thanks to money, much talent, manners, and the kindest heart that ever got its owner into scrapes by trying to get other people out of them, he stood in great danger of being spoiled. Probably he would have been, like many another promising boy, if he had not possessed a talisman against evil in the memory of the kind old man who was bound up in his success, the motherly friend who watched over him as if he were her son, and last, but not least by any means, the knowledge that four innocent girls loved, admired, and believed in him with all their hearts.

"Dovecote" was the name of the little brown house which Mr. Brooke had prepared for Meg's first home. It was a tiny house, with a little garden behind and a lawn about as big as a pocket handkerchief in front. The hall was narrow, the dining room was small, but good taste and good sense had presided over the furnishing, and the result was highly satisfactory. There were no marble-topped tables, long mirrors, or lace curtains in the little parlor, but simple furniture, plenty of books, a fine picture or two, a stand of flowers in the bay window, and, scattered all about, the pretty gifts which came from friendly hands and were the fairer for the loving messages they brought. Beth, alone, had made enough dusters, piece bags, and other such articles to last till the silver wedding came around.

What happy times they had planning together; what solemn shopping excursions, what funny mistakes they made, and what shouts of laughter arose over Laurie's ridiculous bargains! In his love of jokes, this young gentleman, though nearly through college, was as much a boy as ever. His last whim, on his weekly visits, was to bring some new, useful, and ingenious article for Meg, the housekeeper. Now, a bag of remarkable clothespins;

next, a wonderful new nutmeg grater; a knife-cleaner that spoiled all the knives; or a sweeper that picked the nap neatly off the carpet and left the dirt. In vain Meg begged him to stop. John laughed at him, and Jo called him "Mr. Toodles."

Everything was done at last, even to Amy's arranging different colored soaps to match the different colored rooms, and Beth's setting the table for the first meal.

A last tour of the house by Mrs. March and the girls was being made. Tomorrow was the wedding day.

"Do you know, I like this room best of all in my baby house," said Meg as they went upstairs and she looked into her well-stored linen closet.

All laughed as Meg spoke, for that linen closet was a joke. You see, having said that if Meg married "that Brooke" she shouldn't have a cent of her money, Aunt March was rather in a quandary when time had appeased the wrath and made her repent the vow. She never broke her word, and was much exercised in her mind how to get round it, and at last devised a plan whereby she could satisfy herself. Mrs. Carrol, Florence's mamma and the March girls' aunt, was ordered to buy and have made and marked a generous supply of house and table linen, and send it as *her* present. All of which was faithfully done by Mrs. Carrol.

But the secret leaked out and was greatly enjoyed by the family; for Aunt March tried to look utterly unconscious, and insisted that she could give nothing but the old-fashioned pearls, long promised to the first bride.

The next day the June roses over the porch were awake bright and early, rejoicing with all their hearts in the cloudless sunshine, like friendly neighbors, as they were.

Meg looked very like a rose herself; for all that was best and sweetest in heart and soul seemed to bloom in her face that day, making it fair and tender, with a charm more beautiful than beauty.

She had made her wedding gown herself, sewing into it the tender hopes and innocent romances of a girlish heart. Her sisters braided up her pretty hair, and the only ornaments she wore were the lilies of the valley, which "her John" liked best of all the flowers that grew.

"Now I'm going to tie John's cravat for him and then stay a few minutes with Father, quietly in the study." And Meg ran down to perform these little ceremonies.

Jo, Amy, and Beth wore suits of thin, silvery gray, with blush roses in hair and bosom; and all three looked just what they were—fresh-faced, happy-hearted girls, pausing a moment in their busy lives to read with wistful eyes the sweetest chapter in the romance of womanhood.

There was no bridal procession, but a sudden silence fell upon the room as Mr. March and the young pair took their places under the green arch. Mother and sisters gathered close, as if loath to give Meg up; the fatherly voice broke more than once, which only seemed to make the service more beautiful and solemn; the bridegroom's hand trembled visibly, and no one heard his replies; but Meg looked straight up into her husband's eyes and said, "I will!" with such tender trust in her own face and voice that her mother's heart rejoiced and Aunt March sniffed audibly.

Everybody crowded up after that and said something brilliant, or tried to, which did just as well, for laughter is ready when hearts are light. There was no display of gifts, for they were already in the little house, nor was there an elaborate breakfast, but a plentiful lunch of cake and fruit, dressed with flowers.

After lunch people strolled about, by twos and threes, through house and garden, enjoying the sunshine without and within. Meg and John happened to be standing in the middle of the grass plot when Laurie was seized with an inspiration which put all the finishing touches needed to this unfashionable wedding.

"All the married people take hands and dance round the new-made husband and wife, as the Germans do, while we bachelors and spinsters prance in couples outside!" cried Laurie, galloping down the path with Amy, with such infectious spirit and skill that everyone else followed their example without a murmur.

Mr. and Mrs. March and then Aunt and Uncle Carrol began it; others rapidly joined in; even Sallie Moffat, after a moment's hesitation, threw her train over her arm and whisked Ned into the ring. But the crowning joke was Mr. Laurence and Aunt March; for when the stately old gentleman *chasséd* solemnly up to the old lady, she just tucked her cane under her arm and hopped briskly away to join hands with the rest and dance about the bridal pair, while the young folks pervaded the garden like bright butterflies on a warm midsummer day.

"Laurie, my lad, if you ever want to indulge in this sort of thing, get one of these little girls to help you and I shall be perfectly satisfied," said Mr. Laurence, settling himself in his easy chair to rest, after all the excitement of the merry dance.

"I'll do my best to gratify you, sir," was Laurie's unusually dutiful reply as he carefully unpinned the posy Jo had put in his buttonhole.

Then people began to go.

"Thank you all for my happy wedding day!" cried Meg. "Good-bye! Good-bye!"

Later the family stood watching her with faces full of love and hope and tender pride as she walked away, leaning on her husband's arm, with her hands full of flowers and the June sunshine brightening her happy face. And so Meg's married life began.

21 • Experiences

FORTUNE SUDDENLY smiled upon Jo and dropped a good-luck penny in her path.

Quite by accident she read in a paper of a prize of one hundred dollars being offered by that same paper for the best sensational story sent to them in a given period of time. She said nothing of her plan at home but fell to work next day, much to the disquiet of her mother, who always looked a little anxious when "genius took to burning." Jo had never tried this style before, contenting herself with very mild romances for *The Spread Eagle*.

Her story was as full of desperation and despair as her limited acquaintance with those uncomfortable emotions enabled her to make it, and, having located it in Lisbon, she wound up with an earthquake as the most striking and appropriate denouement she could think of.

The manuscript was privately dispatched, together with a note modestly saying that, if the tale didn't get a prize, which the writer hardly dared expect, she would be very glad to receive any sum it might be considered worth.

Six weeks is a long time to wait, and a still longer time for a girl to keep a secret; but Jo did both, and was beginning to give up hope of ever seeing her manuscript again, when a letter arrived which almost took her breath away; for, on opening it, a check for a hundred dollars fell into her lap.

A prouder young woman was seldom seen than she when, having composed herself, she electrified the family by appearing before them with the letter in one hand and the check in the other. There was a great jubilee, and when the story came everyone read and praised it; though after her father had told her that the language was good, the romance fresh and hearty, and the tragedy quite thrilling, he shook his head and said in his unworldly way, "You can do better than this, Jo. Aim at the highest and never mind the money."

"I think the money is the best part of it. What *will* you do with such a fortune?" asked Amy.

"Send Beth and Mother to the seaside for a month."

"Oh, how splendid! No, I can't do it, dear—it would be so selfish," cried Beth, who had clapped her thin hands and taken a long breath, as if pining for fresh ocean breezes, then stopped herself and motioned away the check which her sister waved before her.

"Ah, but you shall go," said Jo determinedly. "I've set my heart on it. That's what I tried for, and that's why I succeeded. Won't it be fun to see you come home plump and rosy again? Hurrah for Doctor Jo, who always cures her patients!"

To the seaside they went, after much discussion; and though Beth didn't come home as plump and rosy as could be desired, she was much better, while Mrs. March declared she felt ten years younger. So Jo was satisfied with the investment of her prize money and fell to work with a cheery spirit, bent on earning more of those delightful checks. She did earn several that year and began to feel herself a power in the house, for, by the magic of a pen, her "rubbish" turned into comforts for them all. "The Duke's Daughter" paid the butcher's bill, "A Phantom Hand" put down a new carpet, and "The Curse of the Coventrys" proved the blessing of the Marches in the way of groceries and gowns.

Little notice was taken of her stories, but they found a market; and, encouraged by this fact, she resolved to make a bold stroke for fame and fortune. Having copied her novel for the fourth time and submitted it with fear and trembling to three publishers, she disposed of it on condition that she cut it down one-third and omit all the parts which she particularly admired.

So, with Spartan firmness, the young authoress laid her firstborn manuscript on her table and chopped it up as ruthlessly as any ogre. It was printed, and she got paid three hundred dollars for it, likewise plenty of praise and blame.

"I don't know whether I have written a promising book or broken all the Ten Commandments," cried poor Jo, turning over a heap of notices, the perusal of which filled her with pride and joy one minute, wrath and dire dismay the next.

"Not being a genius like Keats, it won't kill me," she said stoutly, "and I've got the joke on my side, after all. For the parts that were taken straight out of real life are denounced as impossible and absurd, and the scenes which I made up out of my own silly head are pronounced 'charmingly natural, tender, and true.' So I'll comfort myself with that, and when I'm ready, I'll up and take another."

Like most other young matrons, Meg began her married life with the determination to be a model housekeeper. John should find home a paradise; he should always see a smiling face, should fare sumptuously every day, and never know the loss of a button. She brought so much love, energy, and cheerfulness to the work that she could not but succeed, in spite of some obstacles. Her paradise was not a tranquil one; for the little woman fussed, was overanxious to please, and bustled about like a true Martha, cumbered with many cares. She was too tired, sometimes, even to smile; John grew dyspeptic after a course of dainty dishes and ungratefully demanded plain fare. As for buttons, she soon learned to wonder where they went, to shake her head over the carelessness of men, and to threaten to make him sew them on himself and then see if *his* work would stand impatient tugs and clumsy fingers any better than hers.

They were happy, even after they discovered that they couldn't live on love alone. John did not find Meg's beauty diminished, though she beamed at him from behind the family coffeepot; nor did Meg miss any of the romance from the daily parting, when her husband followed up his kiss with the tender inquiry, "Shall I send home veal or mutton for dinner, darling?" The little house ceased to be a glorified bower, but it became a home, and the young couple soon felt that it was a change for the better. So the months sped by.

Laurie came creeping into the kitchen of the Dovecote one Saturday with an excited face and was received with the clash of cymbals; for Hannah clapped her hands with a saucepan in one and the cover in the other.

"How's the little mamma? Where did everybody go?"

began Laurie in a loud whisper.

"Happy as a queen, the dear! Every soul of 'em is up-stairs a-worshipin'. Now you go into the parlor, and I'll send 'em down to you." And Hannah vanished, chuckling ecstatically.

Presently Jo appeared, proudly bearing a small flannel bundle laid forth upon a large pillow.

"Shut your eyes and hold out your arms," she said invitingly.

Laurie backed into a corner and put his hands behind him with an imploring gesture. "No, thank you! I'd rather not. I shall drop it, or smash it, as sure as fate."

"Then you shan't see your nevvy," said Jo decidedly, turning as if to go.

"I will! I will! Only you must be responsible for damages."

Laurie heroically shut his eyes while something was put into his arms. A peal of laughter from Jo, Amy, Mrs. March, Hannah, and John caused him to open them the next minute, to find himself invested with two babies instead of one.

"Twins, by Jupiter!" was all Laurie said for a minute or two.

"Boy and girl. Aren't they beauties?" said the proud papa.

"We shall call the girl Daisy, so as not to have two Megs, and I suppose the mannie will be Jack, unless we find a better name," said Amy, with auntlike interest.

"Name him Demijohn, and call him 'Demi' for short," said Laurie.

"Daisy and Demi—just the thing!" cried Jo, clapping her hands. And so the babies were named.

As the months flew by, each of the girls was kept busy in her own way. All of Amy's efforts were centered upon becoming a true gentlewoman in mind and manners, of which Aunt Carrol approved to the point that she asked the girl to accompany her and her own daughter Flo on a tour of Europe.

There was not much time for preparation, and the house was in a ferment till the travelers were off. Amy bore up stoutly till the steamer sailed; then, just as the gangway was about to be withdrawn, it suddenly came over her that a whole ocean was soon to roll between her and those who loved her best, and she clung to Laurie, the last lingerer, saying with a sob, "Oh, take care of them for me. And if anything should happen—"

"I will, dear, I will. And if anything happens, I'll come and comfort you," whispered Laurie, little dreaming how soon he would be called upon to keep his word.

22 • Tender Troubles

Jo, I'm ANXIOUS about Beth."

"Why, Mother, she has seemed unusually well since the babies came."

"It's not her health that troubles me now—it's her spirits. I'm sure there is something on her mind, and I want you to discover what it is."

"I'll try, Marmee, I'll try," promised Jo.

"You're a great comfort, Jo," said Mrs. March warmly. "I always feel strong when you are at home, now that Meg is gone. Beth is too feeble and Amy too young to depend upon. But when the tug comes, you are always ready."

Jo warmed under her mother's praise. Later, while apparently absorbed in her own affairs, she watched Beth; and after many conflicting conjectures, finally settled upon one which seemed to explain the change in her. She was affecting to write busily one Saturday afternoon, when she and Beth were alone together; yet, as she scribbled, she kept her eye on her sister, who seemed unusually quiet. Sitting at the window, Beth frequently dropped her work into her lap while she leaned her head upon her hand in a dejected attitude and rested her eyes on the dull autumnal landscape. Suddenly someone passed below, whistling like an operatic blackbird, and a voice called out, "All serene! Coming in tonight."

Beth started, leaned forward, smiled and nodded, watched the passerby till his quick tramp died away, then said softly, as if to herself, "How strong and well and happy that dear boy looks."

"Hum!" said Jo, still intent upon her sister's face; for the bright color faded as quickly as it came, the smile vanished, and presently a tear lay shining on the window ledge. Beth whisked it off and glanced apprehensively at Jo; but she was scratching away at a tremendous rate, apparently engrossed in "Olympia's Oath."

Fearing to betray herself, Jo slipped away, murmuring something about needing more paper.

"Mercy on me, Beth loves Laurie!" she said, sitting down in her own room, pale with the shock of the discovery she believed she had just made. "If he shouldn't love her back again, how dreadful it would be!"

Though Laurie flirted with Amy and joked with Jo, his manner to Beth had always been peculiarly kind and gentle, but so was everybody's. Indeed, a general impression had prevailed in the family of late that "our boy" was getting fonder of Jo, who, however, wouldn't hear a word upon the subject and scolded violently if anybody dared to suggest it.

When Laurie first went to college, he fell in love about once a month; but these small flames were as brief as ardent, did no damage, and much amused Jo. But there came a time when Laurie ceased to worship at many shrines, hinted darkly at one all-absorbing passion, and indulged occasionally in Byronic fits of gloom.

Jo watched Laurie that night as she had never done before. As usual, Beth lay on the sofa and Laurie sat in a low chair close by, amusing her with all sorts of gossip; for she depended on her weekly "spin," and he never disappointed her. Jo fancied that Beth's eyes rested on the lively, dark face beside her with peculiar pleasure. She also fancied, having set her heart upon seeing it, that she saw a certain increase of gentleness in Laurie's manner, that he dropped his voice now and then, laughed less than usual, was a little absentminded, and settled the afghan over Beth's feet with an assiduity that was really almost tender.

Who knows! Stranger things have happened, thought Jo. *I do believe he would love her if the rest of us were out of the way.*

As everyone *was* out of the way but herself, Jo began to feel that she ought to dispose of herself with all speed. But where should she go? And burning to lay herself upon the shrine of sisterly devotion, she sat down to settle that point.

Now the old sofa was a regular patriarch of a sofa— long, broad, well cushioned, and low. It was a family refuge, and one corner had always been Jo's favorite lounging place. Among the many pillows that adorned the venerable couch was one, hard, round, covered with prickly horsehair, and furnished with a knobby button at each end; this repulsive pillow was her especial property, being used as a weapon of defense, a barricade, or a preventive of too much slumber.

Laurie knew this pillow well, and had cause to regard it with deep aversion, having been unmercifully pummeled with it in former days, when romping was allowed, and now frequently debarred by it from taking the seat he most coveted, next to Jo in the sofa corner. If "the sausage," as they called it, stood on end, it was a sign that he might approach and repose; but if it lay flat across the sofa, woe to the man, woman, or child who dared disturb it. That evening Jo forgot to barricade her corner and had not been in her seat five minutes before a massive form appeared beside her, and, with both arms spread over the sofa back, both long legs stretched out before him, Laurie exclaimed with a sigh of satisfaction, "Now *this* is filling at the price!"

"No slang," snapped Jo, slamming down the pillow. But it was too late; there was no room for it, and, coasting on to the floor, it disappeared in a most mysterious manner somewhere in the room.

"Come, Jo, don't be thorny. After studying himself to a skeleton all the week, a fellow deserves petting and ought to get it."

"Beth will pet you. I'm busy."

"No, she's not to be bothered with me. But you like that sort of thing, unless you've suddenly lost your taste for it. Have you? Do you hate your boy, and want to fire pillows at him?"

Mercy on us, this will never do, thought Jo, adding aloud, "Go and sing to me. I'm dying for some music."

"I'd rather stay here, thank you."

"Well, you can't. There isn't room. Go and make yourself useful, since you're too big to be ornamental. I thought you hated to be tied to a woman's apron strings," retorted Jo, quoting certain rebellious words of his own.

"Ah, that depends on who wears the apron!"

"Are you going?" demanded Jo, diving for the pillow.

He fled at once, and the minute it was well "Up with the bonnets of bonnie Dundee" she slipped away, to return no more till the young gentleman had departed in high dudgeon.

Jo lay long awake that night and was just dropping off when the sound of a stifled sob made her fly to Beth's bedside with the anxious inquiry, "What is it, dear?"

"I thought you were asleep," sobbed Beth.

"Is it the old pain, my precious?"

"No, it's a new one, but I can bear it." And Beth tried to check her tears.

"Tell me about it, and let me cure it as I often did the other."

"You can't; there is no cure." There Beth's voice gave way, and, clinging to her sister, she cried so despairingly that Jo was frightened.

"Where is it? Shall I call Mother?"

Beth did not answer the first question; but in the dark one hand went involuntarily to her heart, as if the pain were there; with the other she held Jo fast, whispering eagerly, "No, no, don't call her. I'll be quiet and go to sleep, indeed I will."

Jo obeyed; but as her hand went softly to and fro across Beth's forehead and wet eyelids, her heart was very full, and she longed to speak. But young as she was, Jo had learned that hearts, like flowers, cannot be rudely handled, but must open naturally; so, though she believed she knew the cause of Beth's new pain, she only said, in her tenderest tone, "Does anything trouble you, deary?"

"Yes, Jo!" after a long pause.

"Wouldn't it comfort you to tell me what it is?"

"Not now, not yet."

"Then I won't ask! But remember, Bethy, that Mother and Jo are always glad to hear you and try to help you, if we can."

"I know it. I'll tell you by and by."

Cheek to cheek they fell asleep, and on the morrow Beth seemed quite herself again.

Jo pondered over a project for some days, and then she confided in her mother.

"You asked me the other day what my wishes were. I'll tell you one of them, Marmee," she began as they sat alone together. "I want to go away somewhere this winter."

"Why, Jo?" And her mother looked up quickly.

Jo answered soberly, "I want something new. I feel restless, and anxious to be seeing, doing, and learning more than I am. I brood too much over my own small affairs and need stirring up. So, as I can be spared this winter, I'd like to hop a little way and try my wings."

"Where will you hop?"

"To New York. I had a bright idea yesterday, and this is it. You know Mrs. Kirke wrote to you for some respectable young person to teach her children and sew. It's rather hard to find just the thing, but I think I should suit if I tried."

"But your writing?"

"All the better for the change. I shall see and hear new things, get new ideas, and, even if I haven't much time there, I shall bring home quantities of material for my rubbish."

"I have no doubt of it. But are these your only reasons?"

"No, Mother."

"May I know the others?"

Jo looked up and Jo looked down, then said slowly, with

sudden color in her cheeks, "It may be vain and wrong to say it, but—I'm afraid—Laurie is getting too fond of me."

"Then you don't care for him in the way it is evident he begins to care for you?" And Mrs. March looked anxious as she put the question.

"Mercy, no! I love the dear boy as I always have, and am immensely proud of him. But as for anything more, it's out of the question."

"I'm glad of that, Jo!"

"Why, please?"

"Because, dear, I don't think you are suited to one another. As friends you are very happy, and your frequent quarrels soon blow over. But I fear you would both rebel if you were mated for life. You are too much alike and too fond of freedom, not to mention hot tempers and strong wills, to get on happily together in a relation which needs infinite patience and forbearance as well as love."

"That's just the feeling I had, though I couldn't express it. I think I had better go away before it comes to anything."

"I agree with you, and if it can be managed, you shall go," said Mrs. March quietly. "By the way, Beth seems brighter this last day or two. Have you spoken to her?"

"Yes. She owned she had a trouble and promised to tell me by and by. I said no more, for I think I know it." And Jo told her little story.

Mrs. March shook her head and did not take so romantic a view of the case, but looked grave and repeated her opinion that, for Laurie's sake, Jo should go away for a time.

"Let us say nothing about it to him till the plan is settled. Then I'll run away before he can collect his wits and be tragical. Beth must think I'm going to please myself, as I am, for I can't talk about Laurie to her. But she can pet and comfort him after I'm gone, and so cure him of his romantic notion. He's been through so many little trials of the sort, he's used to it, and will soon get over his love-lornity."

The plan was talked over in a family council and agreed upon; for Mrs. Kirke gladly accepted Jo and promised to make a pleasant home for her. The teaching would render her independent; and such leisure as she got might be made profitable by writing, while the new scenes and society would be both useful and agreeable. Jo liked the prospect and was eager to be gone, for the home nest was growing too narrow for her restless nature and adventurous spirit. When all was settled, with fear and trembling she told Laurie; but to her surprise, he took it very quietly. He had been graver than usual of late, but very pleasant; and, when jokingly accused of turning over a new leaf, he answered soberly, "So I am, and I mean this one shall stay turned."

Jo was very much relieved that one of his virtuous fits should come on just then, and she made her preparations with a lightened heart—for Beth seemed more cheerful—and hoped she was doing the best for all.

"One thing I leave to your special care, Bethy," she said.

"You mean your papers?"

"No—my boy! Be very good to him, won't you?"

"Of course I will. But I can't fill your place, and he'll miss you sadly."

"It won't hurt him. So remember, I leave him to your charge, to plague, pet, and keep in order."

"I'll try to do my best, for your sake," promised Beth,

wondering why Jo looked at her so queerly.

When Laurie said good-bye, he whispered significantly, "It won't do a bit of good, Jo. My eye is on you. So mind what you do, or I'll come and bring you home."

23 · Jo's Journal

DEAR MARMEE AND BETH,

I'm going to write you a regular volume, for I've got lots
to tell, though I'm not a fine young lady traveling on the
continent.

Mrs. Kirke welcomed me so kindly I felt at home at once,
even in that big boardinghouse full of strangers. She gave me
a funny little sky parlor—all she had; but there is a stove in it
and a nice table in a sunny window, so I can sit here and write
whenever I like. A fine view, and a church tower opposite, and
I took a fancy to my den on the spot. The nursery, where I am
to teach and sew, is a pleasant room next Mrs. Kirke's private
parlor, and the two little girls are pretty children—rather
spoiled, I guess, but they took to me after telling them "The
Seven Bad Pigs," and I've no doubt I shall make a model
governess.

I am to have my meals with the children, if I prefer it to the
great table, and for the present I do, for I am bashful, though
no one would believe it.

As I went downstairs that first afternoon, I saw something
I liked. The flights are very long in this tall house, and as I
stood waiting at the head of the third one for a little servant
girl to lumber up, I saw a queer-looking man come along behind her, take the heavy hod of coal out of her hand, carry it
all the way up, put it down at a door, and walk away, saying,
with a kind nod and a foreign accent, "It goes better so. The

195

little back is too young to haf such a heaviness."

Wasn't it good of him? I like such things; for, as Father says, trifles show character. When I mentioned it to Mrs. K. that evening, she laughed and said, "That must have been Professor Bhaer. He's always doing things of that sort."

Mrs. K. told me he was from Berlin; very learned and good, but poor as a church mouse, and gives lessons to support himself and two little orphan nephews whom he is educating here, according to the wishes of his sister, who married an American. Not a very romantic story, but it interested me; and I was glad to hear that Mrs. K. lends him her parlor for some of his scholars. There is a glass door between it and the nursery, and I mean to peep at him, and then I'll tell you how he looks. He's almost forty, so it's no harm, Marmee.

After tea and a go-to-bed romp with the little girls, I attacked the big workbasket, and had a quiet evening chatting with my new friend. I shall keep a journal-letter, and send it once a week; so good night, and more tomorrow.

Tuesday Eve

Had a lively time in my seminary this morning, for the children acted like Sancho; and at one time I really thought I should shake them all around. Some good angel inspired me to try gymnastics, and I kept it up till they were glad to sit down and keep still. After luncheon, the girl took them out for a walk, and I went to my needlework, like little Mabel, "with a willing mind." I was thanking my stars that I'd learned to make nice buttonholes, when the parlor door opened and shut, and someone began to hum "Kennst du das land," like a big bumblebee. It was dreadfully improper, I know, but I couldn't resist the temptation; and lifting one end of the curtain before the glass door, I peeped in. Professor Bhaer was there; and while he arranged his books, I took a good look at him. A regular German—rather stout, with brown hair tumbled all over his head, a bushy beard, droll nose, the kindest eyes I ever saw, and a splendid big voice that does one's ears good, after our sharp or slipshod American gabble. His clothes were rusty, his hands were large, and he hadn't a handsome feature in his face, except his beautiful teeth; yet I liked him, for he had a fine head; his linen was spandy nice, and he looked like a gentleman, though two buttons were off his coat, and there was a patch on one shoe. He looked sober in spite of his humming, till he went to the window to turn the hyacinth bulbs toward the sun and stroke the cat, who received him like an old friend. Then he smiled and, when a tap came at the door, called out in a loud, brisk tone, "*Herein!*"

I was just going to run, when I caught sight of a morsel of a child with a big book, and stopped to see what was going on.

"Me wants my Bhaer," said the mite, slamming down her book and running to meet him.

"Thou shalt haf thy Bhaer. Come, then, and take a goot hug from him, my Tina," said the Professor, catching her up with a laugh.

"Now we mus tuddy my lessin," went on the funny little thing; so he put her up at the table, opened the great dictionary she had brought, and gave her a pencil and paper, and she scribbled away.

Another knock, and the appearance of two young ladies sent me back to my work, and there I virtuously remained through all the noise and gabbling next door. One of the girls kept laughing coquettishly, and the other pronounced her German with an accent that must have made it hard for him to keep sober.

Both seemed to try his patience sorely; for more than once I heard him say emphatically, "No, no, it is *not* so; you haf not attend to what I say"; and once more there was a loud rap, as if he struck the table with his book, followed by the despairing exclamation, "Prut! It all goes bad this day."

Poor man, I pitied him; and when the girls were gone, took just one more peep, to see if he survived it. He seemed to have thrown himself back in his chair, tired out, and sat there with his eyes shut, till the clock struck two, when he jumped up, put his books in his pocket, as if ready for another lesson, and taking little Tina, who had fallen asleep on the sofa, in his arms, he carried her quietly away. I guess he has a hard life of it.

Mrs. Kirke asked me if I wouldn't go down to the five o'clock dinner; and feeling a little bit homesick, I thought I would, just to see what sort of people are under the same roof with me. There was the usual assortment of young men, absorbed in themselves; young couples absorbed in each other; young ladies in their babies; and old gentlemen in politics. I don't think I shall care to have much to do with any of them, except one sweet-faced maiden lady.

Cast away at the very bottom of the table was the Professor, shouting answers to the questions of a very inquisitive, deaf old gentleman on one side, and talking philosophy with a Frenchman on the other. If Amy had been here, she'd have turned her back on him forever, because, sad to relate, he had a great appetite and shoveled in his dinner in a manner that would have horrified "her ladyship." I didn't mind, for I like "to see folks eat with a relish," as Hannah says, and the poor man must have needed a deal of food, after teaching idiots all day.

Thursday

Yesterday was a quiet day, spent in teaching, sewing, and writing in my little room, which is very cozy, with a light and a fire. I picked up a few bits of news; it seems that Tina is the child of the Frenchwoman who does the fine ironing here. The little thing has lost her heart to Mr. Bhaer; Kitty and Minnie Kirke likewise regard him with affection.

The maiden lady is a Miss Norton, rich, cultivated, and kind. She has fine books and pictures, knows interesting persons, and seems friendly.

I was in our parlor last evening when Mr. Bhaer came in with some newspapers for Mrs. Kirke. She wasn't there, but Minnie, who is a little old woman, introduced us very prettily.

I was doomed to see a good deal of him, for today, as I passed his door on my way out, by accident I knocked against it with my umbrella. It flew open, and there he stood, with a big, blue sock on one hand and a darning needle in the other. He said in his loud, cheerful way, "You haf a fine day to make your walk. Bon voyage, mademoiselle."

I laughed all the way downstairs; but it was a little pathetic, also, to think of the poor man having to mend his own clothes.

Saturday

I have made a call on Miss Norton, who has a room full of lovely things, and who was very charming, for she showed me all her treasures and asked me if I would sometimes go with her to lectures and concerts, as her escort, if I enjoyed them. She put it as a favor; but I'm sure Mrs. Kirke told her about us, and she does it as a kindness to me. I'm proud as Lucifer, but such favors from such people don't burden me, and I accepted gratefully.

The Professor and I are very good friends now, and I've begun to take lessons in German. I really couldn't help it, and it all came about in such a funny way that I must tell you. Mrs. Kirke called to me one day as I passed Mr. Bhaer's room, where she was rummaging.

"Did you ever see such a den, my dear? Just come in and help me put it to rights."

I went in, and while we worked I looked about me. Books and papers everywhere; a broken meerschaum and an old flute over the mantelpiece, as if done with; a ragged bird, without any tail, chirped on one window seat and a box of white mice adorned the other; half-finished boats and bits of string lay among the manuscripts. I picked up two heelless socks.

"I will mend these," I said. "I don't mind it, and he needn't know. I'd like to—he's so kind to me about bringing my letters and lending me books."

So I knit heels into two pairs of socks and repaired some of his other clothes, also. Nothing was said, and I hoped he wouldn't find it out, but one day last week he caught me at it.

He laughed and said, "Mees March, I haf a debt to pay," and he pointed to my work. "I haf a heart, and I feel the thanks for this. Come, a little lesson in German now and then, or—no more good fairy works for me."

Of course I couldn't say anything after that, and as it really is a splendid opportunity, I made the bargain, and we began. I took four lessons, and then I stuck fast in a grammatical bog.

The Professor was very patient with me, but it must have been a torment to him, and now and then he'd look at me with such an expression of mild despair, that it was a toss-up with me whether to laugh or cry. I tried both ways; and when it came to a sniff of utter mortification and woe, he just threw the grammar onto the floor and marched out of the room. I felt myself disgraced and deserted forever, but didn't blame him a particle, and was scrambling my papers together, meaning to rush upstairs and shake myself hard, when in he came, as brisk and beaming as if I'd covered my name with glory.

"Now we shall try a new way. You and I will read these pleasant little Märchen together and dig no more in that dry book; that goes in the corner for making us trouble."

He spoke so kindly, and opened Hans Andersen's fairy tales so invitingly before me, that I was more ashamed than ever, and went at my lesson in a neck-or-nothing style that seemed to amuse him immensely. I forgot my bashfulness and pegged away (no other word will express it) with all my might, tumbling over long words, pronouncing according to the inspiration of the minute, and doing my very best.

After that we got on better, and now I read my lessons pretty well; for this way of studying suits me, and I can see that the grammar gets tucked into the tales and poetry, as one gives pills in jelly. I like it very much, and he doesn't seem tired of it yet, which is very good of him, isn't it? I mean to give him something for Christmas, for I don't dare offer money. Tell me something nice, Marmee.

I'm glad that Laurie seems so happy and busy, that he has given up smoking, and lets his hair grow. You see, Beth manages him better than I did. I'm not jealous, dear; do your best, only don't make a saint of him. I'm afraid I couldn't like him without a spice of human naughtiness. Read him bits of my letters. I haven't time to write much, and that will do just as well. Thank Heaven Beth continues comfortable.

January

A happy New Year to you all, my dearest family, which of course includes Mr. L. and a young man by the name of

Teddy. I can't tell you how much I enjoyed your Christmas bundle, for I didn't get it till night and had given up hoping. Your letter came in the morning, but you said nothing about a parcel, meaning it for a surprise; I was disappointed, for I'd had a "kind of a feeling" that you wouldn't forget me. I felt a little low in my mind as I sat up in my room after tea; and when the big, muddy, battered-looking bundle was brought to me, I just hugged it, and pranced. It was so homey and refreshing that I sat down on the floor, and read, and looked, and ate, and laughed, and cried, in my usual absurd way. The things were just what I wanted, and all the better for being made instead of bought. Beth's new "ink-bib" was capital; and Hannah's box of hard gingerbread will be a treasure. I'll be sure and wear the nice flannels you sent, Marmee, and read carefully the books Father has marked. Thank you heaps and heaps!

Speaking of books reminds me that I'm getting rich in that line; for on New Year's Day Mr. Bhaer gave me a fine Shakespeare. It is one he values much, and I've often admired it, set up in the place of honor, with his German Bible, Plato, Homer, and Milton. So you may imagine how I felt when he brought it down and showed me my name that he had written in it, "from your friend Friedrich Bhaer."

Now, don't laugh at his name; it isn't pronounced either Bear or Beer, but something between the two, as only Germans can give it. I'm glad you both like what I tell you about him, and hope you will know him someday. Mother would admire his warm heart, Father his wise head. I admire both, and feel rich in my new "friend Friedrich Bhaer."

Not having much money, nor knowing what he'd like, I got several little things and put them about the room, where he would find them unexpectedly. They were useful, pretty, or funny—a new standish on his table, a little vase for his flower —he always has one or a bit of green in a glass, to keep him fresh, he says—and a holder for his blower, so that he needn't burn up what Amy calls "mouchoirs." Poor as he is, he didn't forget a servant or a child in the house, and not a soul forgot him. I was so glad of that.

They got up a masquerade and had a gay time New Year's Eve. I didn't mean to go down, having no dress; but at the last minute Mrs. Kirke remembered some old brocades, and Miss Norton lent me lace and feathers; so I rigged up as Mrs. Malaprop, and sailed in with a mask on. No one knew me, for I disguised my voice, and no one dreamed that the silent, haughty Miss March (for they think I am very stiff and cool, most of them; and so I am to whippersnappers) could dance, and dress, and burst out into a "nice derangement of epitaphs, like an allegory on the banks of the Nile." I enjoyed it very much; and when we unmasked, it was fun to see them stare at me. I heard one of the young men tell another that he knew I'd been an actress; in fact he thought he remembered seeing me in one of the minor theaters. Meg will relish that joke.

Mr. Bhaer was Nick Bottom, and Tina was Titania—a perfect little fairy in his arms. To see them dance was "quite a landscape," to use a Teddyism.

I had a very happy New Year, after all, and when I thought it over in my room, I felt as if I was getting on a little in spite of my many failures; for I'm cheerful all the time now, work with a will, and take more interest in other people than I used to, which is satisfactory. Bless you all!

Ever your loving
Jo

24 • A Friend

THOUGH VERY happy in the social atmosphere about her, and very busy with the daily work that earned her bread, making it sweeter for the effort, Jo still found time for literary labors. The purpose which now took possession of her was a natural one to a poor and ambitious girl; she saw that money conferred power; money and power, therefore, she resolved to have, not to be used for herself alone, but for those whom she loved more than self. The dream of filling home with comforts, giving Beth everything she wanted, from strawberries in winter to an organ in her bedroom, going abroad herself, and always having *more* than enough, so that she might indulge in the luxury of charity, had been for years Jo's most cherished castle in the air.

She took to writing sensation stories—for in those dark ages even all-perfect America read rubbish. She told no one, but concocted a "thrilling tale" and boldly carried it herself to Mr. Dashwood, editor of *The Weekly Volcano*. She dressed herself in her best and, trying to persuade herself that she was neither excited nor nervous, bravely climbed two pairs of dark, dirty stairs to find herself in a disorderly room, a cloud of cigar smoke, and the presence of three old gentlemen sitting with their heels rather higher than their hats, which articles of dress none of them took the trouble to remove on her appearance. Somewhat daunted by this reception, Jo hesitated on the threshold, murmuring in much embarrassment, "Excuse me. I was looking for *The Weekly Volcano* office. I wished to see Mr. Dashwood."

Down went the highest pair of heels, up rose the smokiest gentleman, and, carefully cherishing his cigar between his fingers, he advanced with a nod and a countenance expressive of nothing but sleep. Feeling that she must get through with the matter somehow, Jo produced her manuscript and, blushing redder and redder with each sentence, blundered out fragments of the little speech carefully prepared for the occasion.

"A friend of mine desired me to offer—a story—just as an experiment—would like your opinion—be glad to write more if this suits."

While she blushed and blundered, Mr. Dashwood had taken the manuscript and was turning over the leaves with a pair of rather dirty fingers and casting critical glances up and down the neat pages.

"Well," he said indifferently, "you can leave it if you want to. We've more of this sort of thing on hand than we know what to do with, at present, but I'll run my eye over it and give you an answer next week."

When she went again, Mr. Dashwood was alone, whereat she rejoiced. Mr. Dashwood was much wider awake than before, which was agreeable, and Mr. Dashwood was not too deeply absorbed in a cigar to remember his manners, so the second interview was a great deal more comfortable than the first.

"We'll take this, if you don't object to a few alterations. It's too long, but omitting the passages I've marked will make it just the right length," he said in a businesslike tone.

Jo hardly knew her own manuscript again, so crumpled and underscored were its pages and paragraphs; but, feeling as a tender parent might on being asked to cut off her baby's legs in order that it might fit into a new cradle, she looked at the marked passages and was surprised to find that all the moral reflections, which she had carefully put in as ballast for much romance, had been stricken out.

"We give from twenty-five to thirty for things of this sort. Pay when it comes out," said Mr. Dashwood.

"Very well. You can have it," said Jo, handing back the story; for, after the dollar-a-column work, even twenty-five seemed good pay.

As she departed, Mr. Dashwood put his feet upon his desk again and remarked, "Poor and proud, as usual, but she'll do."

Following Mr. Dashwood's directions and making Mrs. Northbury her model, Jo rashly took a plunge into the sea of sensational literature; but, thanks to the life preserver thrown her by a friend, she came up again, and not much the worse for her ducking.

She soon became interested in her work, for her emaciated purse grew stout and the little hoard she was making to take Beth to the mountains next summer grew slowly but surely as the weeks passed. One thing disturbed her satisfaction, and that was that she did not tell them at home. She had a feeling that Father and Mother would not approve, and preferred to have her own way first and beg pardon afterward. It was easy to keep her secret, because no name appeared with the stories.

While endowing her imaginary heroes with every perfection under the sun, Jo was discovering a live hero, who interested her in spite of many imperfections. Mr. Bhaer, in one of their conversations, had advised her to study simple, true, and lovely characters, wherever she found them, as good training for a writer; Jo took him at his word, for she coolly turned round and studied—him.

Why everybody liked him was what puzzled Jo at first. He was neither rich nor great, young nor handsome, in no respect what is called fascinating, imposing, or brilliant; and yet he was as attractive as a genial fire, and people seemed to gather about him as naturally as about a warm hearth. He was poor, yet always appeared to be giving something away; a stranger, yet everyone was his friend; no longer young, but as happy-hearted as a boy; plain and odd, yet his face looked beautiful to many and his oddities were freely forgiven for his sake by those who knew him.

Jo watched him, trying to discover the charm, and at last decided it was benevolence which worked the miracle. If he had any sorrow, "it sat with its head under its wing," and he turned only his sunny side to the world. There were lines upon his forehead, but time seemed to have touched him gently. The pleasant curves about his mouth were the memorials of many friendly words and cheery laughs; his eyes were never cold or hard, and his big hand had a warm, strong grasp that was more expressive than words.

"That's it!" said Jo to herself, when she at length discovered that genuine goodwill toward one's fellowmen could beautify and dignify even a stout German teacher.

She began to see that character is a better possession

than money, rank, intellect, or beauty and to feel that if greatness is what a wise man has defined it to be—"truth, reverence, and goodwill"—then her friend Friedrich Bhaer was not only good, but also great.

This belief strengthened daily. She valued his esteem, she coveted his respect, she wanted to be worthy of his friendship; and, just when the wish was sincerest, she came near losing everything. It all grew out of a cocked hat; for one evening the Professor came in to give Jo her lesson, with a paper soldier-cap, made from an old newspaper, on his head. Tina had put it there, and he had forgotten to take it off.

Then suddenly he did take off the hat and caught sight of a picture on it. He unfolded the paper and said with an air of great disgust, "I wish these papers did not come in the house; they are not for children to see, nor young people to read. It is not well, and I haf no patience with those who make this harm."

Jo glanced at the sheet and saw a pleasing illustration composed of a lunatic, a corpse, a villain, and a viper. She did not like it; but the impulse that made her turn it over was not one of displeasure, but fear, because for a minute she fancied the paper was *The Volcano*. It was not, however, and her panic subsided as she remembered that, even if it had been, and one of her own tales in it, there would have been no name to betray her. She had betrayed herself, however, by a look and a blush; for though an absent man, the Professor saw a good deal more than people fancied. He knew that Jo wrote, but as she never spoke of it, he asked no questions, in spite of a strong desire to see her work.

Mr. Bhaer now walked to the fire, crumpling the paper

207

into a tight ball in his hands.

"No," he said, "they have no right to put poison in the sugarplum and let the small ones eat it. They should think a little, and sweep mud in the street before they do this thing."

Jo sat still, looking as if the fire had come to her; for her cheeks burned long after the cocked hat had turned to smoke.

"I should like much to send all the rest after him," muttered the Professor.

Jo thought what a blaze her pile of papers upstairs would make, and her hard-earned money lay rather heavily on her conscience at that minute.

They went on with their lesson, with Jo feeling that the words *Weekly Volcano* were printed in large type on her forehead.

As soon as she went to her room, she got out her papers and carefully reread every one of her stories. The faults of these poor stories now glared at her dreadfully.

"They *are* trash and will soon be worse than trash if I go on, for each is more sensational than the last. I can't read this stuff in sober earnest without being horribly ashamed of it. And what should I do if they were seen at home or Mr. Bhaer got hold of them?"

Jo turned hot at the bare idea and stuffed the whole bundle into her stove.

But when nothing remained of all her work except a heap of ashes, and the money in her lap, Jo looked sober, wondering what she ought to do about her wages.

"I think I haven't done much harm *yet*, and may keep this to pay for my time," she said, after long meditation.

Jo wrote no more sensational stories, deciding that the

money did not pay for her share of the sensation. She produced an intensely moral tale, but found no purchaser for it. She tried a child's story, but found that no editor paid for juvenile literature. So Jo corked up her inkstand and said in a fit of very wholesome humility, "I don't know anything. I'll wait till I do before I try again."

Mr. Bhaer helped her in many ways, proving himself a true friend, and Jo was happy; for while her pen lay idle, she was learning other lessons beside German, and laying a foundation for the story of her own life.

It was a pleasant winter and a long one, for she did not leave Mrs. Kirke till June.

She was going early; so she bade them all good-bye overnight. And when Mr. Bhaer's time came, she said warmly, "Now, sir, you won't forget to come and see us, if you ever travel our way, will you? I'll never forgive you, if you do, for I want them all to know my friend."

"Do you? Shall I come?" he asked, looking down at her with an eager expression that she did not see.

"Yes, come next month. Laurie graduates then, and you'd enjoy commencement as something new."

"That is your best friend, of whom you speak?" he said, in an altered tone.

"Yes, my boy Teddy. I'm very proud of him and should like you to see him."

Jo looked up then, quite unconscious of anything but her own pleasure in the prospect of showing them to one another. Something in Mr. Bhaer's face suddenly recalled the fact that she might find Laurie more than a best friend, and simply because she particularly wished not to look as if anything was the matter, she involuntarily began to blush; and the more she tried not to, the redder she grew.

The Professor saw it, and his own expression changed from that momentary anxiety to its usual expression as he said cordially, "I fear I shall not make the time for that, but I wish the friend much success, and you all happiness. Gott bless you!" And with that he shook hands warmly and went away.

Early as it was, he was at the station next morning to see Jo off; and, thanks to him, she began her solitary journey with the pleasant memory of a familiar face smiling its farewell, a bunch of violets to keep her company, and, best of all, the happy thought, *Well, the winter's gone, and I've written no books and earned no fortune. But I've made a friend worth having, and I'll try to keep him all my life.*

25 · Heartache

LAURIE GRADUATED with honors and gave the Latin oration with the grace of a Phillips and the eloquence of a Demosthenes—so his friends said. They were all there—his grandfather, oh, so proud! Mr. and Mrs. March, John and Meg, Jo and Beth, and all exulted over him.

"I've got to stay for this confounded supper, but I shall be home early tomorrow. You'll come and meet me as usual, girls?" Laurie said as he put the sisters into the carriage after the joys of the day were over. He said "girls," but he meant Jo, for she was the only one who kept up the old custom.

She had not the heart to refuse her splendid, successful boy anything and answered warmly, "I'll come, Teddy, rain or shine, and march before you, playing 'Hail, the Conquering Hero Comes' on a Jew's harp."

Laurie thanked her with a look that made her think, in a sudden panic, *Oh, deary me! I know he'll say something, and then what shall I do?*

Evening meditation and morning work somewhat allayed her fears, and, having decided that she wouldn't be vain enough to think people were going to propose when she had given them every reason to know what her answer would be, she set forth at the appointed time, hoping Teddy wouldn't go and make her hurt his poor little feelings.

But when she saw his stalwart figure looming in the distance, she had a strong desire to turn about and run away.

"Where's the Jew's harp, Jo?" cried Laurie as soon as he was within speaking distance.

"I forgot it." And Jo took heart again, for that salutation could not be called lover-like.

She talked on rapidly about all sorts of faraway subjects, till they turned from the road into the little path that led homeward through the grove.

"It's no use, Jo," said Laurie suddenly and firmly. "We've got to have it out, and the sooner we do it the better it will be for both of us."

"Say what you like, then; I'll listen," said Jo, with a desperate sort of patience.

"I've loved you ever since I've known you, Jo—couldn't help it, you've been so good to me. I've tried to show it, but you wouldn't let me. Now I'm going to make you hear and give me an answer, for I *can't* go on so any longer."

"I wanted to save you this. I thought you'd understand—" began Jo, finding it a great deal harder than she had expected it to be.

"I know you did, but girls are so queer you never know what they mean. They say no when they mean yes, and drive a man out of his wits just for the fun of it," returned Laurie, entrenching himself behind an undeniable fact.

"I don't see why I can't love you as you want me to!" cried Jo. "I've tried but I can't change the feeling, and it would be a lie to say I do when I don't."

"Really, truly, Jo?"

He stopped short and caught both her hands as he put his question with a look that she did not soon forget.

"Really, truly, dear!"

They were in the grove now, close by the stile; as the last words dropped reluctantly from Jo's lips, Laurie dropped her hands and turned as if to go on, but for once in his life that fence was too much for him.

There was a long pause, while a blackbird sang blithely on the willow by the river and the tall grass rustled in the wind. Jo sat down on the step of the stile and said very soberly, "Laurie, I want to tell you something."

"Don't tell me that!" cried Laurie fiercely. "I can't bear it now, Jo!"

"Tell you what?" she asked, wondering at his violence.

"That you love that old man."

"What old man?" demanded Jo, thinking he must mean his grandfather.

"That devilish professor you were always writing about. If you say you love him I know I shall do something desperate"—and he looked as if he might keep his word.

Jo wanted to laugh, but restrained herself and said warmly, "He isn't old, nor anything bad, but good and kind, and the best friend I've got, next to you. I haven't the least idea of loving him or anybody else."

Seeing a ray of hope in that speech, Laurie threw himself down on the grass at her feet, leaned his arm on the lower step of the stile, and looked up at her with an expectant face. Now, that arrangement was not conducive to calm speech or clear thought on Jo's part. She gently turned his head away, saying, as she stroked the wavy hair, "I agree with Mother that you and I are not suited to each other, because our quick tempers and strong wills would probably make us very miserable, if we were so foolish as to—"

Jo paused a little over the last word, but Laurie uttered it with a rapturous expression. "Marry—no, we shouldn't! If you loved me, Jo, I should be a perfect saint, for you can make me anything you like!"

"No, I can't. I've tried it and failed, and I won't risk our happiness by such a serious experiment. We don't agree, and we never shall. So we'll be good friends all our lives, but we won't do anything rash."

"Yes, we will, if we get the chance," muttered Laurie.

Jo ignored that with, "You'll see that I'm right, by and by, and thank me for it."

"I'll be hanged if I do!" cried Laurie. He bounced up off the grass, burning with indignation at the bare idea.

"I've done my best!" cried Jo, losing patience with poor Teddy. "But you *won't* be reasonable. I shall always be fond of you, very fond, indeed, as a friend. But I'll never marry you, and the sooner you believe it, the better it will be for both of us. So now!"

That speech was like fire to gunpowder. Laurie looked at her a minute as if he did not quite know what to do with himself, then turned sharply away, saying in a desperate tone, "You'll be sorry some day, Jo."

"Oh, where are you going?" she cried, for the look on his face frightened her.

"To the devil!" was the consoling answer.

For a minute Jo's heart stood still as he swung himself down the bank toward the river; but it takes much folly, sin, or misery to send a young man to a violent death; and Laurie was not one of the weak sort who are conquered by a single failure. He flung his hat and coat into his boat and rowed away with all his might.

Jo went slowly home, feeling as if she had murdered some innocent thing.

Now I must go and prepare Mr. Laurence to be very kind to my poor boy, she thought. *I wish he'd love Beth. Perhaps he may, in time, but I am beginning to think I was mistaken about her.*

Being sure that no one could do it so well as herself, she went straight to Mr. Laurence, told her story bravely through, and then broke down, crying so dismally over her own insensibility that the kind old gentleman, though sorely disappointed, did not utter a reproach. He found it difficult to understand how any girl could help loving Laurie and hoped she would change her mind, but he knew even better than Jo that love cannot be forced; so he shook his head sadly and resolved to carry his boy out of harm's way.

When Laurie came home, dead tired, but quite composed, his grandfather met him as if he knew nothing, and kept up the delusion very successfully for an hour or two. But when they sat together in the twilight, it was hard work for the old man to ramble on as usual and harder still for the young one to listen. He bore it as long as he could, then went to his piano and began to play.

"I can't stand this," muttered the old gentleman. Up he got, groped his way to the piano, laid a kind hand on either of the broad shoulders, and said, as gently as a woman, "I know, my boy, I know."

Laurie asked, sharply, "Who told you?"

"Jo, herself."

"Then there's an end of it!" And he shook off his grandfather's hands with an impatient motion; for, though grateful enough for the sympathy, his man's pride could not bear a man's pity.

His grandfather understood and said gently, "Take it as a man. Why not go abroad, as you planned, and forget it?"

"I can't."

"But you've been wild to go, and I promised you should, when you got through college."

"Ah, but I didn't mean to go alone!"

Mr. Laurence kept hold of the young man, as if fearful that he would break away, as his father had done before him. He said, "There is business in London that needs looking after. I meant you should attend to it. I will go, too. Things here will get on very well, with Brooke to manage them. My partners do almost everything; I'm merely holding on till you take my place. We can be off at any time."

Now, Laurie felt just then that his heart was entirely broken and the world a howling wilderness; but the broken heart gave an unexpected leap, and a green oasis or two suddenly appeared in the howling wilderness.

"Just as you like, sir," he said quietly. "It doesn't matter where I go or what I do."

Being an energetic individual, Mr. Laurence struck while the iron was hot; and before the blighted being recovered spirit enough to rebel, they were off.

As Jo told him good-bye, she knew that the boy Laurie would never come again.

When Jo came home that spring, she had been struck with the change in Beth. No one spoke of it or seemed aware of it, for it had come too gradually to startle those who saw her daily; but to eyes sharpened by absence it

217

was very plain, and a heavy weight fell on Jo's heart as she saw her sister's face.

When Laurie was gone, this vague anxiety haunted her more and more. She took her savings and with them paid for a trip for herself and Beth, down to the seashore, where they could live much in the open air.

The sisters were always together, as if they felt instinctively that a long separation was not far away. During the quiet weeks, when the shadow grew so plain to her, Jo said nothing of it to those at home, believing that it would tell itself when Beth came back no better.

She wondered if Beth really guessed the hard truth, and what thoughts were passing through her mind during the long hours when she lay on the sand with her head in Jo's lap.

One day Beth told her. Jo thought she was asleep, she lay so still, and, putting down her book, sat looking at her with wistful eyes, trying to see signs of hope in the faint color on Beth's cheeks. But she could not find enough to satisfy her, for the cheeks were very thin, and the hands seemed too feeble to hold even the rosy little shells she had been gathering.

For a minute her eyes were dimmed with tears, and when they were cleared, Beth was looking up at her so tenderly that there was hardly any need for her to say, "Jo, dear, I'm glad you know it. I've tried to tell you, but I couldn't."

Beth tried to comfort and sustain her stronger sister. "I've known it for a good while, dear, and now I'm used to it, it isn't hard to think of or to bear. Try to see it so, and don't be troubled about me, because it's best; indeed it is, Jo."

218

"Is that what made you so unhappy in the autumn, Beth?" asked Jo, refusing to see or say that it *was* best, but glad to know that Laurie had no part in Beth's trouble.

"Yes, I gave up hoping then, but I didn't like to own it. I tried to think it was a sick fancy. But when I saw you all so well and strong and full of happy plans, it was hard to feel that I could never be like you."

"You shall get better, Beth," said Jo with a firmness she did not feel. "I can't let you go. I'll work and pray and fight for you. I'll keep you in spite of everything. There must be ways. It can't be too late. God won't be so cruel as to take you from me."

By and by Beth said, with recovered serenity, "You'll tell them this when we go home?"

"I think they will see it without words," sighed Jo.

She was right. There was no need for any words when they got home, for Father and Mother saw plainly, now, what they had prayed to be saved from seeing. Tired with her short journey, Beth went to bed at once, saying how glad she was to be at home; and when Jo went down, she found that she would be spared the hard task of telling Beth's secret. Her father stood leaning his head on the mantelpiece, and did not turn as she came in; but her mother stretched out her arms as if for help, and Jo went to comfort her without a word.

26 • New Impressions

AT THREE O'CLOCK in the afternoon all the fashionable
world at Nice may be seen on the Promenade des Anglais,
a charming place; for the wide walk, bordered with palms,
flowers, and tropical shrubs, is bounded on one side by
the sea, on the other by the grand drive, lined with hotels
and villas, while beyond lie orange orchards and the hills.
Many nations are represented, many languages spoken,
many costumes worn; and on a sunny day the spectacle is
as gay and brilliant as a carnival.

Here the haughty English, lively French, sober Germans, handsome Spaniards, ugly Russians, meek Jews,
free-and-easy Americans—all drive, sit, or saunter here,
chatting over the news and criticizing the latest celebrity
who has arrived—Ristori or Dickens, Victor Emmanuel or
the Queen of the Sandwich Islands. The equipages are as
varied as the company and attract as much attention, especially the low basket barouches in which ladies drive
themselves, with a pair of dashing ponies, gay nets to
keep their voluminous flounces from overflowing the di-
minutive vehicles, and little grooms standing on the perch
behind.

Along this walk on Christmas Day, a tall young man

walked slowly, with his hands behind him and a somewhat absent expression of countenance. He looked like
an Italian, was dressed like an Englishman, and had the
independent air of an American—a combination which
caused sundry pairs of feminine eyes to look approvingly
after him, and sundry dandies in black velvet suits, with
rose-colored neckties, buff gloves, and orange flowers in
their buttonholes, to shrug their shoulders and then envy
him his inches. There were plenty of pretty faces to admire, but the young man took little notice of them, except
to glance now and then at some blond lady or girl in blue.
Presently he strolled out of the promenade and stood a
moment at the crossing, as if undecided whether to go
and listen to the band in the *Jardin Publique* or to wander
along the beach toward Castle Hill. The quick trot of
ponies' feet made him look up, as one of the little car-
riages, containing a single lady, came rapidly down the
street. The lady was young, blond, and dressed in blue.
He stared a minute, then his whole face woke up and,
waving his hat like a boy, he hurried to meet her.

"Oh, Laurie! Is it really you? I thought you'd never
come!" cried Amy, dropping the reins and holding out
both hands, to the great scandalization of a French mamma, who hastened her daughter's step, lest she should be
demoralized by beholding the free manners of these "mad
English."

"I was detained by the way, but I promised to spend
Christmas with you, and here I am."

"How is your grandfather? When did you come? Where
are you staying?"

"Very well—last night—at the Chauvain. I called at your
hotel, but you were all out."

"I have so much to say and don't know where to begin. Tell me all about yourself. The last I heard of you, your grandfather wrote that he expected you from Berlin."

"Yes, I spent a month there and then joined him in Paris, where he has settled for the winter. He has friends there, and finds plenty to amuse him. So I go and come, and we get on capitally."

They waited for a procession to pass; then Amy touched up her ponies.

"*Que pensez vous?*" she said, airing her French, which had improved in quantity, if not in quality, since she came abroad.

"That *mademoiselle* has made good use of her time, and the result is charming," replied Laurie, bowing, with his hand on his heart, and an admiring look.

At Avigdor's she found precious letters from home, and, giving the reins to Laurie, read them luxuriously as they wound up the shady road between green hedges, where tea roses bloomed as freshly as in June.

"Beth is very poorly, Mother says. I often think I ought to go home, but they all say 'stay.' So I do, for I shall never have another chance like this," said Amy, looking sober over one page.

"I think you are right there. You could do nothing at home, and it is a great comfort to them to know that you are well and happy and enjoying so much, my dear."

He drew a little nearer; the fear that sometimes weighed on Amy's heart was lightened, for the look, the act, the brotherly "my dear," seemed to assure her that if any trouble did come, she would not be alone in a strange land. Presently she laughed and showed him a small sketch of Jo in her scribbling suit, with the bow rampantly

erect upon her cap, and issuing from her mouth the words "Genius burns!"

Laurie smiled, took it, put it in his vest pocket "to keep it from blowing away," and listened with interest to the lively letter Amy read him.

After idling away an hour, they drove home again; and, having paid his respects to Mrs. Carrol, Laurie left them, promising to return in the evening. It must be recorded of Amy that she deliberately "prinked" that night.

"I do want him to think I look well, and tell them so at home," said Amy to herself as she put on Flo's old white silk dress and covered it with a cloud of illusion, out of which her white shoulders and golden head emerged with a most artistic effect. She had sense enough to let her hair alone, after gathering up the thick waves and curls into a Hebe-like knot at the back of her head.

She walked up and down the long salon waiting for Laurie, and once arranged herself under the chandelier, which had a good effect upon her hair; then she thought better of it and went away to the other end of the room. It so happened that she could not have done a better thing, for Laurie came in so quietly she did not hear him; and as she stood at the distant window with her head half turned and one hand gathering up her dress, the slender, white figure against the red curtains was as effective as a well-placed statue.

"Good evening, Diana!" said Laurie, struck with her beauty.

"Good evening, Apollo!" she answered, smiling back at him.

Laurie devoted himself to Amy for the rest of the evening in a most delightful manner; the hours passed swiftly and pleasantly for both of them; this very agreeable change was the result of one of the new impressions which both Laurie and Amy were unconsciously giving and receiving.

Laurie went to Nice intending to stay a week, and remained a month. He was tired of wandering about alone, and Amy's familiar presence seemed to give a homelike charm to the foreign scenes in which she bore a part. He rather missed the "petting" he used to receive, and enjoyed a taste of it again; for no attentions from strangers, however flattering, were half so pleasant as the sisterly adoration of the girls at home. Amy never would pet him like the others, but she was very glad to see him now and quite clung to him, feeling that he was the representative of the dear family for whom she longed more than she would confess.

They naturally took comfort in each other's society and were much together, riding, walking, dancing, or dawdling, for at Nice no one can be very industrious during the gay season. But while apparently amusing themselves in the most careless fashion, they were half consciously making discoveries and forming opinions about each other. Amy rose daily in the estimation of her friend, but he sank in hers, and each felt the truth before a word was spoken. Amy tried to please, and succeeded, for she was grateful for the many pleasures he gave her and repaid him with the little services to which womanly women know how to lend an indescribable charm. Laurie made no effort of any kind, but just let himself drift along as comfortably as possible, trying to forget, and feeling that all women owed him a kind word because one had been cold to him. It cost him no effort to be generous, and he would have given Amy all the trinkets in Nice if she would have taken them; but at the same time, he felt that he could not change the opinion she was forming of him, and he rather dreaded the keen eyes that seemed to watch him with such half-sorrowful, half-scornful surprise.

"All the rest have gone to Monaco for the day. I preferred to stay home and write letters. They are done now, and I am going to Valrosa to sketch. Will you come?" said Amy one lovely day as Laurie lounged in as usual, about noon.

"Well, yes, but isn't it rather warm for such a long drive?" he answered slowly, for the shaded salon looked inviting after the glare without.

"Don't trouble yourself," said Amy sharply. "It's no exertion to me, but perhaps *you* are not equal to it."

Laurie lifted his eyebrows and followed at a leisurely pace as she ran downstairs. They never quarreled; Amy was too well bred, and just now Laurie was too lazy.

Valrosa well deserved its name, for in that climate of perpetual summer, roses bloomed everywhere. They overhung the archway, thrust themselves between the bars of the great gate with a sweet welcome to passersby, and lined the avenue winding through lemon trees and feathery palms up to the villa on the hill. Every shadowy nook, where seats invited one to stop and rest, was a mass of bloom; every cool grotto had its marble nymph smiling from a veil of flowers; and every fountain reflected crimson, white, or pale pink roses, leaning down to smile at their own beauty.

"Did you ever see such roses?" asked Amy, pausing on the terrace to enjoy the view and a luxurious whiff of perfume that came wandering by.

"No, nor felt such thorns," returned Laurie, with his thumb in his mouth, after a vain attempt to capture a solitary flower that grew just beyond his reach.

"Laurie, when are you going to your grandfather?" Amy asked presently as she settled herself on a rustic seat.

"Very soon."

"You have said that a dozen times within the last three weeks."

"I daresay; short answers save trouble."

"He expects you, and you really ought to go."

"Hospitable creature! I know it."

"Then why don't you do it?"

"Natural depravity, I suppose."

"Natural indolence, you mean. It's really dreadful!" And Amy looked severe.

"Not so bad as it seems, for I should only plague him if I went. So I might as well stay and plague you a little longer—you can bear it better. In fact, I think it agrees with you excellently!" And Laurie composed himself for a lounge on the broad ledge of the balustrade.

"Stay as you are," said Amy. "I need a figure in my sketch. I intend to work hard."

"What delightful enthusiasm!"

"What would Jo say if she saw you now?" asked Amy.

"As usual, 'Go away, Teddy, I'm busy.'" He laughed as he spoke, but the laugh was not natural, and a shade passed over his face; for the utterance of the familiar name touched the wound that was not healed yet. Both tone and shadow struck Amy, for she had seen and heard them before; and now she looked up in time to catch a new expression on Laurie's face—a hard, bitter look, full of pain, dissatisfaction, and regret. It was gone before she

227

could study it, and the listless expression back again. She watched him for a moment with artistic pleasure, thinking how like an Italian he looked as he lay basking in the sun with uncovered head and eyes full of Southern dreaminess; for he seemed to have forgotten her and fallen into a reverie.

"What are you going to do when I am gone?" Laurie suddenly came alive.

"Be an ornament to society, if I get a chance," said Amy.

"And here is where Fred Vaughn comes in, I fancy," he teased her.

Amy preserved a discreet silence, but there was a conscious look in her downcast face that made Laurie sit up and say gravely, "Now I'm going to play brother and ask questions. May I?"

"I don't promise to answer."

"Your face will, if your tongue doesn't. You aren't woman of the world enough yet to hide your feelings, my dear. I've heard rumors about Fred and you last year, and it's my private opinion that if he had not been called home suddenly and detained so long, something would have come of it—hey?"

"That's not for me to say," said Amy. But her lips would smile, and there was a traitorous sparkle of the eye which betrayed that she knew her power perfectly well and enjoyed the knowledge.

"You are not engaged, I hope." And Laurie looked very elder-brotherly and grave all of a sudden.

"No."

"But you will be, if he comes back and goes properly down upon his knees, won't you?"

"Very likely."

"Then you are fond of old Fred?"

"I could be if I tried."

"But you don't intend to try until the proper moment? Bless my soul, what unearthly prudence! He's a good fellow, Amy, but not the man I fancied you'd like."

"He is rich, a gentleman, and has delightful manners," began Amy, trying to be quite cool and dignified; but she was feeling a little ashamed of herself in spite of the sincerity of her intentions.

"I understand—queens of society can't get on without money. So you mean to make a good match and start in that way? Quite right and proper as the world goes, but it does sound odd from the lips of one of your mother's girls."

"True, nevertheless!" said Amy sharply. She changed the subject. "Flo and I have got a new name for you. It's 'Lazy Laurence.' How do you like it?"

She thought that would annoy him, but he only folded his arms and said, "That's not bad! Thank you, ladies."

"Do you want to know what I honestly think of you?"

"Pining to be told."

"Well, I despise you."

The grave, almost sad accent of her voice made him open his eyes and ask quickly, "Why, if you please?"

"Because, with every chance for being good, useful, and happy, you are faulty, lazy, and miserable."

"Strong language, *mademoiselle*."

"If you like it, I'll go on."

"Pray do. It's quite interesting."

"You are abominably lazy; you like gossip, and waste time on frivolous things; you are contented to be petted and admired by silly people, instead of being loved and

229

respected by wise ones. With money, talent, position, health, and beauty—with all these splendid things to use and enjoy, you can find nothing to do but dawdle, and instead of being the man you might and ought to be, you are only—" There she stopped, with a look that had both pain and pity in it.

A hand came down over the pages so that she could not draw, and Laurie's voice said, with a droll imitation of a penitent child, "I will be good! Oh, I will be good!"

Amy's keen eyes filled, and when she spoke again, it was in a voice that could be beautifully soft and kind when she chose to make it so.

"I know I have no right to talk so to you, Laurie. And if you weren't the sweetest-tempered fellow in the world, you'd be very angry with me. But we are all so fond and proud of you, I couldn't bear to think they should be disappointed in you at home as I have been, though perhaps they would understand the change better than I do."

"I think they would," came in a grim tone, quite as touching as a broken one.

Now, Laurie flattered himself that he had borne it remarkably well—making no moan, asking no sympathy, and taking his trouble away to live it down alone. Amy's lecture put the matter in a new light, and for the first time it did look weak and selfish to lose heart at the first failure and shut himself up in moody indifference. He felt as if he had suddenly been shaken out of a pensive dream, and found it impossible to go to sleep again.

"May I venture to suggest," he said almost gaily, "that five o'clock is the dinner hour at your hotel?"

Laurie rose as he spoke, and with a bow looked at his watch, as if to remind her that even moral lectures should have an end. He tried to resume his former easy, indifferent air, but it *was* an affectation now, for the rousing had been more efficacious than he would confess. Amy felt the change.

They laughed and chatted all the way home. But both felt ill at ease; the friendly frankness was disturbed, the sunshine had a shadow over it, and despite their apparent gaiety, there was a secret discontent in the heart of each.

"Shall we see you this evening, *mon frère?*" asked Amy as they parted at her aunt's door.

"Unfortunately, I have an engagement. *Au revoir, mademoiselle.*" And Laurie bent as if to kiss her hand, in the foreign fashion, which became him better than many men. Something in his face made Amy say, quickly and warmly, "No, be yourself with me, Laurie, and part in the good old way. I'd rather have a hearty American handshake than all the sentimental salutations in France."

"Good-bye, dear." And with these words, uttered in the tone she liked, Laurie left her, after a handshake almost painful in its heartiness.

Next morning, instead of the usual call, Amy had a note which made her smile at the beginning and sigh at the end.

My dear Mentor,

Please make my adieux to your aunt and exult within yourself, for "Lazy Laurence" has gone to his grandpa like the best of boys. A pleasant winter to you, and may the gods grant you a blissful honeymoon at Valrosa. I think Fred would be benefited by a rouser. Tell him so, with my congratulations.

Yours gratefully,
Telemachus

231

"Good boy! I'm glad he's gone," said Amy, with an approving smile. The next minute her face fell as she glanced about the empty room, adding, with an involuntary sigh, "Yes, I *am* glad—but how I shall miss him!"

27 · The Valley of the Shadow

WHEN THE FIRST bitterness was over, the family accepted the inevitable and tried to bear it cheerfully, helping one another by the increased affection which comes to bind households tenderly together in times of trouble. They put away their grief, and each did his part toward making that last year a happy one.

The pleasantest room in the house was set apart for Beth, and in it was gathered everything that she most loved—flowers, pictures, her piano, the little worktable, and the beloved pussies. Father's best books found their way there, with Mother's easy chair, Jo's desk, Amy's loveliest sketches; and every day Meg brought her babies on a loving pilgrimage, to make sunshine for Aunty Beth. John quietly set apart a little sum, that he might enjoy the pleasure of keeping the invalid supplied with the fruit she loved and longed for; old Hannah never wearied of concocting dainty dishes to tempt a capricious appetite, dropping tears as she worked; and, from across the sea, came little gifts and cheerful letters, seeming to bring breaths of warmth and fragrance from lands that know no winter.

Here, cherished like a household saint at its shrine, sat

Beth, tranquil and busy as ever, for nothing could change the sweet, unselfish nature; and even while preparing to leave life, she tried to make it happier for those who should remain behind. The feeble fingers were never idle, and one of her pleasures was to make little things for the schoolchildren daily passing to and fro—to drop a pair of mittens from her window for a pair of purple hands, a needle book for some small mother of many dolls, penwipers for young penmen toiling through forests of pothooks, scrapbooks for picture-loving eyes, and all manner of pleasant devices, till the reluctant climbers up the ladder of learning found their way strewn with flowers, as it were, and came to regard the gentle giver as a sort of fairy godmother, who sat above there, and showered down gifts miraculously suited to their tastes and needs. If Beth wanted a reward, she found it in the bright little faces always turned up to her window with nods and smiles, and the droll little letters which came to her, full of blots and gratitude.

It was well for all that this peaceful time was given them as preparation for the sad hours to come, for by and by Beth said the needle was "so heavy" and put it down forever; talking wearied her, faces troubled her, pain claimed her for its own, and her tranquil spirit was sorrowfully perturbed by the ills that vexed her feeble flesh. Ah, me! Such heavy days, such long, long nights, such aching hearts and imploring prayers, when those who loved her best were forced to see the thin hands stretched out to them beseechingly, to hear the bitter cry, "Help me, help me!" and to feel that there was no help. A sad eclipse of the serene soul, a sharp struggle of the young life with death; but both were mercifully brief, and then,

the natural rebellion over, the old peace returned, more beautiful than ever. With the wreck of her frail body, Beth's soul grew strong; and, though she said little, those about her felt that she was ready, saw that the first pilgrim called was likewise the fittest, and waited with her on the shore, trying to see the Shining Ones coming to receive her when she crossed the river.

Jo never left her for an hour since Beth had said, "I feel stronger when you are here." She slept on a couch in the room, waking often to renew the fire, to feed, lift, or wait upon the patient creature who seldom asked for anything and "tried not to be a trouble." All day she haunted the room, jealous of any other nurse, and prouder of being chosen then than of any honor her life ever brought her. Precious and helpful hours to Jo, for now her heart received the teaching that it needed; lessons in patience were so sweetly taught her that she could not fail to learn them: charity for all, the lovely spirit that can forgive and truly forget unkindness, the loyalty to duty that makes the hardest easy, and the sincere faith that fears nothing, but trusts undoubtingly.

Often when she woke, Jo found Beth reading in her well-worn little book, heard her singing softly to beguile the sleepless night, or saw her lean her face upon her hands, while tears dropped through the transparent fingers; and Jo would lie watching her, with thoughts too deep for tears, feeling that Beth, in her simple, unselfish way, was trying to wean herself from the dear old life and fit herself for the life to come, by sacred words of comfort and the music she loved so well.

Seeing this did more for Jo than the wisest sermons, the saintliest hymns, the most fervent prayers that any voice could utter; for, with eyes made clear by many tears and a heart softened by the tenderest sorrow, she recognized the beauty of her sister's life—uneventful, unambitious, yet full of the genuine virtues which "smell sweet and blossom in the dust," the self-forgetfulness that makes the humblest on earth remembered soonest in heaven, the true success which is possible to all.

One night, when Beth looked among the books upon her table to find something to make her forget the mortal weariness that was almost as hard to bear as pain, she turned the leaves of her old favorite *Pilgrim's Progress* and found a little paper scribbled over in Jo's hand. The name caught her eye, and the blurred look of the lines made her sure that tears had fallen on it.

Poor Jo, she's fast asleep. So I won't waken her to ask leave. She shows me all her things, and I don't think she will mind if I look at this, thought Beth, with a glance at her sister, who lay on the rug with the tongs beside her, ready to wake up the minute the log fell apart.

It was a poem, faulty and feeble in line, written by Jo in the tenderest of language. It was entitled "My Beth," and extolled the virtues of her dearest little sister.

The words brought a look of inexpressible comfort to Beth's face, for her one regret had been that she had done so little; and this seemed to assure her that her life had not been useless, that her death would not bring the despair she feared. As she sat with the paper folded between her hands, the charred log fell asunder. Jo started up, revived the blaze, and crept to the bedside, hoping Beth slept.

"Not asleep, dear, but so happy. See, I found this and read it. I knew you wouldn't care.

"Have I been all that to you, Jo?" she asked with wistful, humble earnestness.

"Oh, Beth, so much, so much!" And Jo's head went down upon the pillow beside her sister's.

"Then I don't feel as if I'd wasted my life. I'm not so good as you make me, but I *have* tried to do right. And now, when it is too late to begin even to do better, it's such a comfort to know that someone loves me so much and feels as if I'd really helped her."

"More than anyone in the world, Beth. I used to think I couldn't let you go. But I'm learning to feel that I don't lose you, that you'll be more to me than ever and death can't part us, though it seems to."

"I know it cannot, and I don't fear it any longer, for I'm sure I shall be your Beth still, to love and help you more than ever. You must take my place, Jo, and be everything to Father and Mother when I'm gone. They will turn to you—don't fail them. And if it's hard to work alone, remember that I don't forget you, and that you'll be happier in doing that than writing splendid books or seeing all the world. For love is the only thing that we can carry with us when we go, and it makes the end so easy."

"I'll try, Beth." And then and there Jo renounced her old ambition, pledged herself to a new and better one, acknowledging the poverty of other desires, and feeling the blessed solace of a belief in the great immortality of love.

So the spring days came and went, the sky grew clearer, the earth greener, the flowers were up fair and early, and all the birds came in time to say good-bye to Beth, who, like a tired but trustful child, clung to the hands that had led her all her life, as Father and Mother guided her tenderly through the valley of the shadow and gave her up to God.

As Beth had hoped, the "tide went out easily"; and in the dark hour before the dawn she quietly drew her last, with no farewell but one loving look and a little sigh.

When morning came, for the first time in many months the fire was out and Jo's place was empty. But a bird sang blithely on a budding bough close by, the snowdrops blossomed freshly at the window, and the spring sunshine streamed in like a benediction over the placid face upon the pillow—a face so full of painless peace that those who loved it best smiled through their tears and thanked God that Beth was well at last.

28 • Learning to Forget

LAURIE BROUGHT himself to confess that he *had* been selfish and lazy; he felt that his blighted affections were quite dead now. Jo *wouldn't* love him, but he might *make* her respect and admire him by doing something which should prove that a girl's "no" had not spoiled his life. He had always meant to do something, and Amy's advice was quite unnecessary. He had only been waiting till the aforesaid blighted affections were decently interred; that being done, he felt that he was ready to "hide his stricken heart, and still toil on."

As Goethe, when he had a joy or a grief, put it into song, so Laurie resolved to embalm his love-sorrow in music by composing a requiem which should harrow up Jo's soul and melt the heart of every hearer. But, whether the sorrow was too vast to be embodied in music, or music too ethereal to lift up a mortal woe, he soon discovered that the requiem was beyond his power to compose.

Then he tried an opera, but here, again, unforeseen difficulties beset him. He wanted Jo for his heroine, and called upon his memory to supply him with tender recollections and romantic visions of his love. But memory turned traitor; he could only recall Jo's oddities, faults, and freaks; he had to give her up with a "Bless that girl, what a torment she is!" and a clutch at his hair, as became a distracted composer.

When he looked about him for another and a less intractable damsel to immortalize in melody, memory produced one with the most obliging readiness. This phantom wore many faces, but it always had golden hair, was enveloped in a diaphanous cloud, and floated airily before his mind's eye in a pleasing chaos of roses, peacocks, white ponies, and blue ribbons. He did not give the complaisant wraith any name, but he took her for his heroine and grew quite fond of her, as well he might, for he gave her every gift and grace under the sun and escorted her, unscathed, through trials which would have annihilated any mortal woman.

Thanks to this inspiration, he got on swimmingly for a time, but gradually the work lost its charm, and finally he forgot to compose.

"Now what shall I do?" he asked himself. He began to wish he had to work for his daily bread.

Laurie thought that the task of forgetting his love for Jo would absorb all his powers for years; but to his great surprise, he discovered it grew easier every day. He refused to believe it at first, got angry with himself, and couldn't understand it. He carefully stirred up the embers of his lost love, but they refused to burst into a blaze; there was only a comfortable glow that warmed and did him good. There was left a brotherly affection which would last unbroken to the end.

As the word "brotherly" passed through his mind in one of these reveries, he smiled and glanced up at the picture of Mozart that was before him. *Well, he was a*

great man, and when he couldn't have one sister, he took
the other one and was happy.

Laurie did not utter the words, but he thought them,
and the next instant he said to himself, "No, I won't! I
haven't forgotten—I never can. I'll try once more, and if
that fails, why then—"

He seized pen and paper and wrote to Jo, telling her
that he could not settle to anything while there was the
least hope of her changing her mind. Couldn't she,
wouldn't she, and let him come home and be happy?
While waiting for an answer, he did nothing, but he did
it energetically. The answer came at last: Jo couldn't and
wouldn't.

Laurie opened his desk, as if writing to Amy had been
the proper conclusion of the sentence he had left unfinished some weeks before.

The letter went very soon and was promptly answered,
for Amy was homesick and confessed it in the most delightfully confiding manner. The correspondence flourished famously, and letters flew to and fro with unfailing
regularity all through the early spring.

Laurie wanted desperately to go to Nice, but would not
till he was asked; and Amy would not ask him, for just
then she was having little experiences that she did not
wish "our boy" to see.

Fred Vaughn had returned and put the question to
which she had once decided to answer, "Yes, thank you";
but now she said to Fred, "No, thank you," kindly but
steadily.

Amy never lectured Laurie now; she asked his opinion
on all subjects; she was interested in everything he did,
made charming little presents for him, and sent him two

letters a week, full of lively gossip, sisterly confidences, and captivating sketches of the lovely scenes about her. She grew a little pale and pensive that spring, lost much of her relish for society, and went out sketching alone a great deal.

Her aunt thought that she regretted her answer to Fred; Amy left her to think what she liked, but took care that Laurie should know that Fred had gone to Egypt.

While these changes were going on abroad, trouble had come at home. Amy bore the news of Beth's death very well, and quietly submitted to the family decree that she should not shorten her visit. But her heart was very heavy —she longed to be at home, and every day looked wistfully across the lake, waiting for Laurie to come and comfort her.

He did come very soon, with a heart full of joy and sorrow, hope and suspense.

As soon as the boat touched the little quay, he hurried along the shore to La Tour, where the Carrols were living *en pension*.

A pleasant old garden on the borders of the lovely lake, with chestnuts rustling overhead, ivy climbing everywhere, and the black shadow of the tower falling far across the sunny water. At one corner of the wide, low wall was a seat, and here Amy often came to read or work, or console herself with the beauty all about her. She was sitting here that day, leaning her head on her hand, with a homesick heart and heavy eyes, thinking of Beth, and wondering why Laurie did not come. She did not hear him cross the courtyard beyond, nor see him pause in the archway that led from the subterranean path into the garden where she sat.

He stood a minute, looking at her with new eyes, seeing what no one had ever seen before—the tender side of Amy's character. Everything about her mutely suggested love and sorrow—the blotted letters in her lap, the black ribbon that tied up her hair, the womanly pain and patience in her face; even the little ebony cross at her throat seemed pathetic to Laurie, for he had given it to her, and she wore it as her only ornament. If he had any doubts about the reception she would give him, they were set at rest the minute she looked up and saw him; for, dropping everything, she ran to him, exclaiming in a tone of unmistakable love and longing, "Oh, Laurie! Laurie! I knew you'd come to me!"

They stood together quite silent for a moment, with the dark head bent down protectingly over the light one, Amy feeling that no one could comfort and sustain her so well as Laurie, and Laurie deciding that Amy was the only woman in the world who could fill Jo's place and make him happy.

The quaint old garden had sheltered many pairs of lovers, and seemed expressly made for them, so sunny and secluded was it, with nothing but the tower to overlook them and the wide lake to carry away the echo of their words as it rippled by below. For an hour this new pair walked and talked, or rested on the wall, enjoying the sweet influences which gave such a charm to time and place; and when an unromantic dinner bell warned them away, Amy felt as if she left her burden of loneliness and sorrow behind her in the chateau garden.

The moment Mrs. Carrol saw the girl's altered face she was illuminated with a new idea, and exclaimed to herself, "Now I understand it all! The child has been pining for young Laurence. Bless my heart! I never thought of such a thing!"

Laurie had rather imagined that the denouement would take place in the chateau garden by moonlight, and in the most graceful and decorous manner; but it turned out exactly the reverse, for the matter was settled on the lake, at noonday, in a few blunt words.

They had been talking of Bonnivard as they glided past Chillon, and of Rousseau as they looked up at Clarens, where he wrote his *Héloïse*. Neither Amy nor Laurie had read it, but they knew it was a love story, and each privately wondered if it was half as interesting as their own. Amy had been dabbling her hand in the water during the little pause that fell between them, and when she looked up, Laurie was leaning on his oars, with an expression in his eyes that made her say hastily, merely for the sake of saying something, "You must be tired. Rest a little, and let me row. It will do me good, for since you came I have been altogether lazy and luxurious."

"I'm not tired, but you may take an oar if you like. There's room enough, though I have to sit nearly in the middle, else the boat won't trim," returned Laurie, as if he rather liked the arrangement.

Feeling that she had not mended matters much, Amy took the offered third of a seat, shook her hair over her face, and accepted an oar. She rowed as well as she did many other things; and though she used both hands and Laurie but one, the oars kept time, and the boat went smoothly along.

"How well we pull together, don't we?" said Amy, who objected to silence just then.

"So well that I wish we might always pull in the same

boat. Will you, Amy?" very tenderly.

"Yes, Laurie!" very low.

Then they both stopped rowing and unconsciously added a pretty little tableau of human love and happiness to the dissolving views reflected in the lake.

29 • All Alone

Poor Jo! These were dark days to her, for something like despair came over her when she thought of spending all her life in that quiet house, devoted to humdrum cares, a few poor little pleasures, and the duty that never seemed to grow any easier. "I can't do it. I wasn't meant for a life like this, and I know I shall break away and do something desperate if somebody doesn't come and help me," she said to herself, when her first efforts failed, and she fell into the moody, miserable state of mind which often comes when strong wills have to yield to the inevitable.

But someone did come and help her, though Jo didn't recognize her good angels at once, because they wore familiar shapes and used the simple spells best fitted to poor humanity.

Jo went to her father and told him her troubles, the resentful sorrow for her loss, the fruitless efforts that discouraged her, the want of faith that made life look so dark, and all the sad bewilderment which we call despair. She gave him entire confidence, he gave her the help she needed, and both found consolation in the act; for the time had come when they could talk together not only as father and daughter, but as man and woman, able and glad to serve each other with mutual sympathy as well as mutual love. Happy, thoughtful times there in the old study, which Jo called "the church of one member," and from which she came with fresh courage, recovered cheerfulness, and a more submissive spirit, for the parents who had taught one child to meet death without fear were trying now to teach another to accept life without despondency or distrust, and to use its beautiful opportunities with gratitude and power.

Other helps had Jo, humble, wholesome duties and delights, that would not be denied their part in serving her, and which she slowly learned to see and value. Brooms and dishcloths never could be as distasteful as they once had been, for Beth had presided over both; and something of her housewifely spirit seemed to linger round the little mop and the old brush that were never thrown away. As she used them, Jo found herself humming the songs Beth used to hum, imitating Beth's orderly ways, and giving the little touches here and there that kept everything fresh and cozy, which was the first step toward making home happy, though she didn't know it till Hannah said, with an approving squeeze of her hand, "You thoughtful creeter, you're determined we shan't miss that dear lamb ef you can help it. We don't say much, but we see it, and the Lord will bless you for't, see ef He don't."

As they sat sewing together, Jo discovered how much improved her sister Meg was; how well she could talk; how much she knew about good, womanly impulses, thoughts, and feelings; and how happy she was in husband and children.

"Marriage is an excellent thing, after all. I wonder if I should blossom out half as well as you have, if I tried it, always 'perwisin'' I could," said Jo as she constructed a kite for Demi in the topsy-turvy nursery.

"It's just what you need to bring out the tender, womanly half of your nature, Jo. You are like a chestnut burr, prickly outside but silky-soft within, and a sweet kernel, if one can only get at it. Love will make you show your heart someday, and then the rough burr will fall off."

Jo had got so far, she was learning to do her duty, and to feel unhappy if she did not; but to do it cheerfully—ah, that was another thing!

Providence had taken her at her word; here was the task, not what she had expected, but better, because self had no part in it; now, could she do it? She decided that she would try, and in her first attempt she found the helps I have suggested. Still another was given her, and she took it, not as a reward but as a comfort, as Christian took the refreshment afforded by the little arbor where he rested as he climbed the hill called Difficulty.

"Why don't you write? That always used to make you happy," said her mother once, when the desponding fit overshadowed Jo.

"I've no heart for it, and if I had, nobody cares for the things I write."

"We do. Write something for us, and never mind the rest of the world. Try it, dear. I'm sure it would do you good and please us very much."

"Don't believe I can." But Jo got out her desk and began to overhaul her half-finished manuscripts.

Jo never knew how it happened, but something got into her next story that went straight to the hearts of those who read it; for when her family had laughed and cried over it, her father sent it, much against her will, to one of the popular magazines; and to her utter surprise, it was not only paid for, but others requested. Letters from several persons, whose praise was honor, followed the appearance of the little story; newspapers copied it, and strangers as well as friends admired it. For a small thing, it was a great success; and Jo was more astonished than when her novel was commended and condemned all at once.

"What *can* there be in a simple little story like that to make people praise it so?" she asked, bewildered.

"There is truth in it, Jo—that's the secret. Humor and pathos make it alive, and you have found your style at last," said her father. "You put your heart into it, my daughter. Do your best and grow as happy as we are in your success."

So, taught by love and sorrow, Jo wrote her little stories and sent them away to make friends for themselves and her.

When Amy and Laurie wrote of their engagement, Mrs. March feared that Jo would find it difficult to rejoice over it, but her fears were soon set at rest; for, though Jo looked grave at first, she took it very quietly and was full of hopes and plans for "the children."

"It is so beautiful to be loved as Laurie loves me," Amy wrote. "He isn't sentimental, doesn't say much about it, but I see and feel it in all he says and does, and it makes me so happy and so humble that I don't seem to be the same girl I was. I never knew how good and generous and tender he was till now, for he lets me read his heart, and I find it full of noble impulses and hopes and purposes, and am so proud to know it's mine. Oh, Mother, I never knew how much like heaven this world could be,

when two people truly love and live for one another and no one else!"

"And that's our cool, reserved, and worldly Amy! Truly love does work miracles. How very, very happy they must be!" And Jo laid the rustling sheets together with a careful hand, as one might shut the covers of a lovely romance which holds the reader fast till the end comes, and he finds himself alone in the workaday world again.

By and by Jo roamed upstairs, for it was rainy and she could not walk. A restless spirit possessed her, and the old feeling came again, not bitter as it once was, but a sorrowfully patient wonder why one sister should have all she asked, the other nothing. It was not true; she knew that and tried to put it away, but the natural craving for affection was strong, and Amy's happiness woke the hungry longing for someone to "love with heart and soul, and cling to, while God let them be together."

Up in the garret, where Jo's unquiet wanderings ended, stood four little chests in a row, each marked with its owner's name, and each filled with relics of the childhood and girlhood ended now for all. Jo glanced over them, then, when she came to her own, leaned her chin on the edge and stared absently at the chaotic collection, till a bundle of old exercise books caught her eye. She drew them out, turned them over, and, looking through them, relived that pleasant winter at kind Mrs. Kirke's.

She smiled at first, then looked thoughtful, next sad, and, when she came to a little message written in the Professor's hand, her lips began to tremble, the books slid out of her lap, and she sat looking at the friendly words as if they took a new meaning and touched a tender spot in her heart.

"Wait for me, my friend. I may be a little late, but I shall surely come."

Oh, if he only would! So kind, so good, so patient with me always—my dear old Fritz. I didn't value him half enough when I had him, but now I should love to see him, for everyone seems going away from me and I'm all alone.

Holding the little paper fast, as if it were a promise yet to be fulfilled, Jo laid her head down on a ragbag and cried, as if in opposition to the rain pattering on the roof.

Was it all self-pity, loneliness, or low spirits? Or was it the waking up of a sentiment which had bided its time as patiently as its inspirer? Who shall say?

30 · Surprises

Jo WAS ALONE in the twilight, lying on the old sofa, looking at the fire, and thinking.

An old maid—that's what I'm going to be. A literary spinster, with a pen for a spouse, a family of stories for children, and twenty years hence a morsel of fame, perhaps, when, like poor Johnson, I'm old, and can't enjoy it, solitary, and can't share it, independent, and don't need it. Well, I needn't be a sour saint nor a selfish sinner, and, I daresay, old maids are very comfortable when they get used to it, but— And there Jo sighed, as if the prospect was anything but inviting.

She dozed off. Then, suddenly, Laurie's ghost seemed to stand before her. A substantial, lifelike ghost, leaning over her with the look he used to wear when he felt a good deal and didn't like to show it. He stooped and kissed her. Then she knew him and flew up, crying joyfully, "Oh, my Teddy! Oh, my Teddy!"

"Dear Jo, you are glad to see me, then?"

"Glad! My blessed boy, words can't express my gladness. Where's Amy?"

"Your mother has got her, down at Meg's. We stopped there by the way, and there was no getting my young wife out of their womanly clutches."

"You've gone and got married?"

"Yes, please, but I never will again." And he went down upon his knees with a penitent clasping of hands, and a face full of mischief, mirth, and triumph. "Now, really, Jo, you ought to treat me with more respect."

"How can I, when the mere idea of you, married and settled, is so irresistibly funny that I can't keep sober?" answered Jo. They had another laugh and then settled down for a good talk, quite in the pleasant old fashion.

"When, where, how?" asked Jo in a fever of feminine interest and curiosity, for she could not realize it yet, this marriage.

"Six weeks ago, at the American consul's in Paris—a very quiet wedding, of course, for even in our happiness we didn't forget dear little Beth."

Jo put her hand in his and said, "Why didn't you let us know afterward?"

"We wanted to surprise you. We thought we were coming directly home, at first, but the dear old gentleman, as soon as we were married, found he couldn't be ready under a month, at least, and sent us off to spend our honeymoon wherever we liked. Amy had once called Valrosa a regular honeymoon home. So we went there, and were as happy as people are but once in their lives. My faith, but wasn't it love among the roses!"

Jo tried to draw away her hand, but Laurie held it fast and said, with a manly gravity she had never seen in him before, "Jo, dear, I want to say one thing, and then we'll put it by forever. As I told you in my letter, I shall never stop loving you. But the love is altered, and I have learned to see that it is better as it is. Will you believe it, and go

255

back to the happy old times, when we first knew one another?"

"I'll believe it with all my heart. But, Teddy, we never can be boy and girl again—the happy old times can't come back, and we mustn't expect it. We can't be playmates any longer, but we will be brother and sister, to love and help one another all our lives, won't we, Laurie?"

He did not say a word, but took the hand she offered him, and laid his face down on it for a minute, feeling that out of the grave of a boyish passion there had risen a beautiful, strong friendship to bless them both.

Amy's voice was heard calling, "Where is she? Where's my dear old Jo?"

In trooped the whole family, and everyone was hugged and kissed all over again, and after several vain attempts, the three wanderers were set down to be looked at and exulted over. Mr. Laurence, hale and hearty as ever, was quite as much improved as the others by his foreign tour, for the crustiness seemed to be nearly gone, and the old-fashioned courtliness had received a polish which made it kindlier than ever. It was good to see him beam at "my children," as he called the young pair. It was better still to see Amy pay him the daughterly duty and affection which completely won his old heart.

Amy's face was full of the soft brightness which betokens a peaceful heart, her voice had a new tenderness in it, and the cool, prim carriage was changed to a gentle dignity, both womanly and winning.

"Love has done much for our little girl," said her mother softly.

"She has had such a good example before her all her life, my dear," Mr. March whispered back, with a loving look at the worn face and gray head beside him.

Daisy found it impossible to keep her eyes off her "pitty aunty," and attached herself like a lapdog to the wonderful chatelaine full of delightful charms. Demi paused to consider the new relationship before he compromised himself by the rash acceptance of a bribe, which took the tempting form of a family of wooden bears from Berne.

"Blest if she ain't in silk from head to foot! Ain't it a relishin' sight to see her settin' there as fine as a fiddle, and hear folks calling little Amy Mrs. Laurence?" muttered old Hannah, who could not resist frequent peeks from the kitchen. "Will Miss Amy ride in her coop (coupé) and use all them lovely silver dishes that's stored away over yander?" she asked eagerly, when Jo went to the kitchen for something.

"Shouldn't wonder if she drove six white horses, ate off gold plates, and wore diamonds and point lace every day. Teddy thinks nothing is too good for her," returned Jo, with infinite satisfaction.

"No more there is! Will you have hash or fishballs for breakfast?" asked Hannah, who wisely mingled poetry and prose.

"I don't care," answered Jo, just as a knock came at the porch door.

Jo opened it with hospitable haste, and started as if another ghost had come to surprise her, for there stood a stout, bearded gentleman, beaming in on her from the darkness.

"Oh, Mr. Bhaer, I *am* so glad to see you!" cried Jo.

"And I to see Miss Marsch—but no, you haf a party—" And the Professor paused.

"No, we haven't—only the family. My brother and sister

257

have just come home, and we are all very happy. Come in, and be one of us."

Though a very social man, I think Mr. Bhaer would have gone decorously away, and come again another day; but how could he when Jo shut the door behind him and bereft him of his hat?

"Father, Mother, this is my friend, Professor Bhaer," she said with a face and tone of such irrepressible pride and pleasure that she might as well have blown a trumpet and opened the door with a flourish.

If the stranger had had any doubts about his reception, they were set at rest in a minute by the cordial welcome he received. Everyone greeted him kindly, for Jo's sake, at first, but very soon they liked him for his own. They could not help it, for he carried the talisman that opens all hearts, and these simple people warmed to him at once, feeling even the more friendly because he was poor. Mr. Bhaer sat looking about him with the air of a traveler who knocks at a strange door, and when it opens, finds himself at home. Daisy and Demi went to him like bees to a honeypot. Establishing themselves on his knees, they proceeded to captivate him by rifling his pockets, pulling his beard, and investigating his watch, with juvenile audacity. The women telegraphed their approval to one another, and Mr. March, feeling that he had got a kindred spirit, opened his choicest stores for his guest's benefit, while silent John listened and enjoyed the talk, but said not a word, and Mr. Laurence found it impossible to doze off.

If Jo had not been otherwise engaged, Laurie's behavior would have amused her; for a faint twinge, not of jealousy but of something like suspicion, caused that gentleman to stand aloof at first and observe the newcomer with brotherly circumspection. But it did not last long. He got interested in spite of himself, and before he knew it was drawn into the circle; for Mr. Bhaer talked well in this genial atmosphere and did himself justice.

He seldom spoke to Laurie but looked at him often, and a shadow would pass across his face, as if he regretted his own lost youth as he watched the young man in his prime. Then his eyes would turn to Jo so wistfully that she would have surely answered the mute inquiry if she had seen it. But Jo had her own eyes to take care of, and feeling that they could not be trusted, she prudently kept them on the little scarf she was knitting, like a model maiden aunt.

A stealthy glance now and then refreshed her like sips of fresh water after a dusty walk, for the sidelong peeps showed her several propitious omens. Mr. Bhaer's face had lost the absentminded expression and looked all alive with interest in the present moment, actually young and handsome, she thought, forgetting to compare him with Laurie as she usually did strange men, to their great detriment. Then, he seemed quite inspired, though the burial customs of the ancients, to which the conversation had strayed, might not be considered an exhilarating topic.

Jo quite glowed with triumph when Laurie got quenched in an argument, and thought to herself, as she watched her father's absorbed face, *How he would enjoy having such a man as my Professor to talk with every day!*

Lastly, Mr. Bhaer was dressed in a new suit of black, which made him look more like a gentleman than ever. His bushy hair had been cut and smoothly brushed, but

259

didn't stay in order long, for in exciting moments he rumpled it up in the droll way he used to do; and Jo liked it rampantly erect better than flat, because she thought it gave his fine forehead a Jove-like aspect. Poor Jo, how she did glorify that plain man as she sat knitting away so quietly, yet letting nothing escape her, not even the fact that Mr. Bhaer actually had gold sleeve-buttons in his immaculate wristbands!

"Dear old fellow! He couldn't have got himself up with more care if he'd been going a-wooing," said Jo to herself. Then a sudden thought, born of the words, made her blush so dreadfully that she had to drop her ball and go down after it to hide her face.

Nobody knew where the evening went to. Hannah skillfully abstracted the babies, nodding like two rosy poppies, at an early hour, and Mr. Laurence went home to rest. The others sat round the fire, talking away, utterly regardless of the lapse of time till Meg, whose maternal mind was impressed with a firm conviction that Daisy had tumbled out of bed and Demi had set his nightgown afire studying the structure of matches, made a move to go.

"We must have our sing, in the good old way, for we are all together once more," said Jo, feeling that a good shout would be a safe and pleasant vent for her jubilant emotions.

They were not *all* there. But no one found the words thoughtless or untrue; for Beth still seemed among them, a peaceful presence, invisible but dearer than ever, since death could not break the household league that love made indissoluble. The little chair stood in its old place; the tidy basket, with the bit of work she left unfinished

when the needle grew "so heavy," was still on its accustomed shelf; the beloved instrument, seldom touched now, had not been moved; and above it Beth's face, serene and smiling as in the early days, looked down upon them, seeming to say, "Be happy. I am here."

"Play something, Amy. Let them hear how much you have improved," said Laurie, with pardonable pride.

But Amy whispered, with full eyes, as she twirled the faded stool, "Not tonight, dear. I can't show off tonight."

But she did show something better than brilliancy and skill, for she sang Beth's songs with a tender music in her voice which the best master could not have taught had he tried.

"Now we must finish with Mignon's song, for Mr. Bhaer sings that," said Jo. And Mr. Bhaer cleared his throat with a gratified "hem" as he stepped into the corner where Jo stood, saying, "You will please sing with me? We go excellently well together."

A pleasing fiction, by the way, for Jo had no more idea of music than a grasshopper. But she would have consented if he had proposed to sing a whole opera, and warbled away blissfully regardless of time and tune. It didn't much matter, for Mr. Bhaer sang like a true German, heartily and well, and Jo soon subsided into a subdued hum, that she might listen to the mellow voice that seemed to sing for her alone.

Later Laurie said in his most gracious manner as they parted, "My wife and I are very glad to meet you, sir. Please remember that there is always a welcome waiting for you over the way."

Then the Professor thanked him so heartily, and looked so suddenly illuminated with satisfaction, that Laurie thought him the most delightfully demonstrative fellow he ever met.

"I, too, shall go. But I shall gladly come again, if you will gif me leave, dear madame, for a little business in the city will keep me here some days."

He spoke to Mrs. March, but he looked at Jo; and the mother's voice gave as cordial an assent as did the daughter's shining eyes.

"I suspect that is a wise man," remarked Mr. March, with satisfaction, from the hearthrug, after the guests had gone.

"I know he is a good one," added Mrs. March with decided approval as she wound up the clock.

"I thought you'd like him," was all Jo said as she slipped away to her bed.

She wondered what the business was that brought Mr. Bhaer to the city, and finally decided that he had been appointed to some great honor somewhere but was far too modest to mention the fact. If she had seen his face when, safe in his own room, he looked at the picture of a severe and rigid young lady, with a good deal of hair, who appeared to be gazing darkly into futurity, it might have thrown some light upon the subject, especially when he turned off the gas and kissed the picture in the dark.

31 · My Lord and Lady

"PLEASE, MADAM MOTHER, could you lend me my wife for half an hour? The luggage has come, and I've been making hay of Amy's Paris finery, trying to find some things I want," said Laurie, coming in the next day to find Mrs. Laurence sitting in her mother's lap, as if being made "the baby" again.

"Certainly. Go, dear. I forget that you have any home but this." Mrs. March pressed the white hand that wore the wedding ring.

"I shouldn't have come over if I could have helped it; but I can't get on without my little woman any more than a—"

"Weathercock can without wind," suggested Jo as he paused for a simile. Jo had grown quite her own saucy self again since Teddy came home.

"Exactly, for Amy keeps me pointing due west most of the time, with only an occasional whiffle round to the south, and I haven't had an easterly spell since I was married. Don't know anything about the north, but am altogether salubrious and balmy, hey, my lady?"

"Lovely weather so far. I don't know how long it will last, but I'm not afraid of storms, for I'm learning how to sail my ship. Come home, dear, and I'll find your boot-jack. I suppose that's what you are rummaging after among my things. Men are *so* awfully helpless, Mother," said Amy, with a matronly air that delighted her husband.

"What are you going to do with yourselves after you get settled?" asked Jo, buttoning Amy's cloak as she used to button her pinafores.

"We have our plans," answered Laurie. "We don't mean to say much about them yet, because we are such very new brooms, but we don't intend to be idle. I'm going into business with a devotion that shall delight Grandfather and prove to him that I'm not spoiled. I need something of the sort to keep me steady. I'm tired of dawdling and mean to work like a man."

"And Amy, what is she going to do?" asked Mrs. March, well pleased at Laurie's decision and the energy with which he spoke.

"After doing the civil all round and airing our best bonnet, we shall astonish you by the elegant hospitalities of our mansion, the brilliant society we shall draw about us, and the beneficial influence we shall exert over the world at large. That's about it, isn't it, Madame Récamier?" asked Laurie with a quizzical look at Amy.

"Time will show. Come away, Impertinence, and don't shock my family by calling me names before their faces," answered Amy. But she was resolving to herself that there should be a home with a good wife in it before she set up a *salon* as a queen of society.

"How happy those children seem together!" observed Mr. March after the young couple had gone.

"Yes, and I think it will last," added Mrs. March, with

the restful expression of a pilot who has brought a ship safely into port.

"I know it will. Happy Amy!" sighed Jo. Then she smiled brightly as Mr. Bhaer opened the gate with an impatient push.

Later in the evening, when his mind had been set at rest about the bootjack, Laurie spoke suddenly to his wife, who was flitting about, arranging her new art treasures.

"Mrs. Laurence."

"My lord!"

"That man intends to marry our Jo!"

"I hope so. Don't you, dear?"

"Well, my love, I consider him a trump, in the fullest sense of that expressive word, but I do wish he was a little younger and a good deal richer."

"Now, Laurie, if they love one another it doesn't matter a particle how old they are, nor how poor. Women *never* should marry for money—"

Amy caught herself up short as the words escaped her and looked at her husband, who replied with malicious gravity.

"Certainly not, though you do hear charming girls say they intend to do it. If my memory serves me right, you once thought it your duty to make a rich match; that accounts, perhaps, for your marrying a good-for-nothing like me."

"Oh, my dearest boy, don't, don't say that! I forgot you were rich when I said 'Yes.' I'd have married you if you hadn't a penny, and I sometimes wish you *were* poor, that I might show how much I love you!" And Amy, who was very dignified in public and very fond in private, gave convincing proofs of the truth of her words.

"You don't really think I am such a mercenary creature as I tried to be once, do you? It would break my heart if you didn't believe that I'd gladly pull in the same boat with you, even if you had to get your living by rowing on the lake!"

"Am I an idiot and a brute? How could I think so, when you refused a richer man for me, and won't let me give even half I want to now, when I have the right?" Laurie paused, for Amy's eyes had an absent look, though fixed still upon his face.

"You are not listening to my remarks at all, Mrs. Laurence."

"Yes, I am, and admiring the dimple in your chin at the same time. I don't wish to make you vain, but I must confess that I'm prouder of my handsome husband than of all his money. Don't laugh, but your nose is *such* a comfort to me." And Amy softly caressed the well-cut feature with artistic satisfaction.

Laurie had received many compliments in his life, but never one that suited him better, as he plainly showed.

Then Amy said slowly, "May I ask you a question, dear?"

"Of course you may."

"Shall you care if Jo does marry Mr. Bhaer?"

"Oh, that's the trouble, is it? I thought there was something in the dimple that didn't suit you. Not being a dog in the manger but the happiest fellow alive, I assure you I can dance at Jo's wedding with a heart as light as my heels. Do you doubt it, my darling?"

Amy looked up at him and was satisfied. Her last little

267

jealous fear vanished forever, and she thanked him with a face full of love and confidence.

"I wish we could do something for that capital old professor. Couldn't we invent a rich relation, who shall obligingly die out there in Germany and leave him a tidy little fortune?" said Laurie, when they began to pace up and down the long drawing room, arm in arm, as they were fond of doing in memory of the chateau garden.

"Jo would find us out and spoil it all. She is very proud of him just as he is, and said yesterday that she thought poverty was a beautiful thing."

"Bless her dear heart! She won't think so when she has a literary husband and a dozen little professors and professorins to support. We won't interfere now, but watch our chance, and do them a good turn in spite of themselves."

"How delightful it is to be able to help others, isn't it? That was always one of my dreams, to have the power of giving freely. And thanks to you, the dream has come true."

"Oh, we'll do quantities of good!" said Laurie. "There's one sort of poverty that I particularly like to help. Out-and-out beggars get taken care of, but poor gentlefolks fare badly, because they won't ask and people don't dare to offer charity."

"I knew something of that," said Amy, "before you made a princess of me. People have been very kind to me. And whenever I see girls struggling along as we used to do, I want to put out my hand and help them, as I was helped."

"And so you shall!" cried Laurie.

"It's a bargain, and we shall get the best of it!"

So the young pair shook hands upon it, and then paced happily on again, feeling that their pleasant home was more homelike because they hoped to brighten other homes.

32 • Under the Umbrella

WHILE LAURIE and Amy were taking conjugal strolls over velvet carpets as they set their house in order and planned a blissful future, Mr. Bhaer and Jo were enjoying promenades, too, along muddy roads and sodden fields.

"I always do take a walk toward evening, and I don't know why I should give it up just because I often happen to meet the Professor on his way out," said Jo to herself, after two or three encounters. Though there were two paths to Meg's, whichever one she took she was sure to meet him, either going or returning. He was always walking rapidly and never seemed to see her till quite close, when he would look as if his shortsighted eyes had failed to recognize the approaching lady till that moment. Then, if she was going to Meg's, he always had something for the babies; if her face was turned homeward, he had merely strolled down to see the river and was just about returning, unless they were tired of his frequent calls.

Under the circumstances, what could Jo do but greet him civilly and invite him in? If she *was* tired of his visits, she concealed her weariness with perfect skill and took care that there should be coffee for supper, "as Friedrich —I mean Mr. Bhaer—doesn't like tea."

By the second week everyone knew perfectly well what was going on, yet everyone tried to look as if they were stone-blind to the changes in Jo's face—never asked why she sang about her work, did up her hair three times a day, and got so blooming with her evening exercise; and no one seemed to have the slightest suspicion that Professor Bhaer, while talking philosophy with the father, was giving the daughter lessons in love.

For a fortnight the Professor came and went with lover-like regularity; then he stayed away for three whole days, and made no sign—a proceeding which caused everybody to look sober and Jo to become pensive at first, and then, alas for romance, very cross.

"Disgusted, I daresay, and gone home as suddenly as he came. It's nothing to me, of course, but I *should* think he *would* have come and bid us good-bye, like a gentleman," she said to herself, with a despairing look at the gate as she put on her things for the customary walk one afternoon.

"You'd better take the little umbrella, dear. It looks like rain," said her mother, observing that she had on her new bonnet, but not alluding to the fact.

"Yes, Marmee. Do you want anything in town? I've got to run in and get some paper," returned Jo, pulling out the bow under her chin.

"Yes, I want some twilled silesia, a paper of number nine needles, and two yards of narrow lavender ribbon. Have you thick boots on and something warm under your cloak?"

"I believe so," answered Jo absently.

"If you happen to meet Mr. Bhaer, bring him home to tea. I quite long to see the dear man," added Mrs. March.

Jo heard *that*, but made no answer except to kiss her mother and walk rapidly away, thinking, with a glow of gratitude in spite of her heartache, *How good she is to me! What do girls do who haven't any mothers to help them through their troubles?*

The dry-goods stores were not down among the counting houses, banks, and wholesale warerooms, where gentlemen mostly congregate; but Jo found herself in that part of the city before she did a single errand, loitering along as if waiting for someone, examining engineering instruments in one window and samples of wool in another, with most unfeminine interest. A drop of rain on her cheek recalled her thoughts from baffled hopes to ruined ribbons; for the drops continued to fall, and being a woman as well as a lover, she felt that, though it was too late to save her heart, she might her bonnet. Now she remembered the little umbrella, which she had forgotten in her hurry to take off; but regret was unavailing, and nothing could be done but borrow one or submit to a drenching.

"It serves me right! What business had I to put on all my best things and come philandering down here, hoping to see the Professor? Jo, I'm ashamed of you! No, you shall *not* go there to borrow an umbrella or find out where he is from his friends. You shall slop away and do your errands in the rain; and if you catch your death and ruin your bonnet, it's no more than you deserve. Now then!"

With that she rushed across the street so impetuously that she narrowly escaped annihilation from a passing truck, and precipitated herself into the arms of a stately old gentleman, who said, "I beg pardon, ma'am," and looked mortally offended. Somewhat daunted, Jo righted herself, spread her handkerchief over the beloved ribbons, and, putting temptation behind her, hurried on, with increasing dampness about the ankles, and much clashing of umbrellas overhead. The fact that a somewhat dilapidated blue one remained stationary above the unprotected bonnet attracted her attention; and, looking up, she saw Mr. Bhaer looking down.

"I feel to know the strong-minded lady who goes so bravely under many horse noses, and so fast through the mud. What do you down here, my friend?"

"I'm shopping."

Mr. Bhaer smiled as he glanced from the pickle factory on one side to the wholesale hide and leather concern on the other; but he only said politely, "You haf no umbrella. May I go also, and take for you the bundles?"

"Yes, thank you."

Jo's cheeks were as red as her ribbon, and she wondered what he thought of her; but she didn't care, for in a minute she found herself walking away, arm in arm with her Professor, feeling as if the sun had suddenly burst out with uncommon brilliancy, that the world was all right again, and that one thoroughly happy woman was paddling through the wet that day.

"We thought you had gone," said Jo hastily, for she knew he was looking at her. Her bonnet wasn't big enough to hide her face, and she feared he might think the joy it betrayed was most unmaidenly.

"Did you believe that I should go with no farewell to those who haf been so heavenly kind to me?" he asked so reproachfully that she felt she had insulted him by the suggestion.

She answered heartily, "No, I didn't. I knew you were

busy about your own affairs, but we rather missed you—
Father and Mother especially."

"And you?"

"I'm always glad to see you, sir."

In her anxiety to keep her voice quite calm, Jo made
it rather cool, and the frosty little monosyllable at the
end seemed to chill the Professor, for his smile vanished
as he said gravely, "I thank you, and come one time more
before I go."

"You *are* going, then?"

"I haf no longer any business here. It is done."

"Successfully, I hope," said Jo, for the bitterness of
disappointment was in that short reply of his.

"I ought to think so, for I haf a way opened to me so I
can make my bread and gif my *Junglings* much help."

"Tell me, please! I like to know all about the—the boys,"
said Jo eagerly.

"That is so kind, I gladly tell you. My friends find for
me a place in a college, where I teach as at home, and
earn enough to make the way smooth for Franz and Emil.
For this I should be grateful, should I not?"

"Indeed you should! How splendid it will be to have
you doing what you like, and be able to see you often, and
the boys—" cried Jo, clinging to the lads as an excuse for
satisfaction she could not help betraying.

"Ah, but we shall not meet often, I fear. This place is
at the West."

"So far away!" And Jo left her skirts to their fate, as it
didn't matter now what became of her clothes or herself.

But the next minute she said, like one entirely absorbed
in the matter, "Here's the place for my errands. Will you
come in? It won't take long."

Jo prided herself upon her shopping capabilities, and particularly wished to impress her escort with the neatness and dispatch with which she would accomplish the business. But, owing to the flutter she was in, everything went amiss; she upset the tray of needles, gave the wrong change, and covered herself with confusion by asking for lavender ribbon at the calico counter.

All the while, Mr. Bhaer stood by, watching her blush and blunder; and as he watched her, his own bewilderment seemed to subside, for he was beginning to see that on some occasions women, like dreams, go by contraries.

When they came out, he put the parcel under his arm with a more cheerful aspect and splashed through the puddles as if he rather enjoyed it, on the whole.

"Should we not do a little what you call shopping for the babies, and haf a farewell feast tonight if I go for my last call at your so pleasant home?" he asked, stopping before a window full of fruit and flowers.

"What will we buy?" said Jo, ignoring the latter part of his speech and sniffing the mingled odors with an affectation of delight as they went in.

"May they haf oranges and figs?" asked Mr. Bhaer, with a paternal air.

"They eat them when they can get them."

"Do you care for nuts?"

"Like a squirrel."

"Hamburg grapes! Yes, we shall surely drink to the Fatherland in those!"

Jo frowned upon that piece of extravagance and asked why he didn't buy a frail of dates, a cask of raisins, and a bag of almonds, and done with it? Whereat Mr. Bhaer confiscated her purse, produced his own, and finished the marketing by buying several pounds of grapes, a pot of rosy daisies, and a pretty jar of honey. Then, distorting his pockets with the knobby bundles and giving her the flowers to hold, he put up the old umbrella and they traveled on again.

"Miss Marsch, I haf a great favor to ask you," began the Professor, after a moist promenade of half a block.

"Yes, sir." And Jo's heart began to beat so hard she was afraid he would hear it.

"I am bold to say it in spite of the rain, because so short a time remains to me."

"Yes, sir." And Jo nearly crushed the small flowerpot with the sudden squeeze she gave it.

"I wish to get a little dress for Tina, and I am too stupid to go alone. Will you kindly gif me a word of taste and help?"

"Yes, sir." And Jo felt as calm and cool, all of a sudden, as if she had stepped into a refrigerator.

"Perhaps also a shawl for Tina's mother; she is so poor and sick and the husband is such a care. Yes, yes, a thick, warm shawl would be a friendly thing to take the little mother."

"I'll do it with pleasure, Mr. Bhaer," Jo answered. *I'm going very fast and he's getting dearer every minute*, she added to herself. Then, with a mental shake, she entered into the business with an energy which was pleasant to behold.

Mr. Bhaer left it all to her; so she chose a pretty gown for Tina and then ordered out the shawls. The clerk, being a married man, condescended to take an interest in the couple, who appeared to be shopping for their family.

"Your lady may prefer this—it's a superior article, a

most desirable color, quite chaste and genteel," he said, shaking out a warm gray shawl and throwing it over Jo's shoulders.

"Does this suit you, Mr. Bhaer?" she asked, turning her back to him and feeling deeply grateful for the chance of hiding her face.

"Excellently well. We will haf it," answered the Professor, smiling to himself as he paid for it, while Jo continued to rummage the counters like a confirmed bargain hunter.

"Now shall we go home?" he asked, as if the words were very pleasant to him.

"Yes. It's late, and I'm *so* tired." Jo's voice was more pathetic than she knew, for now the sun seemed to have gone in as suddenly as it came out, and the world grew muddy and miserable again. For the first time she discovered that her feet were cold, her head ached, and her heart was even colder and fuller of pain. Mr. Bhaer was going away; he only cared for her as friend, it was all a mistake, and the sooner it was over the better. With this idea in her head, she hailed an approaching omnibus with such a hasty gesture that all of the daisies flew out of the pot.

"This is not our omniboos," said the Professor, waving the loaded vehicle away and stooping to pick up the poor little flowers.

"I beg your pardon, I didn't see the name distinctly. Never mind, I can walk. I'm used to plodding in the mud," returned Jo, winking hard because she would have died rather than openly wipe her eyes.

Mr. Bhaer saw the drops on her cheeks, though she turned her head away; the sight seemed to touch him very much, for, suddenly stooping down, he asked in a tone that meant a great deal, "Heart's dearest, why do you cry?"

Jo, with an irrepressible sob, answered, "Because you are going away."

"Ah, my Gott, that is *so* good!" cried Mr. Bhaer, managing to clasp his hands in spite of the umbrella and the bundles. "Jo, I haf nothing but much love to gif you. I came to see if you could care for it, and I waited to be sure that I was something more than a friend. Am I? Can you make a little place in your heart for old Fritz?" he added, all in the same breath.

"Oh, yes!" said Jo, and he was quite satisfied, for she folded both her hands over his arm, and looked up at him with an expression that plainly showed how happy she would be to walk through life beside him, even though she had no better shelter than the old umbrella, if he carried it.

For a year Jo and her Professor worked and waited, hoped and loved; met occasionally and wrote such voluminous letters that the rise in the price of paper was accounted for, Laurie said. The second year began rather soberly, for their prospect didn't brighten, and Aunt March died suddenly. But when their sorrow was over—for they loved the old lady dearly in spite of her sharp tongue—they found they had cause for rejoicing, for she had left Plumfield to Jo, which made all sorts of joyful things possible.

"I know what we shall do!" cried Jo happily. "We shall open a good, happy, homelike school for boys, with me to take care of them and Fritz to teach them."

Mrs. March held out her hand to Jo, who took it, smiling, with tears in her eyes, and went on in the old enthusiastic way, which they had not seen for a long while.

"I have told my plan to Fritz, and he said it was just what he would like, and agreed to try it. We can live at Plumfield and have a flourishing school. There's plenty of room for dozens inside, and splendid grounds outside. They could help in the garden and orchard—Fritz can train and teach in his own way, and Father will help him. I've always longed for boys, and never had enough. Now I can fill the house, and revel in the little dears to my heart's content. Think what luxury—Plumfield my own, and a wilderness of boys to enjoy it with me!"

Almost before she knew where she was, Jo found herself married and settled at Plumfield. Then a family of six or seven boys sprang up like mushrooms and flourished surprisingly—poor boys, as well as rich, for Mr. Laurence was continually finding some touching case of destitution, and begging the Bhaers to take pity on the child and he would gladly pay a trifle for its support.

The years went on, and two little lads of her own came to increase Jo's happiness—Rob, named for Grandpa, and Teddy, a happy-go-lucky baby, who seemed to have inherited his papa's sunshiny temper as well as his mother's lively spirit. How they ever grew up alive in that whirlpool of boys was a mystery to their grandma and aunts; but they flourished like dandelions in spring, and their rough nurses loved and served them well.

There were a great many holidays at Plumfield, and one of the most delightful was the yearly apple-picking, for then the Marches, Laurences, Brookes, and Bhaers turned out in full force and made a day of it. Five years after Jo's wedding one of these fruitful festivals occurred.

Mr. March was there, strolling placidly about, quoting Tusser, Cowley, and Columella to Mr. Laurence, while enjoying "the gentle apple's winey juice."

The Professor charged up and down the green aisles like a stout Teutonic knight, with a pole for a lance, leading on the boys. Laurie devoted himself to the little ones, rode his small daughter in a bushel basket, took Daisy up among the birds' nests, and kept adventurous Rob from breaking his neck. Mrs. March and Meg sat among the apple piles like a pair of Pomonas, sorting the contributions that kept pouring in, while Amy sketched the various groups.

Jo was in her element that day and rushed about with her gown pinned up, her hat everywhere but on her head, and her baby tucked under her arm, ready for any lively adventure which might turn up.

After all the apples had been gathered and lunch was over with, the boys dispersed for a final lark, leaving Mrs. March and her daughters sitting together on the grass under a gnarled old tree.

"Jo, I think your harvest will be a good one," said Mrs. March, frightening away a big black cricket that was staring Teddy out of countenance.

Jo knew that her meaning was deeper than her words.

"Not half so good as yours, Mother," she cried, with the loving impetuosity which she never could outgrow. "Here it is, and we can never thank you enough for the patient sowing and reaping you have done!"

"I hope there will be more wheat and fewer tares every year," said Amy softly.

"A large sheaf, but I know there's room in your heart

for it, Marmee, dear," added Meg's tender voice.

Touched to the heart, Mrs. March could only stretch out her arms, as if to gather children and grandchildren to herself, and say, with face and voice full of motherly love, gratitude, and humility, "Oh, my girls, however long you may live, I never can wish you a greater happiness than this!"